When **Virginia Heath** was a little girl it took her ages to fall asleep, so she made up stories in her head to help pass the time while she was staring at the ceiling. As she got older the stories became more complicated—sometimes taking weeks to get to their happy ending. One day she decided to embrace her insomnia and start writing them down. Virginia lives in Essex, with her wonderful husband and two teenagers. It still takes her for ever to fall asleep...

Also by Virginia Heath

Her Enemy at the Altar
That Despicable Rogue
The Discerning Gentleman's Guide
Miss Bradshaw's Bought Betrothal

The Wild Warriners miniseries

A Warriner to Protect Her
A Warriner to Rescue Her

Discover more at millsandboon.co.uk.

HIS MISTLETOE WAGER

Virginia Heath

MILLS & BOON

First published in Great Britain 2017
by Mills & Boon, an imprint of HarperCollins*Publishers*
1 London Bridge Street, London, SE1 9GF

Large Print edition 2018

© 2017 Susan Merritt

ISBN: 978-0-263-07458-1

MIX
Paper from
responsible sources
FSC™ C007454

This book is produced from independently certified
FSC™ paper to ensure responsible forest management.
For more information visit www.harpercollins.co.uk/green.

Printed and bound in Great Britain
by CPI Group (UK) Ltd, Croydon, CR0 4YY

For Nicole Locke.

My first-ever writing buddy. Thanks for adopting me and showing me the ropes.

Prologue

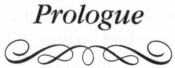

St George's Church, Hanover Square—
June 1815

Every pew was taken. No mean feat in a church as large and grand as this one, yet hardly a surprise when this was the wedding of the Season: the day when the darling of society, the beautiful only daughter of the Earl of Upminster, married her handsome peer.

Even the sun had come out to celebrate and was cheerfully streaming through the imposing stained-glass windows in an exceedingly pleasing fashion and causing a kaleidoscope of colours to decorate the floor. The air hung heavy with the fragrance of lilacs, Lizzie's favourite flower, and tall vases and boughs festooned the aisle she would soon walk down.

Her wedding dress was embroidered subtly to

match and her dainty bonnet decorated with beautiful silk replicas, scaled down to sit in a pleasing fashion. Just as she had always imagined.

In fact, to her complete delight, everything about her wedding to the Marquess of Rainham was exactly as she had imagined it. After all, she had been planning it all since she was ten, right down to the minutest of details because it was the most important day of her life. The beginning of her perfect, happily ever after, exactly six months on from her first meeting with the man she loved with all her heart.

Many in society were surprised by the match, her own dear parents included. Charles did have a reputation as a bit of a rake and had broken more than one heart before he had found his one true love. But as she was prone to point out whenever he was criticised—something which happened with annoying regularity—everybody knew rakes made the very best husbands once they found the right woman, and Lizzie was very definitely the right woman for him.

Dear Charles told her so every single day. From their very first dance he had been the most ardent and attentive suitor, and although Lizzie came with a substantial dowry, he made it quite plain that he did not give two figs for the money. The money meant nothing because he would happily take her with nothing. In rags if need be. Dowries were of no consequence when his heart beat only for her. They were destined to be together for ever. All he cared about was her. Something he proved time and time again with his effusive compliments and daringly longing gazes. It was all so wonderfully romantic. A courtship which had made her the envy of her peers and now she was having the perfect wedding, too. The first bride of June.

'I shall give him a stern piece of my mind later! Be assured of that!' For the second time in as many minutes her father snapped his pocket watch open and stared impatiently at the dial. 'It is the bride's prerogative to be late, not the groom's. To leave us here, hiding in the vestry like common criminals, is beyond the pale, Lizzie. I have no idea what the bounder can be thinking to insult us so grievously.'

She smiled reassuringly at him. At the Foreign Office he was used to being in charge and far too much of a stickler for timekeeping than was necessary, and he had been very vocal with his misgivings about her choice of husband. She had spent much of the last two months reassuring him that everything was destined to be wonderful and her Marquess was not at all what everyone believed. 'Calm down, Papa. Nobody in the congregation is aware that we have arrived, so it hardly matters. There is probably a perfectly good reason Charles has been delayed. He will be here.' Last night, just before he had crept out of her bedchamber window and scrambled down the wisteria, he had blown her a kiss and told her how he was counting the seconds until they took their vows. What difference did a few minutes of tardiness make in the grand scheme of things? Especially when they were about to embark on a lifetime together.

Instinctively, her hand fluttered towards her belly and she suppressed the grin which threatened to bloom. Her father would hit the roof if he knew what she had kept secret from everyone for the last week.

Later tonight, when they were all alone, she would tell Charles about the baby. Her wedding present to him. Made in love almost two months ago, when she had gladly given him her innocence as there seemed little point in prolonging the agony of withholding it unnecessarily. 'We are engaged,' he had said teasingly the first time he had clambered up the wisteria and surprised her in her bedchamber. 'What difference do a few more weeks make? Besides, when a love is as deep and abiding as ours is, a wedding ceremony is merely a formality. I am already married to you in my heart.' As was she. Lizzie knew he would be overjoyed by the news. The perfect end to the most perfect year of her life.

It was the ashen face of her brother Rafe, over half an hour later, which caused the first real doubts to creep in. He came in through a side door, quietly closed it behind him and simply stood, slightly slumped before her.

'He's gone, Lizzie.'

The finality in his voice made her fear the worst. Her darling fiancé was dead? Surely not. She could not bear it. 'What do you mean he's gone? What has happened?' He had been in fine fettle a few scant hours ago. Ardent. No sign of illness or fever. Tears were already streaming down her cheeks as the panic made her heart hammer wildly in her chest. 'Did he have an accident?' Please God, make him not have suffered.

Her brother shook his head and it was then she saw the fierce anger in his eyes.

Anger and pity. For her.

'No, poppet. Nothing so noble, I'm afraid. I don't quite know how to tell you this, so I shall just say it straight out. The scoundrel is marrying someone else.'

Lizzie's knees gave way and her father supported her as she stumbled backwards on to a chair. 'You are mistaken.' The walls started to spin as nausea threatened. 'Charles would not do that to me. He loves me.'

'He left a letter...' A letter that her brother had obviously already read because the seal was broken and the open missive hung limply in his hand.

Callously, it was addressed to no one in particular and had been left on the mantelpiece in his bachelor lodgings at the Albany. Conversationally, it informed the reader that he was bound, with all haste, for Gretna Green with the Duke of Aylesbury's daughter. A drastic step taken because her father had forbidden their courtship a full year before. Of course, they had tried to fight the fierce attraction which had consumed them. However, his love for the obscenely wealthy Duke's plain and awkward youngest daughter was *'deep and abiding'* and for the longest time he had already been *'married to her in his heart'*. Their vows were just a formality because, and this was the most crushing blow, *'his heart beat for her alone'*.

The familiar words cut deeply, slicing through her initial disbelief and shock more effectively than anything else could have. What a dreadful way to discover words which had meant so very much to her had ultimately been meaningless to him all along.

'If we act in all haste, Rafe, we might be able to mitigate the scandal.'

Ever the pragmatist, her father's conversation wafted over her. A message was dispatched to the Duke of Aylesbury. Fevered plans were set in place. Her papa's government connections and high place in society would all be utilised to make everything all right, they would close ranks around her to protect her flawless reputation—yet how could things ever be all right again? She had been jilted.

Jilted!

With every meticulous and carefully laid plan for her perfect future made so thoroughly for so long, she had failed to foresee this terrible scenario. Lizzie had been the silly fool who had fallen for the charming Marquess until a much richer prospect had come along. The pregnant, silly fool who had stood waiting patiently for him at the church, who had believed all his calculated seductions, all his blatant flattery, so blinkered by her love for him that she had not heeded all the well-meant words of caution from nearly everyone in her acquaintance including her own family. The trusting, needy, idiot who did not even warrant the courtesy of a letter of her own from the treacherous scoundrel who had deflowered her, nor a mention in the one her brother had found. Written by the same duplicitous hands which had been all over her body only hours before. Charles must have known he was eloping when he had climbed into her bedroom window, but had used her regardless. Like the true libertine and shameless rake he was. Their fairy-tale courtship and all of his apparently heartfelt declarations whispered intimately in her virgin's bed stood for naught. It had all been a pack of lies and she had fallen for every single one.

Her hand automatically went to her belly again. All at once, the sickly smell of lilacs threatened to overpower her, or maybe it was the catastrophic ramifications of her now-dire situation. Or perhaps that was merely the bitter taste of humiliation and utter, complete betrayal. Total devastation. Willingly, she had given a man her tender, young heart and he had blithely returned it to her bludgeoned.

Shredded into irreparable pieces.

Chapter One

A London ballroom—St Nicholas's Day,
6th December 1820

Hal twisted the sprig of mistletoe idly between his fingers and took another cleansing breath of the cold night air. The heat in the tedious Renshaw ballroom was stifling, but then again, as it was quite the crush inside no doubt everyone would laud the evening as a resounding success. There was nothing guaranteed to cause more excitement in town than two hundred sweating aristocrats stuffed into their winter finery and all forcing themselves to be cheerful in deference to the season.

For Hal, it also signalled the start of a month of sheer hell, as now he was the Earl of Redbridge he would be expected to attend every single one of the festive functions between now and Twelfth

Night. It was, apparently, a Redbridge tradition, and the only one his mother was determined to continue even though her tyrannical husband was mouldering in the ground, and she had happily ignored all his other edicts since his death last year. In fact, she was so looking forward to it, Hal couldn't bring himself to complain, even though it culminated in him hosting the final, most opulent and eagerly anticipated ball of all at his Berkeley Square house on the sixth of January. Twelfth Night. The official end of the Christmas season.

In previous years, he had always managed to make a hasty exit from the short but frenetic festive season. He had danced and flirted with a few game girls, then disappeared to his club or to a gaming hell or to the bedchamber of whatever willing widow or wayward wife he happened to be enjoying at that particular time. Now he was stuck. Shackled by an ingrained sense of duty to his mother, who was enjoying life to the full now that she finally had her freedom and her period of mourning was over. Although like him, she hadn't seemed to mourn much. His father had been a mean-spirited, dictatorial curmudgeon who criticised absolutely everything his wayward children did. But he had made Hal's gentle mother's life a misery.

Hal had lost count of the number of times he had heard her crying, all alone in her bedchamber, because of yet another cruel or thoughtless thing his sire had done to her. However, if he went to her when she was crying, she would pretend nothing was amiss. 'Pay it no mind, Hal. Marriage is meant to be filled with trials and tribulations.' Something which did not make the prospect of it particularly enticing.

If he went to his father and called him on it, after the tirade of abuse which always accompanied such impertinence, his father would shrug it off as the way of things. A wife was a means of getting heirs. Nothing more. That duty discharged, they were merely doomed to tolerate each other. That was the inevitable way of things. And surely it was long past time Hal stopped sowing wild oats, settled down to do his duty to the house of Stuart and begat some heirs of his own to continue the legacy? And whilst he was about it, he needed to start learning about estate management and how to do *proper* business, which in his father's world usually meant ruining people and feasting off their carcasses in order to amass an even larger fortune than he already had.

'The world runs on coin, Henry, nothing else matters. Or do you intend to be a shocking and scandalous disappointment to me for ever?'

A silly question, seeing as Hal had no appetite for either cruelty or *proper* business. Instead, he had made it his life's mission to thoroughly disappoint his father at every given opportunity as a point of principal, and the single most thorough way of doing that was to be creating frequent scandals. Hal enjoyed the spectacle of his livid father's purple face as much as he did bedding a succession of wholly unsuitable, and gloriously unmarriageable, women. Reckless wagers at the card table came a close second. His father abhorred the careless use of good money on anything so frivolous and unpredictable. Money was for making more money to add to the heaps and heaps they had already, because money meant power and his father adored being powerful above all else. Even if that meant making everybody else miserable or his only son hate everything his father stood for. As the years passed, the gulf between the Earl and his scandalous only son had widened so much there might as well have been a whole ocean between them. A state of affairs which suited Hal just fine. Being scandalous had become so ingrained, such an intrinsic part of his own character, now his father was dead he actually *missed* misbehaving. It was as if a part of him was missing.

It was not the only thing in his life which had changed since he had inherited the title. He also had to run the enormous estate he now owned, something he never expected to relish, and the vast and varied business investments were a constant source of amusement. Because it turned out Hal had a natural talent for making more money by considering investment opportunities his father would never have dared touch, and without having to resort to those abhorrent *proper* business tactics his dreadful father had used, Hal had been feeling a trifle odd for months now. Yet could not quite put his finger on why.

The sad truth was simply having fun really wasn't fun any more. Since he had become the Earl of Redbridge he had found the gaming hells had lost their appeal, as had the bawdy widows and wayward wives. Instead, he found himself wanting to dive into his new ledgers rather than a willing woman's bed. He enjoyed reading the financial news and, to his utter dismay and total disgust, found the debates in the Lords fascinating. All the things his father had wanted him to take an interest in, the very things he had avoided resolutely for all of his twenty-seven years, now called to him and Hal was uncharacteristically inclined to listen. It was beyond disconcerting.

To begin with, he assumed this odd malaise was a temporary condition, brought about by the lack of need to vex his father and the shock of taking on his mantle, but the odd mood had persisted way beyond those unfamiliar, tentative first months. In fact, he hadn't been between anyone's sheets but his own in an age, and apparently out of choice rather than lack of opportunity. The last time he had engaged in a bit of bed sport, Hal had had to force himself and then found the whole interlude wholly unsatisfying. Almost as if something was missing although he could not say what. The widow had been passionate and lustful—two things he had always enjoyed in a woman—yet Hal had not been able to get out of her bed quickly enough and certainly had no intentions of ever going back to it. All in all, his lack of libido was becoming quite worrying. As was his lack of risky, devil-may-care behaviour.

If he did not find a way to combat it, Hal was in danger of turning into his cold, dour father and that would never do.

'Are you hoping to find a willing young lady on this terrace to steal a kiss from?' His brother-in-law, next-door neighbour and best friend in the world, Aaron Wincanton, Viscount Ardleigh, stared pointedly at the green sprig in Hal's hand. 'And if you are, should I make myself scarce? I can happily hide somewhere else if I am interrupting a potential tryst.' His friend held aloft two generously filled brandy glasses and did a poor job of blending into the background.

'By all means, join me. There is nobody here I want to kiss.' Too many seasons spent in too many ballrooms had made him quite jaded. Each crop of new debutantes seemed to become sillier than the previous ones, not one of them could converse on any topics other than the banal and he found their blatant, simpering new interest in him since he acquired his title irritating. Especially when they wouldn't give him the time of day beforehand. He had been far too scandalous. But now, he was an earl and they all wanted to be the one to give him his father's longed-for heirs.

'Oh, dear. Have things got that bad?'

'It's all right for you. You are no longer an eligible bachelor. You can breeze in and out of any ballroom unencumbered. I can scarcely make it to the refreshment table without some hungry young miss trying to get her matrimonial claws in me. And do not get me started on the mothers!'

'You are an earl, tolerably handsome, I am told, and a rich one to boot. I doubt you will need the mistletoe, I dare say most of them will happily kiss you quite enthusiastically without it. Even with your womanising reputation.' Hal groaned and stared mournfully in to his brandy, something which made his brother-in-law laugh. 'Is there really no one you find even slightly intriguing?'

'It is hard to be intrigued when they are all so frightfully eager.'

His friend nearly choked on his brandy. 'A travesty indeed! Poor you. All these eager women and no inclination to indulge.' Good grief! Had it become *that* obvious? Things were clearly direr than Hal had imagined if other people were beginning to notice, and that was beyond embarrassing. 'I think I know what ails you?'

'You do?'

'Yes, indeed. Your lack of interest in the opposite sex can easily be explained. You miss the thrill of the chase. We men are born with the inherent desire to hunt for what we need.'

'I hate hunting.' Hal's father had thoroughly enjoyed it and had forced his reluctant little boy to accompany him on far too many of them. He still recalled the first time he had seen a poor, terrified fox ripped to pieces by a pack of dogs and how frightened and appalled he had been when his father had soaked his handkerchief in the still-warm entrails and smeared the sticky blood all over Hal's face. A hunting tradition, apparently, and one he still could not understand. 'You know I hate hunting.'

Aaron rolled his eyes. 'Not foxes, you fool, women! You cannot deny you are a hunter of women. A lone and fearless predator. When they are all so depressingly eager and happy to fall at your feet, you miss the thrill of seducing them.'

'Perhaps.' Without thinking he turned his body to gaze through the windows back into the ballroom and watched the sea of swirling silk-clad young women on the dance floor to see if just one of them stood out to him and inspired him to go seduce them. Then sighed when none did.

'The trouble is,' his friend continued, far too

cheerfully for Hal's liking, 'you grew up with Connie.'

'And what, pray tell, does my tempestuous sister have to do with this?'

'She has set a standard you have come to expect from all women.'

'Are you suggesting I yearn for a foul-tempered, flouncing termagant of a woman? Because really, Aaron, I love my dear sister to distraction, but the idea of being married to someone similar terrifies me.' Not that he was looking for a wife. Heaven forbid! The idea of being shackled for life in matrimonial disharmony, like his parents, filled him with dread. Besides, he was still too young to sacrifice himself to the parson's trap. His father had often said all respectable gentlemen had a duty to be married before they were thirty. Hal had another three years to go to thwart that edict and had no immediate desire to become respectable. Not when he still had far too many wild oats to sow. And he would, as soon as he shook off his odd mood. He had every intention of making the man spin in his grave for a considerate amount of time as penance for being so awful. At least another decade.

'Fear not, it takes a *real* man to deal with a

woman like your sister and you are not in my league, dear fellow. What I mean is merely this. All those eager girls do not present a challenge to you, which is why you are so out of sorts.' He waved his hand dismissively in the direction of the dancers. 'Therefore I am prepared to set you an *interesting* challenge out of family loyalty, to restore some of your missing vigour. A bit of fun to liven up this laboriously festive social season for the both of us, seeing as Connie has decreed we spend it here with your mother, and your mother has such *exuberance* for society again. Wouldn't you relish a decent challenge? For our usual stakes, of course.'

'I suppose…' It was a sorry state of affairs if a man in his prime was without vigour, yet the plain and simple truth was Hal had not encountered a single woman in well over a year who did not bore him to tears. Even the unsuitable, corruptible ones he favoured were leaving him cold. Although he was prepared to concede fun would be good, if nothing else, as it had been a bit thin on the ground of late. 'What sort of challenge?'

'How many berries are on that sprig of parasitic vegetation you are clutching like an amulet?'

'Five—why?' Because Aaron had a particular gleam in his eye and as their usual stakes involved the loser mucking out the other's stables single-handed, or when in town just Hal's, as Aaron had cheerfully sold his house years before, he was understandably wary. Being bored and being consigned to shovelling excrement for his brother-in-law's amusement were two very different things entirely.

'Five berries equal the five separate kisses I challenge you to steal. Each one in a different location and all five before Twelfth Night. Let us call it The Mistletoe Wager, in a nod to the season.' Their bets always had names and there had been some momentous ones. The North Road Race. The Serpentine Swim. The Fisticuffs Experiment and the ill-conceived and often-lamented Naked Night in Norfolk, when they both nearly froze to death trying to brave the winter weather sitting out in the elements on the exposed beach of Great Yarmouth. They had hastily agreed to end that one early when they simultaneously lost feeling in their gentlemen's areas. The Mistletoe Wager certainly sounded a lot more pleasant than all its painful predecessors.

Hal felt himself grin at the thought. Five kisses! He could do that in his sleep. 'To be frank, I think it is only fair to point out I am so confident of my appeal, I believe you will be ensconced in my well-stocked stable tomorrow. Challenge accepted!'

'Hold your fire, my arrogant young friend. I have not set out my full terms yet. There is one more thing I must insist upon.'

'Which is?'

'I get to choose whom you have to kiss.'

Hal felt his eyes narrow suspiciously. 'No nuns. No dowagers or ladies in their dotage and for pity's sake spare me Lady Daphne Marsh. I must insist that the ladies selected have teeth! Rumour has it those clattering dentures she wears are made with teeth chiselled out of the corpses on the battlefield at Waterloo.'

'Really? I had heard they were carved out of a single walrus tusk… Either way, I agree they are distasteful.' Aaron held up his palm solemnly. 'You have my word. Only eligible, pretty ladies I would have chased after myself, before I had the great good fortune to be forced into marriage with your sister, qualify. What do you say? Shall we shake on it to seal the wager?'

For a few seconds Hal dithered, before he realised dithering was reminiscent of something his staid father would have done. 'On one condition. The ladies you choose can only be selected from within the very ballroom we are currently avoiding. Those are my particular terms.' That would ensure no ridiculous women were chosen. Aaron did like to best him and he would not put it past him to select five girls in the remotest corners of the British Isles just to vex him.

'Agreed!'

Hal thrust out his hand and the two men did their level best to out-shake and out-squeeze the other, as was their custom, for a solid thirty seconds before they stepped back. 'Five stolen kisses in five entirely different locations with five very lucky ladies.' He turned towards the French doors and grinned triumphantly. 'Choose away, dear brother. I feel guilty for accepting such a ridiculously easy bet.'

'Your arrogance astounds me! Do you honestly believe every proper young lady in that room would allow *you* to steal a kiss?'

Hal actually laughed, because really, it was just too funny. 'There will be no need for stealing, I can assure you. I am the single most eligible man at this ball. I am phenomenally wealthy, devilishly handsome, totally charming and, as you have quite rightly pointed out, I'm an *earl*. There isn't a young lady in that ballroom who would *not* welcome my advances. In fact, I dare say a few of them might try to steal a kiss from me with precious little effort on my part this very evening.' Which ironically was part of his current problem. They really were all so predictably eager.

'I refuse to believe you. As the father to two tenacious daughters and husband to a wife of supreme intelligence, I believe you are grossly underestimating the female sex. There must be at least a dozen young ladies currently in the ballroom who are in possession of good sense and taste, and thereby would never consider attaching their lips to yours.'

Hal watched with mounting amusement as Aaron carefully scanned the crowds, his frustration with the eager young ladies beyond becoming more apparent with every passing second. After a full minute, his intense perusal became a trifle desperate, then he straightened and nearly sighed with relief. When he turned back to Hal there was definite mischief in his expression, yet it did not daunt him. 'Who is the lucky first of the five?' Because he fully intended to pluck off one of those white mistletoe berries tonight in front of Aaron's eyes and then ceremonially place it in his hand.

'I don't recall stating there would be five different ladies, old boy.' Aaron was grinning smugly from ear to ear. It was a familiar tactic. Each time one of them proposed a ridiculous wager, the devil was in the detail of the language. Like attorneys they always quibbled about the minutiae of the terms. Hal went back over their conversation himself, preparing to counter, and experienced the first trickle of unease when he realised his irritatingly smug relative was right. There had been no mention of five *different* young ladies which shifted the parameters of the challenge significantly. To steal a kiss from a young lady once was a relatively simple task, by and large. More than that involved actual wooing and Hal had always been scrupulously careful about where and to whom he wooed. And Aaron knew it, too.

'I shall not be selecting five young ladies. In fact, there is only the one. All you need to do is find suitable opportunities and locations to kiss her five times.' He turned and pointed triumphantly through the condensation covered window to the solitary figure sat alone in a corner. 'I choose Lady Elizabeth Wilding.'

'Sullen Lizzie?'

'Now, now. You of all people should know how unfair nicknames can be here in the *ton*. Wasn't your own dear sister known as the Ginger Amazonian for years? A dreadful name which was most unfortunate. If people overhear you calling the poor girl that, the name might stick.'

Hal could almost smell the horse manure and realised he had been ambushed. 'As I recall, dear brother-in-law, it was you who gave my sister that unfortunate nickname, so don't try to use that against me. Besides, she *is* sullen. The sullenest woman in Mayfair. Why, she barely casts me a disdainful glance if we happen to pass on the street. You picked her on purpose, you snake! Everybody knows Lady Elizabeth Wilding loathes all men!'

'How can you say that when the chit was engaged once?'

'And callously called it off on the morning of her wedding without a thought to the poor groom's feelings!' Everyone remembered that juicy titbit of gossip. It had caused quite a scandal, from what he recalled, as the announcement was made to the congregation as they had waited for the bride and groom to take their vows.

'Marriage is for life, Hal. I believe it shows how sensible she is to have refrained from making the wrong choice. And even you have to concede that the dissolute Rainham was a bad choice. Nobody has seen the fellow in years—probably had to run away from all his creditors. *Brava* to her, I say. It hardly makes her a man-hater to have realised Rainham was a mistake at the last minute—merely choosy. When one has the largest dowry of any young lady in the *ton*, one has to be *very* careful.'

'Ha! By all accounts the dowry is so sweet because her personality is so sour. Her poor father must be so desperate to marry her off to have offered such a ridiculous sum. How many Seasons has she been out now?' Hal prodded Aaron in the chest. 'I shall tell you. Too many and that in itself tells me everything I need to know. Even with the dowry she is resolutely dour. She has not, to the best of my knowledge, entertained the overtures of a suitor in years. Her mouth curls in distaste every time she converses with a single gentleman. And when was the last time she accepted an invitation to dance?' Sullen Lizzie positively glared at any fellow brave enough to get within ten feet of her. Despite her famed beauty, Hal had never bothered being one of them. Gently bred young ladies with pristine reputations were not his type and he sincerely doubted scandalous earls were hers. Kissing the frosty Lady Elizabeth once would be a huge achievement. Managing to do it five times would be a miracle.

'Are you conceding the challenge then, because if you are I shall send a note to my stable master immediately, instructing him to cease all shovelling for the night. I want you to have a decent pile in the morning. We did shake on the wager, after all, and I must remind you that you are both a gentleman and a peer of the realm, and as such duty bound to honour your word. It is a great shame, though. I had hoped you were made of sterner stuff. Lady Elizabeth is a very beautiful woman and, as you previously stipulated, one who is in possession of all of her own teeth.'

Male pride, Hal mused, was a dangerous thing. Everything about the wager told him he would lose so why bother. However, a bigger, primal part of him wanted to best his cocky friend and in truth Lady Elizabeth was a stunningly beautiful woman and it would be no great hardship to kiss her. Unsociable. Unapproachable. Unreachable. Very definitely a challenge for only the finest, most skilled of hunters, and only where women were concerned he was undoubtedly that. 'I wouldn't dream of conceding.'

He watched Aaron's face fall before staring back at him stunned. 'Really? Are you completely sure?' And now his friend sounded nervous, as if he regretted his own choice, too, but was also too stubborn to back down.

'I shall kiss Sullen Lizzie five times in five different locations before Twelfth Night. And you, Aaron, are going to move a veritable mountain once I win and I am going to crack open a bottle of my finest port and watch, gloating, while you do it!' The more he thought about it, the more Hal was convinced Lady Elizabeth Wilding was the perfect candidate to test his superior powers of seduction on. At least she wasn't eager and surely that had to be a point in her favour. Hal would have to be resourceful and tenacious. Like a hunter of old. Already, he could feel the previously sluggish, hot male blood coursing through his veins at the prospect. He clinked his glass against his flabbergasted friend's.

'Let the Mistletoe Wager commence!'

Chapter Two

Lizzie gazed wistfully at the ormolu clock on the Renshaws' opulent fireplace and stifled a groan when she saw the time. It would be at least another hour before her father relented and allowed her to summon the carriage. His insistence that she maintain this silly façade after five long years was beyond tiresome. Initially, he had insisted she return to society to maintain appearances. Her continued presence gave credence to the lie that she had chosen to terminate her engagement to Rainham, as was a woman's prerogative, and therefore she had nothing to be ashamed of. It was necessary, he explained, to keep her scandalous, dirty secret a secret.

Back then, she had readily agreed to keep her baby a secret and spare her family the scandal. The wonderful Wildings had rallied around her, fiercely protective, and their loyalty was something she would always be grateful for. So many girls 'in trouble' were cast out and shunned by their families, even more had to suffer the horrendous grief of giving up their child and never seeing or daring to mention the poor thing again. Fortunately, she had been spared both of those ordeals. For the first year she stayed largely at the family estate in Cheshire with her brother, his wife and their young son Frederick, venturing back into town to keep up the necessary appearances when the need arose, but after her mother had died, Lizzie and George were summoned back to Mayfair to live with her father, something she had agreed to do temporarily because she could not stand the thought of him being all alone.

Aside from the bothersome London Season and the shorter Christmas one, where she was forced into a society which would instantly turn on her if they were ever appraised of the truth, she got to live her life exactly as she wanted to.

Almost.

Yet to all intents and purposes, little George did not exist outside their Mayfair house. Small children, it turned out, were very easy to conceal from the prying eyes of the world. For the longest time it had been surprisingly easy to behave in public as if nothing untoward was going on. Back when he was a baby, Lizzie had only been too pleased to comply. It would have caused the most horrendous scandal for both their family and the Government to have done otherwise. As the most senior man at the Foreign Office, the King's chief advisor on the delicate art of global diplomacy, her father had to be seen to be above reproach and she had not wanted to bring his ambitions to a shuddering halt because of her foolish indiscretion. She had returned to society after her clandestine confinement and nobody was any the wiser. All in all, they had done such a good job that even now, remarkably, her pristine reputation was still intact and, to all intents and purposes, she was just another single young lady on the marriage mart.

Except she wasn't.

Despite her father's steadfast refusal to give up the hope Lizzie would find a suitable man to marry, there was nothing which would ever tempt her to take a trip down the aisle again. Once bitten, twice shy, and Lizzie had been bitten too hard. So hard she was certain she still bore the treacherous Rainham's teeth marks. From the outset, she had rebelled against her papa's misguided belief she would soon snare another man who could be convinced, or bribed by his powerful father-in-law, into claiming the new-born child as his own. Instead, she actively repelled any man who dared to come within six feet of her. And, for good measure, any woman, too. The last thing she needed was allowing anyone to get too close, just in case she inadvertently let slip something which might embarrass her family or, more importantly, bring unwarranted shame and censure on her son.

Heaven forbid she would consider the alternative and marry a man who was shallow enough to be bribed to take on her child. Georgie deserved better than that and Lizzie would never allow him to be an inconvenience to a husband who would prefer her delightful little boy did not exist at all. As a wife, she would be bound by her husband's edicts. What if Georgie was banished to boarding school or some remote property to be brought up by strangers? Unloved and all alone. She would protect him from that with the last breath in her body. No, indeed. The very last thing she could ever risk, for the sake of her beautiful boy, was marriage.

However, her dear papa refused to acknowledge her fears or that the trusting, foolish girl she had been had died the day Rainham had jilted her. What had emerged from the wreckage was a stronger, harder woman who would never be seduced into the merry dance of courtship again, no matter how charming or handsome her would-be suitor was. If she could thank the scoundrel Marquess for something, other than the fruit of his lying, deceitful loins, then it would be for opening her eyes to the harsh realities of life. Lizzie had been a hopeless dreamer then; now she was a realist. Her papa called it pessimism. It was much better to always expect the worst, that way you were guaranteed never to be disappointed. Being at the mercy of fate, or fickle men, was not a situation she would ever allow again.

And, on the subject of plans, soon she would put her most audacious one into action. This would be her last foray into polite society. One more month of maintaining this ridiculous charade for the sake of propriety, and her dear papa's career, before she withdrew from the *ton* for ever. Georgie was not a baby any more. He could run around, talk and asked an increasing amount of questions about everything, the most consistent one causing her the most sleepless nights. *Where is my papa?* There was only so long her darling boy would accept her blithe answer of *far, far away* without complaint, yet she knew she was being unfair to him by keeping him the dark.

Her little boy needed to go to school and experience the sort of childhood all little boys deserved. He needed to play outside, not be restricted to twice-weekly jaunts to Richmond Park with his mother. The infrequent visits with her brother's son were not enough and, as good a grandpapa as her dear father was to George, or no matter how many hours he spent playing with him, her son needed to be with children his own age, not adults. She wanted him to grow up feeling confident and secure in who he was. It was hardly his fault he was the Wildings' dirty little secret.

Her dirty little secret.

After Christmas was done and dusted, and after she had found the right words to tell her beloved father of her decision, Lizzie was going to leave the sheltered safety of their Mayfair house. The spacious cottage in Yorkshire had already been purchased in the name of Mrs Smith with the small inheritance she had been left from her grandmother and via an attorney sworn to secrecy. It was already decorated and comfortably furnished in readiness. The well-paid attorney had seen to that, too. In a few short weeks, Lizzie would, to all intents and purposes, cease to be Lady Elizabeth Wilding for as much of her life as possible.

Instead, she would pretend to be a young widow—lord knew there were enough of them thanks to the carnage of decades of war—and Georgie would grow up like a normal boy, free from the stain of illegitimacy. Nobly fatherless because of Napoleon. Just the two of them. In quiet, peaceful, utter bliss. No more questions. No more lies—all bar that one.

Even so, she dreaded telling her father. He had stepped into the breach all those years ago and still believed his protection was necessary, until she learned to trust again and found a man to relieve him of the duty. Hence, she was at the Renshaw Ball at her misguided papa's request, miserable and beyond bored, and would no doubt have to attend all manner of so-called similar entertainments for the next, interminable, miserable month.

In desperation, he had even taken to approaching potential husbands on her behalf. Sensible, staid men who were nothing but upright and no doubt he had significantly inflated her dowry as bait. Luring them with the enticing scent of money, encouraging them to come and talk or ask her to dance. Refusing to believe her insistence that she was done with men and never wanted another one, no matter how dull, staid and annoyingly persistent the fellows he selected were.

So pathetically, because she could not bear to hurt her papa's feelings, she was hiding in the furthest chairs reserved for the most committed of wallflowers, attempting to be invisible. A sorry state of affairs, indeed, but easier than upsetting her father with yet another argument.

Why couldn't he see that time was running out and the scandal he had vehemently suppressed for years was in danger of blowing wide open? They could not keep George sequestered in the house for ever, or wire his talkative mouth shut, and hell would have to freeze over before she would allow the rest of society to judge her innocent baby based on the circumstances of his birth. Lizzie would never regret George, regardless of how he had come to be in her life, and she was so very tired of hiding him. Poor Papa. His eagerness to find her a husband was beginning to drive a wedge between them and that broke her heart as well. The last five years of nonsense could not be allowed to continue much longer.

'A penny for your thoughts?'

The deep male voice from behind startled her, yet Lizzie hid it instinctively. Sometimes, particularly arrogant young bucks still attempted to flirt with her for sport. Something which was always ruthlessly nipped in the bud. A slow, calculated glance to the side revealed Henry Stuart, the newly minted Earl of Redbridge. Handsome as sin and with a sinful reputation to match. She did not bother hiding her irritation at recognising him.

'Do not trouble yourself, my lord. I can assure you that whatever misguided impulse sent you my way, it was most assuredly futile. I am in no mood to engage in polite conversation or anything else this evening.' She flicked her eyes back towards the dance floor and turned her body away from his, allowing the uncomfortable seconds to tick by. Men were like wasps. If you ignored them, they eventually went away.

She heard the slight creaking protest of wood and realised he had eased his big body into the chair alongside. She gave him her best unwelcoming frown and curtest tone. 'I do not recall inviting you to sit.' This insect clearly needed swatting.

Looking decidedly bored, the Earl glanced at the rows of empty chairs around them and shrugged. 'These seats have been expressly placed here by our hostess to rest upon. I do not recall being told I needed anyone's permission to sit in them. Please ignore me, Lady Elizabeth and, in turn, I shall ignore you as you have made it quite plain you would prefer me to. Believe me, there are a million places I would rather be as well.'

As she could think of no immediate retort to such blatant indifference, Lizzie stared resolutely at the dance floor and her unwelcome companion did the same. Neither spoke. After a full five minutes, she actively considered standing and moving to the opposite side of the room. His continued presence rattled her, although she could not say why. Men did not linger when they had been rejected. As a rule. But moving would alert him to her discomfort and that would never do. 'You can sit there all night. I still will not talk to you.'

'Yet here you are, talking regardless.' He stifled a yawn. 'Fear not, fair maiden, like you, I am hiding. I find these events tiresome.'

'There are many other places to hide, my lord,

perhaps you should retire to one of those and leave me in peace. I was here first and, in case I have not made it obvious enough, I am not desirous of either your company or your attentions.'

Only his eyes turned to look at her and they were inscrutable. Very green. Very bored. 'Clearly you have an inflated sense of your own appeal if you have construed my sitting as evidence of my interest in you.' Lizzie instantly smarted at the insult, yet quashed the urge to show it. She could hardly go around dismissing men curtly from her presence, then become offended when one was blessedly uninterested.

'I should still prefer you to sit elsewhere.'

'Believe me, under normal circumstances I would be only too happy to comply with your request. However, drastic times call for drastic measures. I find myself in the unpleasant position of *having* to endure your company and, as I have specifically chosen to sit with you, you might try to be a little honoured by the accolade.'

'Honoured?' Despite the affront, he did, devil take him, have her intrigued. 'And why, pray tell, do you *have* to endure me of all people, when there is a positive ocean of other, more agreeable people here to annoy?'

He gave the room a dismissive scan, then his sea-green eyes locked with hers far more impertinently than any eyes had in quite some time. 'May I be brutally frank with you, Lady Elizabeth?'

He was still regarding her blandly and, much as it pained her, Lizzie nodded. 'Honesty? From a renowned rake? This I have to hear.'

He heaved an irritated sigh, although clearly more at his own situation than at her rudeness, and stared at the dance floor with an expression of complete distaste. 'Since I came into the earldom, I find myself in the hideous position of being *eligible*. Earls, apparently, need wives, and there are a vast number of eager candidates for the position keen to push themselves forward—I confess, I am finding it all rather tiresome.'

'From what I know of your reputation, sir, I would have thought you would relish so much *opportunity*.'

His dark brows drew together and his top lip wrinkled in disgust. 'Opportunity? Are you quite mad, Lady Elizabeth? The only opportunity this whole sorry situation offers me is the opportunity to be caught soundly in the parson's trap! A place, I can assure you, I have no desire to be. Any decent rake worth his salt does not dally with *nice* girls. Everybody knows that!' He shuddered and Lizzie found herself smiling before she stopped herself. At least he *was* being honest.

'All very tragic, yet I am still none the wiser as to why you have singled out this particular corner of the ballroom to hide in, or more specifically why you have to endure being here. With me. Or why I should feel *honoured* in the process.'

He lent sideways to whisper, as if he were imparting some great secret, and his warm breath tickled her ear. It was, surprisingly, a wholly pleasant sensation. 'It is well known, my dear lady, that your *charming* disposition and *sociable* nature are not for the faint hearted. Especially during this joyous festive season.' She watched the hint of a smile linger for a moment on his face, a hint of a smile which was every bit as roguish as he was, saw his broad chest rise, then fall slowly under his crossed, irritatingly muscled arms and felt her pulse flutter at the magnificent sight of him. Her bizarre reaction made her scowl at him in anger. Something which obviously amused him greatly, because the half-smile turned into a full rakish grin, and to her complete shame, that grin did strange things to her insides.

'You have *quite* the reputation, Lady Elizabeth,

thank goodness, as I cannot tolerate people *without* a bad reputation. All that goodness makes me nervous. However, I digress, it is your reputation for ill-humoured and barely concealed dislike of polite society which I am in dire need of. A deterrent, as it were. *You*, madam, are the perfect foil for a man in my position. A sullen shield to defend me against my hordes of eager admirers. Nobody will dare to come and talk to me when I am sat here with you. I shall be spared every crushing bore, every ambitious mama and every nimble, nubile, pathetically eager yet dreadfully dull, potential bride.'

When he had first approached her, Hal was determined to charm her out of her perpetual frown. However, at the very last moment he had realised the beautiful and frosty Lizzie would probably be immune to such overt flattery. With her pale golden hair and cornflower-blue eyes, she must have heard every compliment ever uttered and, as Aaron had warned, she was definitely a woman far too intelligent to be won over by flowery words.

At the last second he had changed tack, because he always came up with the best ideas on the hop, and failed to be charming and was now very glad that he had. It had been exactly the right move and one which cemented his belief in his ability to understand women better than most men. Sullen Lizzie was responding to his casual uninterest with far more interest than he had ever witnessed her display before, when really he was only being honest.

Sort of.

He *was* finding the hordes of admirers tiresome and he genuinely *did* have no intention of marrying any time soon, what with all the wild oats which had so vexed his father still in urgent need of sowing whilst he diligently avoided being respectable.

Her pretty blue eyes, which had been narrowed in annoyance just a few minutes ago, regarded him with wary curiosity. 'Have you been encouraged to come speak to me at the bequest of my father?'

'Not at all. I cannot recall the last time I had cause to speak to the Earl of Upminster.' An interesting snippet. Clearly her father disapproved of her solitary tendencies if he was actively directing suitors towards her. 'I take it he is trying to marry you off?' For effect, he scrunched up his face at the word marry and, without thinking, she nodded before she stopped herself. The change was quite spectacular. Her slim shoulders stiffened and her back straightened. Her eyes went icy blue. Her expression became bland. Cold. Even her character seemed to withdraw deep inside herself until all that was left was determined, stony indifference. It was like watching the drawbridge go up on a castle. Hal could not remember a time when he had spoken to a woman quite so…guarded before. Getting past all her layers of defences was not going to be easy and already his conscience was niggling him that something about this situation was very wrong, but a wager was a wager and, if nothing else, he needed to prove something to himself as well as to Aaron. 'My father used to drive me mad with his demands that I marry.' More truth. What the blazes had got into him?

'I notice you managed to resist him.'

'As have you.'

'My father means well.' There was a note of exasperation in her tone. He watched her lovely eyes wander towards the Earl of Upminster and soften instinctively at the sight of him. There was love there. Loyalty. Then he noticed the way she winced when her father grinned back encouragingly. Clearly he assumed the fact she was talking to a man was a good sign. Even if the man happened to be him. Without realising it, she had shown Hal her Achilles' heel. 'He just does not understand…' She stopped herself. Her plump lips sealed in a flat line.

'He just does not understand that you are not inclined towards marriage. Most people do not understand such a thing could be possible, I suppose, especially for a woman, when procuring a husband is meant to be at the very top of her list of priorities.'

'It does not even feature on my list of priorities.' This was said with such fierceness she quite forgot to put her guard up for a moment. There was fire beneath all the ice, too. Interesting.

'Mine either. No doubt I shall have to succumb one day. Produce the obligatory heir and a spare, but I am only twenty-seven and far too young to settle down.'

'Hence you are using me as a shield to ward off the eager hordes.' The ghost of a smile touched her lips and Hal experienced a strange flutter in his chest at being the cause of it. For some reason, he sensed the stare of another and, when he looked towards it, saw her father watching their interactions like a hawk. 'I wish I had a shield to protect me from my father's enthusiasm for finding me suitors. But alas, he is beyond determined and I fear I am doomed to suffer regardless.'

'Perhaps I can return the favour?' The words were out before he could stop them. However, the opportunity was there, ripe for the picking, and a true seducer took advantage of the moment. Thinking on his feet. 'I notice your father appears to be interested in you talking to me.'

The shutters came down again and her expression became unreadable. 'He will get over it.'

Tread carefully, Hal. 'I think it is fairly safe to say we both have an aversion to marriage. Your father wants you to find a man and half of this ballroom wants me to be the man for them. Why don't we form an alliance against them all?'

'I am not sure I follow, my lord.'

'The way I see it, this dreadful Christmas season is stuffed with potentially awkward and bothersome social functions which we are both duty-bound to attend. Your father is going to bore you with a succession of would-be suitors and, because my mother is determined to enjoy life and I must be her escort, I am going to have to spend a great many hours hiding from the hordes on freezing terraces, if tonight's experiences are anything to go by. Therefore, why don't we pretend to be interested in one another? Your father will be thrilled you have selected a suitor of your own accord, thus one would hope he will leave you alone to allow romance to blossom, and your legendary sullen disposition and my most *obvious* attentions towards you will deter other young ladies from coming after me. And at the very least, we will both have someone like-minded to talk to during all those long interminable hours of enforced gaiety. These affairs can be so dreadfully dull.'

Hal allowed the silence to stretch as he watched her mull over his proposal. To his complete surprise, he did feel a little guilty at how he was trying to manipulate her, but that was far outweighed by the benefits of their unlikely partnership. Even if he lost the bet, which of course he wouldn't, Lady Elizabeth would be an effective deterrent from all those eager young ladies and that, in itself, would make the next month far less painful even if he did end up having to take up the shovel.

'No, thank you, my lord.'

'I wouldn't be so quick to dismiss it out of hand if I were you. Such an arrangement benefits both of us and I suspect the pair of us would rub along quite well. We are both obviously jaded and have a healthy disregard for all this nonsense around us. Think of all the fun we could have.'

'I said no!' The barricade went up again and this time it was unyielding. She sat stiffly, staring away from Hal resolutely. Their brief, enlightening conversation was clearly at an end. Something about her demeanour made him reluctant to push further. He had the distinct feeling if he continued to attempt to whittle down her defences he would do more harm than good. Sullen Lizzie was going to be a stubbornly tough nut to crack and therefore Hal would have to use subtle persistence to get her to voluntarily lower the drawbridge rather than a battering ram to breach the enormous walls she had placed around herself. He sat quietly beside her. Just in case she had a change of heart.

After an age, she stood and he watched, fascinated, as her eyes once again sought her father. The sigh of frustration was audible when the Earl of Upminster beamed at her expectantly across the room and beckoned to her to come and meet the gentleman stood ramrod-straight and eager at his elbow. A far more suitable and sensible suitor than Hal.

'Are you sure I cannot tempt you into an alliance?'

Her step faltered and it was then that he realised he might still stand a chance. 'Absolutely not. The idea is preposterous.' But she was tempted. And for now, that was enough.

Chapter Three

Her father could barely contain his excitement in the carriage ride home. 'Although your choice of fellow leaves a great deal to be desired, it was encouraging to see you finally talking to a gentleman, Lizzie. Are you finally warming to the idea of courting again?'

Of course she wasn't, but she could see the benefits of the outrageous proposal. Having a pretend beau would certainly make the next month bearable. Perhaps refusing him had been a hasty decision? And then again, she had survived five interminable Seasons and five miserable Christmases by herself; she could jolly well manage one last month on her own. 'It was a conversation, Papa. Please do not read anything more into it than that. I am quite indifferent to the Earl of Redbridge's charms.'

Besides, Lizzie had already decided never to converse with the man again despite the allure of a month of peace. He had been far too solid and too tall, smelled far too nice and, for some inexplicable reason, he interested her in a way no man had since her traitorous former fiancé. The lack of charm and flattery had been refreshing. A little too refreshing, and she had found herself breaking her own rules by talking to him. And he was astute. He had immediately worked out her father wanted her to wed, yet he had understood her reluctance to comply. Without thinking, Lizzie had let things slip unguarded out of her mouth. At one point, she had to remind herself midsentence that Henry Stuart was cut from the same cloth as Rainham. A handsome rake. A charmer. Something worth bearing in mind when her pulse kept racing every time he had gazed down at her. As soon as she had reassured herself she was still uninterested, talking to him had been almost entertaining.

Almost. Which was a worry.

The man had a very impertinent way of conversing with her which she had decided she did not like. Leaning close and talking in that hushed, deep whisper had made several pairs of nosy eyes stare at them intently. Something which was made all the more uncomfortable by the irritating fact the whispering had been unsettling, too. Lizzie had not been that close to a man since the last time her wretched former fiancé had scrambled down the wisteria and had no desire to ever be again. Unfortunately, her traitorous body seemed to have other ideas and had covered itself in hundreds of goose bumps when his lips had hovered close to her ear. She sincerely doubted her unexpected reaction had anything to do with the Earl of Redbridge, more likely they were caused by five years of blissful isolation from all things male.

'I know it was just a conversation, Lizzie, however as it was the first conversation you have deigned to grant a man of your own accord in years, and because I saw you smiling once or twice, you will forgive me for marking its significance. Regardless of your indifference towards Redbridge—which I heartily approve of, by the way—your change of heart towards the opposite sex *in general* warms mine. Who knows? You might meet a nice man whom you are not indifferent towards. I know plenty of sterling fellows who would suit you perfectly. One more suitable than Redbridge, of course, as his reputation is unacceptable.' His face clouded briefly as they both inadvertently thought of Rainham. 'I want you to marry, Lizzie. Someone safe and dependable. I promised your mother on her death bed that I would see you settled with a good man after what that blackguard did to you. We both hoped you would find someone sooner rather than later.'

'But I have no desire to marry anyone, Papa. Mama would understand if she could see how happy Georgie is. Throwing a new husband into the mix at this stage in his life would unsettle him.'

'The boy needs a father.'

'No. He doesn't. And certainly not one who would tolerate him at best, or hide him away on some distant estate at worst. Forgive me for disagreeing—but he does not need a father. He has a wonderful grandfather instead.'

She watched his eyes go all misty for a moment before he cleared his throat to try to disguise his emotion by pretending to clear away a speck of imaginary dust. 'But I am not getting any younger. You know how much I worry about you being left all alone in the world when I am gone.' The guilt turned sour in her mouth. He would be devastated when she finally plucked up the courage to tell him she intended to be all alone sooner rather than later and would leave him all alone in the process. They would visit, of course, but it would hardly be the same. 'And the right husband would bring my grandson up as his own. I would make it a stipulation in the settlements.'

Wouldn't that be dandy? Poor Georgie's place in his mother's house would be an enforced legality and no doubt the source of a great deal of resentment. 'Does that honestly strike you as the best outcome? Because it doesn't to me. I am quite capable of looking after myself and my son unaided, Papa. I do wish you would stop worrying about us.'

'Tell me, Lizzie, as a parent yourself, can you ever envisage a time when you will not be concerned with little Georgie's welfare?' He had her there. Probably never was the answer. 'Now be a good daughter and indulge this old man for once. I know what is good for you and I refuse to give up on your mother's last wish. You deserve the love of a good man.' He patted her hand affectionately, his mind made up regardless.

As always. Exactly why she had been forced to go behind his back.

'I have high hopes of this festive season. High

hopes indeed.' He had kissed her cheek and practically skipped up the stairs to bed. A very bad sign as he had that twinkle in his eye. The one which he always got when he was intent on matchmaking and, as he had only recently increased her dowry, his buoyant mood did not bode well.

More guilt was piled on afresh and she spent all night questioning the logic of her impulsive decision to refuse Redbridge. Such a bargain only served to give her father hope where none existed and that seemed cruel. Being duplicitous, although it was something she had been forced to do for five long years, was not something which sat well with her, especially when she was doing it to her family rather than the rest of the world. However, her father's attempts at marrying her off were becoming overt in the extreme. Very overt and very extreme. He meant well, she reminded herself. He meant well and he loved her. For that alone she would grit her teeth and endure whatever challenges he threw at her in their final month with as much good grace as she could muster.

Lizzie managed to catch about two hours of sleep before she was woken at dawn by her maid with a steaming cup of chocolate and a report of the weather. 'It's freezing outside, my lady, but it doesn't look like rain.'

'Can you tell the nanny to ensure little Georgie is bundled up against the cold and tell her to inform him if he refuses to put on his gloves again then he will not be flying his kite. And I am sure they have already thought of it, but check the carriage is packed with a few extra blankets.' Knowing her son, he would get cold once he had tired himself out dashing around Richmond Park and if he was too chilly he would not nap on the way home. Something which always made him surly in the afternoons.

As it was every Tuesday and Thursday morning, breakfast was on the table before seven and Georgie was already bouncing in his chair with excitement. 'Come along, young man. Eat your porridge. You know your mama will not leave until the bowl is empty.' Her father was an indulgent grandparent and insisted on eating with them every morning, even if that meant getting up twice a week at such an ungodly hour.

The drive to Richmond took over an hour and the streets were nicely deserted at such an unsociable hour. As the remote park would be, too. Lizzie would be able to spend a blissful few hours outdoors with her son miles away from London and away from prying eyes and be safely back home by early afternoon when the fashionable residents of Mayfair went out. They had visited the huge parkland at Richmond twice weekly for the last six months for the sake of both her own and her son's sanity. It was not as if the pair of them could wander around Hyde Park or St James's. Georgie had never been to either in case he was seen and the scandal erupted. He loved to run free in the countryside, loved to explore wooded nooks and crannies and delighted in all God's creatures, whether that be the smallest woodlouse or the majestic red deer that roamed wild in the open parkland of Richmond.

Soon he would be able to do this every single day and as happy as that prospect made her, it was bittersweet. Part of the reason her son enjoyed these jaunts so very much was regaling the excursion in great detail to his grandpapa afterwards. As soon as they arrived home, her son would boisterously run into her father's study, clamber on his knee and describe every beetle, every twig, the exact strength of the breeze and the hue of the sky. Then he would lie for at least an hour under her father's desk while the pair of them worked in companionable silence—her father on important affairs of state; Georgie sketching childish depictions of animals in the expensive coloured chalks his grandpapa had bought him for that express purpose. She was dreading telling them those days were now numbered, despite the fact it was ultimately for the best.

Her son shovelled in the last spoonful of porridge. 'Come along, Mama! I hope we see the deer again today. Do you know that the Latin name for the red deer is *cervus elaphus*? Grandpapa found it in one of his books. They mainly eat grass and twigs—but apparently they are also partial to moss.'

'Really? Well, that is interesting. What else did you learn about them?' She wrestled him into his coat, then took his hand. Listening to his incessant, excited chatter Lizzie resolutely banished all thoughts of her father's meddling and the Earl of Redbridge's increasingly tempting offer from her mind.

Aaron had been gloating over breakfast. As soon as the ladies left them to their newspapers, he had grinned smugly across the table and recounted the magnificent way Lady Elizabeth

Wilding had given him short shrift at the Renshaw ball. 'All that practised charm, your fortune, title and apparent good looks did nothing to sway the lady. You do not stand a chance of winning this bet, Hal. You have no idea what a good mood that puts me in.'

Hal took it all gracefully, but seethed inside. Aaron took the word competitive to new levels and was a gloating victor. The best Christmas present Hal could give to himself was the splendid sight of his brother-in-law wielding a shovel and, by Jove, he had to do whatever it took to ensure it happened. Sullen Lizzie had been interested in his proposition. He had seen it with his own eyes and an alliance between them was the best way forward to fulfil the terms of the Mistletoe Wager. All he had to do was convince her of the benefits. There was a chance that might be better achieved in private than in a public social setting.

An hour later he found himself striding jauntily up the front steps of the Earl of Upminster's Grosvenor Square town house, a house which had always been but a stone's throw from his own, but might have well been on the moon for all the dealings he had had with its occupants, an enormous bunch of flowers in his arms.

He rapped the brass knocker smartly and stood tall, his most charming smile firmly in place and his thick hair freshly combed. The large, imposing butler was a bit of a shock. The fellow looked more suited to prize fighting than domestic service. He positively filled the door frame. 'Good morning. I have come to call on Lady Elizabeth. Please tell her I am here.' Hal handed over his calling card, but kept the flowers. He wanted to see her face when she saw those as he had picked the blooms specifically.

'Lady Elizabeth is not at home, my lord. I shall tell her that you called.' The heavy front door began to close.

'Now, now, my good man, we both know how this game is played. It is barely eleven o'clock so I am sure she *is* home. Nobody goes out this early. Not in Mayfair.' Unless they were on the hunt for the perfect bunch of flowers to give to a guarded yet intriguing occupant of this very house. Hal had had to travel to Covent Garden directly after breakfast for the cream roses. 'Inform Lady Elizabeth that I intend to remain rooted to this front step until she grants me an audience.'

The giant butler sighed. 'Suit yourself, sir, although I must warn you, it will be a waste of your time. Lady Elizabeth is *genuinely* not at home this morning.' The door went to close again and Hal began to suspect that the man might be telling the truth.

'Can you tell me where she is then?'

'I am afraid not, my lord.'

'Will she be back this afternoon?'

'Yes, my lord. However, she is never *at home* in the afternoons, if you get my meaning.' The butler stared impassively. 'Nor will she be at home tomorrow morning as she is never *at home* in the mornings either.'

'Then you admit that she is, as I suspect, currently *at home* as we speak, yet resolutely *not at home* to all callers regardless as to who they might happen to be.'

'Not at all, my lord. Lady Elizabeth is *genuinely* not at home on Tuesday and Thursday mornings, and not at home *any* other time.'

This clearly called for a different tactic. 'Can I ask what your name is?'

'You can, my lord. I am Stevens, his lordship's butler.'

'You are a vexing fellow, Stevens.'

'I do try, my lord.'

Hal dipped his hand into his pocket and fished out the silver crown he always kept there for emergencies. Covertly, beneath the enormous bouquet he held, Hal flashed the coin at the butler. 'Be a good chap and tell Lady Elizabeth I am here to see her.'

Stevens glanced down at the coin, scowled and promptly closed the door. Hal couldn't help admiring him for it. He liked a man who could not be bribed, it said a great deal about his character. But not all men were as moral, so he wandered around to the mews instead.

However, it soon became apparent that the Earl of Upminster had possibly the most moral staff in Mayfair. With his bribes increasing from a crown to a guinea to a colossal five pounds, he was similarly turned down by the stable boys, a footman and scullery maid who had been sent out to buy beeswax. In fact, their lips were sealed tighter than Stevens's, who had at least informed Hal she was *genuinely* out and would be back this afternoon—although not for him.

That left him with a bit of a quandary. He was too tenacious to give up, but too lazy to stand guard in the square until she came home. Living less than a sedate ten-minute walk away he did not have to. This afternoon suggested *after* midday and *later* this afternoon suggested after one. He would stand guard from one, bouquet in hand, and meet her when she arrived home. She could hardly tell him she was not at home when facing him, could she?

The Upminster carriage turned in to the square a little past two to Hal's enormous relief. Over an hour of sentry duty in December had rendered his feet and fingers frozen solid, but the expensive flowers thankfully still looked impressive as he walked towards the holly-wreathed front door to greet her.

However, the carriage did not slow and sped past him, its elusive occupant hidden from his view by the tightly drawn curtains, and turned down towards the mews. Hal quickly followed, rounding the corner just in time to see the impressively tall, wooden rear gates slam shut. Frustrated, he dashed back to the front door and knocked again.

After an age, Stevens opened it.

'I know she is at home Stevens, I just saw the carriage return. Kindly tell her I am here.'

'Lady Elizabeth has been made aware of your

presence, my lord, and of the fact you have been loitering outside for most of the day. She has asked me to convey a message and was most particular it was issued verbatim.' For effect, he coughed gently, then scowled and bellowed, 'Go away, Redbridge! You are as welcome as a dog with fleas.'

'She said that?'

'She did, my lord. And in that exact tone.'

'Ah.' Seeing as his only option was to try and overpower the butler, something which he was not entirely certain he could do and which would ruin the line of Hal's coat significantly, he had no choice but to admit defeat. 'Can you see that Lady Elizabeth gets these, Stevens.' He thrust the flowers forward. 'And as you are so good at delivering messages verbatim, would you kindly tell her exactly this. My *tempting* invitation still stands.' He winked at the giant saucily and watched the big man's eyes widen. 'Please make sure you wink, Stevens, as that is part of the message, too. Good day to you. It has been a pleasure.'

Chapter Four

The following evening, within half an hour of their arrival at the Benfleet soirée, Lizzie's resolve not to argue with her father lifted surprisingly swiftly and was soon replaced with raging, clawing anger. Because this time, her dear, meddling papa had gone too far.

'I have taken the liberty of filling your dance card for you.'

He had said this so blithely, in the midst of a crowd, which made calling him on it impossible. He had also made sure her partner for the next dance was stood right next to him as well, effectively trapping her because the calculated old politician knew full well she would rather not cause a scene. The 'lucky' gentleman, a slightly rotund fellow with no discernible chin, appeared terrified as he held out his hand, making it obvious to one and all he had been press-ganged into service and was there only on sufferance. She was tempted to feel sorry for him.

With gritted teeth, she allowed him to lead her to the dance floor, all the while shooting daggers at her father. Once this dance was done, they would be having words, and when those words were said she fully intended to go home.

However, being skilled in the art of diplomacy, her dear papa had already anticipated her intent and had successfully managed to render himself invisible. For over an hour she danced stiffly with man after man, trying to catch a glimpse of him, her mood deteriorating significantly every time he failed to materialise. To make matters worse, he had apparently found the dullest men in the whole of Christendom to saddle her with. All so crushingly safe and dependable they blended into the wallpaper. All depressingly in want of a wife with a substantial dowry. When the ancient Earl of Ockendon came to claim her, Lizzie pretended to need to visit the retiring room, fled on to the terrace and shivered behind a statue. Freezing to death was infinitely preferable to dancing with him.

'Isn't it a little cold to be stood out here without a shawl?'

Lizzie spun around and saw the Earl of Redbridge lounging against the balustrade, smiling smugly and looking effortlessly gorgeous. 'Where have you been!' Instantly, she clamped her silly jaws shut. He did not need to know she had been frantically looking out for him.

'Be still my beating heart. You sound astoundingly pleased to see me.' His words grated. 'In fairness,' he said as he shrugged out of his coat, 'I only arrived a few minutes ago. I saw you dancing with someone, looking more sullen than usual, and had been waiting for the opportune moment to rescue you because I am a charitable soul, by and large. But you disappeared out here at speed. At one point, I was certain you were going to break into a run.' He solicitously placed the warm garment over her shivering shoulders. It smelled of him and, despite her better judgement, Lizzie snuggled into it gratefully. He might well be an irritant and a rake to boot, but his thoughtful gesture was kind and not at all what she would have expected from a man like him.

'My father has filled my dance card and I blame you for it!'

'How can I be to blame? I wasn't even here.'

'I chatted with you last night. Then you sent me flowers. It set a precedent and it has given him ideas. He has lined up every dullard from here to Land's End, hoping I will take to one of them.' She tried, and failed, not to notice the way the soft linen of his shirt clung to his upper arms or the way his waistcoat emphasised his broad chest and shoulders. He reached out and plucked the ribbon of her dance card from her wrist and scanned the names.

'Good grief! What a shockingly dour bunch.' To her consternation he then picked up her hand and gently threaded the ribbon back over it. His fingers were warm. Too warm. They were giving her skin ideas. 'As I alluded cryptically to your charming butler yesterday, my offer still stands. I am prepared to lend myself to you as your decoy beau to ward off this sea of dullards if you agree to protect me from my ocean of eager hordes.'

This must have been what Adam felt like when Eve offered him a bite of her apple and, curse him, his proposition was attractive. 'I suppose… for the sake of a month of peace, I could pretend to be a little interested in you.' Good gracious. Lizzie could not quite believe those words had just come out of her mouth, but thanks to her father, what other choice did she have? Her stubborn papa was vehemently determined to get her wed with unacceptable over-zealousness. She was heartily ashamed at being so weak-willed in the face of such temptation. 'But only on the strict understanding that it is all a sham and I would never *really* entertain you as a suitor.' Of its own accord, one of her fingers was jabbing him pointedly in the chest. It was alarmingly solid. His reaction was to smile down at her, unoffended by her insult.

'That's the spirit. I hope you have a talent for acting because nobody will believe it if you continue to glare at me as if I am something offensive stuck to the bottom of your shoe.'

Now that he came to mention it, her facial muscles were beginning to ache from the exertion of her frown. As they always did at these unwelcome social functions. Lizzie scrunched up her face to loosen them and then stared back at him blandly. 'I do not wish to give my father false hope. I should prefer it if you appear more keen than me in his presence. That way, once I terminate our acquaintance he won't be too upset.'

'Agreed. I shall be a simpering, fawning lapdog

in front of your father and an amorous suitor in front of your dullards.'

She did not like the sound of that. 'Not too amorous!'

'My dear, you know nothing about the ways of men. When a young lady is being courted and appears uninterested, it means she is still fair game and only spurs the other fellows on. Men are a competitive bunch. It is in our nature. However, when the lady is obviously keen on another, they will retreat. As gentlemen, they are duty bound to do so. It's in the gentleman's code somewhere. Besides, nothing will cool their ardour quicker than the sight of you fawning over another man. We have our pride.'

'My father has increased my dowry to make me more attractive.' Pride and duty would hardly stop the greedy from coveting the money she came with.

'Even more reason why you must encourage my amorous advances in front of them. I am disgustingly rich and, as I obviously do not need your money, they will assume we are *in love*.' She stiffened then and her outraged reaction clearly amused him. 'I understand your reluctance. Really, I do. You are frightened you might forget our arrangement is all a sham and genuinely fall in love with me. A perfectly understandable fear. I am irresistible, after all, and you are bound to develop romantic *feelings*.'

The snort of laughter escaped before she could stop it, because he was amusing if nothing else and that knowing, rakish grin he perpetually sported did suit him. 'There is no danger of *that*, my lord!'

'Then tonight we shall begin our ruse and by the end of the evening we will be the source of much-fevered speculation.'

Lizzie huffed as reality dawned. 'Thanks to my over-zealous father, I am doomed to dance with a card full of dullards, unless I conveniently freeze to death first.'

'Fear not, fair maiden, once we go back inside I will shamelessly monopolise you. You'll be spared dancing with another dullard this evening and every evening henceforth. From this point on, the only man you will dance with is me.'

'I thought I was to be spared another dullard.' She frowned belligerently and he met it with another roguish smile. It tempted her to smile back. Almost.

'Careful, Lizzie. If you are going to be mean to me I shall have my coat back.'

Automatically, her frozen fingers clutched at the garment possessively. Even for December, it was particularly cold. The statue next to them positively glittered with frost. 'I did not give you leave to call me Lizzie.'

'Yet I have called you it anyway. As a special treat, you can call me Hal. Henry is far too formal, especially when a couple is as besotted as us.'

'We are not besotted.' The set-down had less impact with her teeth chattering together. Both his hands came up and began to briskly rub the warmth back into her arms through the fabric of his coat. She wanted to chastise him for his impertinence, but it did feel marvellous. Escaping into the icy night air had been foolhardy in sleeveless silk.

'Heaven forbid! However, we must give off enough of the appearance of it if we are to be left alone. The *ton* loves to watch a blossoming love affair from afar. It makes it easier for them to gossip about it. If we orchestrate this charade correctly, we are guaranteed at least three yards of space at every function from now until Twelfth Night.'

Something which sounded very tempting.

'Where did you find roses in December.'

'I know a fellow in Covent Garden who can get any bloom for a price. Roses, freesias, tulips, lilacs...'

'I loathe lilacs. Be sure to never buy me those when you are pretending to court me.'

'Understood. No lilacs. Not that I would have bought you lilacs, of course, they don't suit you at all. The flowers in your bouquet were chosen specifically because they reminded me of you.'

Lizzie pulled a face. 'Don't tell me—the cream roses symbolise my alabaster skin?'

He grinned back, unoffended. 'Indeed they did, while the tiny pink rosebuds echoed the beautiful sweetness of those luscious lips I *ache* to kiss.'

'How clichéd. And the holly? Your joy at falling hopelessly in love with me at Christmas?'

'Not at all. They are reminiscent of your charming personality. Sharp and prickly.'

She liked the fact he was not trying to flatter her. Since Rainham, she had greatly distrusted it and found herself grinning at his cheek. 'Lady Elizabeth?' A voice called from the French doors. Her persistent dance partner had clearly tracked her down. The unladylike groan she gave made Hal laugh. Lizzie felt the intimate timbre all the way to her frozen toes.

'Dear me…if my ears do not deceive me, I do believe the Earl of Ockendon is ready for his dance. Tell me, is his breath still rancid? Last time I got too close to him, I swear it singed my eyebrows.'

'My father believes I need a safe, sensible man. Upright and above reproach.'

'And to be that he needs to be hurtling towards seventy?'

'I believe the Earl is fifty-something.'

'Good gracious! The man must have had a very hard life.'

'Lady Elizabeth? Are you out here?' The voice was getting closer and instinctively Lizzie went to dart behind her statue again, only to find herself rooted to the spot by her companion's surprisingly strong arms.

'Hiding is not the answer. He will merely bide his time and hunt you down later. Everyone knows Ockendon is desperate for an heir. Lucky you, by the way. To be favoured with his attentions must be the pinnacle of every young lady's romantic ambitions. You need to brazen it out.'

'Surely you are not suggesting I grin and bear it!' The thought of a few minutes twirling in the pungent wake of the man's breath was already turning her stomach.

'Of course not. Remember what I told you. We need to let him see dancing with you is futile… seeing as your heart is already engaged elsewhere. I do believe this is one of those occasions which warrants my *amorous* attentions.'

Lizzie was nowhere near ready for that. There had been no time to prepare. Instinctively, she took a step back. 'I don't think so.'

He quickly closed the distance and whispered again, far too close to her ear. Goose bumps covered her arms. 'Think, Lizzie. Here we are. The stars are twinkling up above. You are wearing my coat…' Those strong arms slowly snaked around her waist and pulled her closer. 'If you gaze up at me with convincing longing, the old fool will assume we are having a tryst.'

Arguing against his logic was prevented by the ominously close sound of another call from her unwelcome beau. 'Lady Elizabeth! Is that you?'

With the most limpid expression she could manage in a blind panic, Lizzie stared longingly up at Hal. He winked encouragingly, then, to her complete shock, dipped his head and pressed his lips to hers.

The sky tilted. Or perhaps it was the floor. Either way, the experience knocked her off kilter. His arms tightened around her and his mouth moved slowly over hers. It might well have been a pretend kiss, done to give credence to the idea they were engaged in a tryst, but it felt dangerously real to Lizzie. She did not attempt to try and push him away, justifying her actions as a way of discouraging the persistent old Earl rather than enjoying the heady taste of the younger one who held her so possessively. Unconsciously, her own lips began to respond, her eyelids fluttered closed and she found herself rising on tiptoes to press her body against his. More worryingly, she was reluctant to prise herself away. Later, she knew, she would claim this was all part of her act, but for now she was prepared to acknowledge it for what it was.

A revelation.

Because kissing Hal was really, quite something. Not at all how she remembered it with her traitorous fiancé and dangerously addictive.

* * *

He was a scoundrel. A rogue. An opportunity had presented itself and, despite the nagging guilt he could not explain, he had seized it. Regardless of the circumstances, Hal's reaction to the kiss was completely unexpected. Every kiss before this had always been merely a prelude. Pleasant, but not earth-shattering. A means to a more passionate and satisfying end. Lizzie's lips were different. Almost as if they had been infused with something addictive, like opium or absinthe, because the moment they had touched his he had quite lost all sense of everything except her. It had nothing to do with passion or attraction, although undoubtedly he was overwhelmed by both of those emotions, and everything to do with a sense of rightness. They melted together, melded and, for once, a kiss was not merely a prelude but a significant event in its own right. Hal had no idea if Ockendon had seen them, if the man still stood there or if he was loudly expounding his outrage. Everything had disappeared except the woman in his arms. It was all strangely overwhelming.

She broke the contact by taking one step smartly back and to his chagrin appeared decidedly underwhelmed by the whole episode. 'I did not give you leave to kiss me.'

'Yet I did it anyway.' Feeling peculiarly shaky, Hal scanned the vicinity. 'I thought it would convince the amorous Ockendon you were unavailable.' Not strictly true. Yes, they had a bargain, but he had been thinking of his wager with Aaron—then had forgotten it instantly the second their mouths had touched.

'The Earl has gone.' Obviously, it had not had the same impact on Sullen Lizzie, because not only was she heartily unimpressed, she was also briskly removing his coat as if she found it as offensive as his kiss. She thrust it at him unceremoniously. 'Never do that again!'

'Perhaps I was a tad over-zealous.' He forced a rakish grin to cover his disappointment at her reaction.

'I am certain there are other ways to bestow your amorous attentions on me without having to resort to that. We should go back inside. The very last thing I want, aside from dancing with foul-smelling old men, is to be ruined by *you*.' She shuddered and then marched back towards the French doors, before stopping briefly to rally him. 'Come along, *Hal*, let's go put on a show.'

Hal tried not to feel offended. He had only sought her out because of the wager, sort of. There had been an odd part of him which had been desperate to seek her out the moment he had arrived at the Benfleet soirée, however he had put that down to his excitement at winning the bet and besting Aaron. Although Hal was trying not to think about the bet because every time he did he experienced something akin to indigestion, churning up his gut and making him feel uncomfortable about the way he was deliberately deceiving her. Then again, his conscience did feel lighter knowing she was also benefiting from the situation, albeit in a roundabout way. He was doing her a favour and favours were noble. Yet despite all that, he had been unexpectedly moved by the kiss. It hadn't been particularly long and by his standards it had been remarkably chaste, yet it had affected him.

Affected him? Now there was something to ponder, he thought miserably as he trailed behind her back into the crowded ballroom. Something was undoubtedly wrong with him. First a lack of vigour, the bizarre allure of controlling his father's estate, the gnawing constant niggle which hinted dangerously at a lack of real fulfilment in his life and now he was going all pie-eyed and wobbly over one silly kiss with a woman who was, at best, ambivalent to him. Or perhaps that was exactly what was wrong. Her unenthusiastic reaction had dented his male pride, ergo he was feeling unsteady.

Hal took a deep breath and let it out slowly. He was overthinking things and that was also very unlike him. Hal preferred to think on his feet. On a positive note, he was one kiss down and she hadn't slapped his face or severed their fledgling alliance upon receiving it. Which in turn meant there would be another opportunity to steal a kiss from her over Christmas. Poor Aaron would be spitting teeth later.

That thought buoyed him and, by the time he got to the refreshment table, Hal was feeling normal. Thankfully, Lizzie spotted an ambitious-looking matron and her daughter a few seconds before he did and slipped her hand possessively through his arm. It had the most staggering effect. One minute they had been prowling towards him with definite intent, the next they suddenly veered off to the right, pretending they were looking for someone else.

'Well saved, my lady. That was close. An eligible man must keep his wits about him at all times. I knew you would be a sterling deterrent.'

'I am glad I could be of service.' She smiled tightly, her eyes locked on something in the distance and gripping his arm with far more force than was necessary. 'I would greatly appreciate it if the favour was immediately reciprocated.' The smile was now so false it might have been painted on to a mask. Hal followed her eyes and spotted a determined gentleman scurrying in her direction and tried not to smile when the first bars of the waltz began. More by luck than judgement, fate was working in his favour.

'I believe this waltz is mine.' The interloper shot daggers at Hal when he saw her arm still looped through his. There was far too much pomade in the fellow's thin hair, either that or it had not been washed in the last week. Patches of his bald pate shone through the greasy strands and the poor chap was at least two inches shorter than Lizzie, a feat in itself when she was barely a few inches above five feet.

'I'm afraid there has been a mistake, old chap. The lady has already promised this dance to me.'

The bald man was outraged. 'It was arranged with the Earl of Upminster himself. I watched him write my name down on her card.' He puffed out his pigeon chest in indignation. 'We are colleagues at the Foreign Office!' One effeminate hand, more suited to clerical work than seduction, shot out and lunged for the card hanging from Lizzie's wrist, but Hal was closer and grabbed it before the upstart did.

For the most part, being blessed with height was something he was always mindful of. Those less fortunate tended to become a little intimidated if one loomed and he was too good natured to want to make others uneasy. However, occasionally a situation called for it. This one did. Pulling himself up to his full six feet and three impressive inches, Hal glowered down at the irritating fellow before him, forcing him to crane his neck up to look directly into his steely glare. 'This dance is mine.'

'No, it isn't. I specifically asked for the waltz. Upminster pencilled me in for it. I demand to see that card!' The pigeon's chest was now so puffed the buttons on his coat were straining around the heavy padding. 'Hand it over immediately!'

There was no need for any words. They were causing enough of a scene without further unseemly conversation. Rather splendidly, Aaron was paying them particular attention behind a potted palm. Hal tried not to look at his brother-in-law. Already, in less than a day since they'd struck the wager, he had stolen one kiss and secured the possibility of many different locations to kiss his lady again. Now all he had to do was choose the right opportunities to do so. That would take finesse. Clumsy, eager overtures would not be welcomed, of that Hal was quite certain. This fair, prickly ice maiden was too guarded. Wary and suspicious of everything, including him. However, she had just insisted he return the favour and save her from another man and that had nothing whatsoever to do with his bet and everything to do with his fortuitous alliance with Lizzie.

With deliberate slowness, Hal lifted it with a smile and slowly tore the offensive dance card into tiny pieces, then sprinkled them like confetti into Mr Pigeon's outstretched hand. He turned towards his fairly startled-looking new ally and made a great show of kissing her hand.

'You promised me this dance, Lady Elizabeth.'

Chapter Five

There was challenge and amusement in his eyes. Half of the ballroom were watching them, whilst pretending not to. The fevered whispering behind so many hands and raised fans nearly drowned out the orchestra, yet she quite admired the bare-faced audacity of the man. Even though he had already left her completely unsettled after the kiss, and knowing the very last place she would ever find her missing equilibrium was in his arms again, dancing with him was infinitely preferable to the sorry specimen her father had sent. And this was all a charade after all. To her ultimate benefit. The perfect decoy for a month of blissful peace. Her last month of pretence.

'Yes, *Hal*, I did.'

His warm palm came to rest affectionately on her hand. The possessive all-male gesture sending a clear message to everyone in the room.

She's mine.

Lizzie's corset suddenly felt tight at the tingle of excitement it gave her and nerves began to jump in her tummy. Hal took his time leading her to the middle of the floor, obviously used to being the centre of attention and enjoying the spectacle they presented. A tiny part of her did, too—the rest of her was frankly terrified by it all. This was all so bizarre and out of character. She never danced, nor did she ever show any interest in any men, yet here she was, being escorted into the parting sea of obviously shocked couples by possibly the most eligible bachelor in the room. Amongst the openly curious onlookers, she felt the weight of several pairs of female eyes as they glared at her with outright hostility. His hordes. Judging by the amount of dismayed expressions, there were quite a number of them.

'You're supposed to look besotted, not like you are being led to your execution.' The subtle hint from her smiling partner reminded Lizzie theirs was a mutually beneficial arrangement. They were supposed to be protecting each other. She could do this. For peace from her father for their one, final society Christmas. Lizzie forced herself to relax and beamed at him as he took her in his arms.

Once she had got over the fact every eyeball in the Benfleet ballroom was locked on them, dancing with him was quite heady. Of course, she hadn't waltzed in five long years, she reasoned as he glided her effortlessly around the floor, and the waltz was meant to be heady. It had nothing to do with the arrogant, yet amusing, Earl of Redbridge. Despite being completely immune and impervious to men, Lizzie could see what his hordes found so appealing. He was a fine specimen of manhood. Beneath his coat she felt actual muscle—not padding—and he was exceptionally handsome. The dark hair had deep auburn strands running through it, which predictably the chandeliers picked out perfectly. However, both of those things paled into insignificance when one looked deep into his eyes.

Hal had a way of gazing at her which made Lizzie nervous. As if those mossy depths saw right through her. She did not faze him, when she proudly terrified every other man who had tried to get near her, and that was disturbing and strangely thrilling. In fact, if anything, Lizzie was rather enjoying their new little secret just as she had enjoyed the way he had effectively neutralised her father's matchmaking in one fell swoop by tearing up her dance card so publicly. His menacing glare was like a warning shot. She sincerely doubted any more dullards would venture towards her again this evening. The handsome Earl was the perfect deterrent. Even the prospect of remaining at this ball for the duration no longer seemed tiresome now that he would be close by.

Hal woke in a fabulous mood. It made no difference that he had crawled into bed in the small hours or that his troublesome nieces were playing noisily outside his bedchamber door. He had succeeded in kissing Sullen Lizzie once. How marvellous an achievement was that?

Except, if he was honest with himself, he had thoroughly enjoyed spending time with her. After their waltz, they had stood for the better part of an hour near the refreshment table, both revelling in the pithy comments they were parrying back and forth about the dullards and the hordes. The woman had an excellent sense of humour when she let her ironclad guard down, he had to give her credit for that, and was extremely knowledgeable on a wide range of subjects from literature to politics. The latter was fascinating and proved to be a topic she felt safe discussing. She stopped frowning and became animated. Her father's elevated position in the Foreign Office gave her insights Hal had never considered before and he asked her a million questions to gently pry her out of the hard shell she hid within. For once, he did not flirt or flatter, knowing such things would be wasted on her. Instead they talked to each other as equals and retired back to the wallflower chairs for another hour until her father came to claim her.

The Earl of Upminster had greeted Hal unenthusiastically. He had looked him up and down, narrowed his eyes and then told his daughter he remembered all the names of the *other* gentleman who still wanted to dance with her should she require them. As he had promised, Hal behaved like an ardent and besotted potential suitor while she largely appeared indifferent to him until her father had ostensibly left them to their own devices when his daughter showed no desire to comply. However, in reality this meant he took himself to a spot less than twenty feet away and made no secret of the fact he was watching Hal closely.

The pair of them had subtly laughed about it afterwards and then watched the festive nonsense whirl around them from their blissfully solitary position at the furthest edge of the ballroom. It had been strangely fun conversing with a woman and not trying to bed her—not that he would have minded bedding her if she had been inclined. Enjoying intelligent conversation with her did not render him blind to her feminine charms. If anything, her obvious intelligence and rapier wit made her more attractive.

Lizzie was intriguing. Interesting as well as caustically witty, still very guarded which bizarrely gave her an enticing aura of the mysterious, and she was undeniably the single most beautiful woman in the ballroom. The corkscrew golden curls and animated cornflower-blue eyes tended to draw his gaze, as did her lush mouth when she spoke. Even without the wager those plump, pink lips would tempt him to kiss them. He would still win it, but they both benefited from the association as Lizzie was plainly delighted at successfully thwarting her father's matchmaking attempts. A great weight off Hal's newly discovered conscience regarding women. Or more particularly, his conscience regarding one woman. Her.

Dressed and shaved, Hal had a jaunty spring in

his step as he left his bedchamber and scooped up each of his irritating red-haired nieces to hold them wriggling and giggling under each arm. As was his prerogative as naughty uncle, he deposited each one on the ornate curved banister, cocked a long leg over himself, to sit behind them lest they fall off, and began to slide the three of them downstairs.

'Henry!' The ominous tones of his sister Connie did not faze him and he grinned at her as they whizzed past at speed. 'How many times have I told you not to teach them to behave like hellions? The girls are boisterous enough without your help.'

Hal came to a sedate stop at the ostentatious gold acorn at the bottom of the stairs and gave his sister a peck on the cheek. 'As I recall, it was you, dear Sister, who taught me the quickest route down these stairs.'

'We were children.'

'As are Grace and Prudence. Although why you called these two monsters after such ladylike virtues is beyond me.'

'At some point, you need to grow up, Hal.'

He winked at his nieces. 'Never.' For good measure, and to vex his sister further, he roughly

tossed a squealing Grace over his shoulder before picking up Prudence by her foot and carrying her upside down into the breakfast room.

'Good morning, Aaron! And if I may say so,
what a *splendid* morning it is.'

His brother-in-law glared at him through narrowed eyes over the top of his newspaper while
his sister poured them all tea.

'Somebody is particularly jovial this morning. I
couldn't help noticing you spent most of the evening intimately ensconced with Lady Elizabeth
Wilding. Does she have a bearing on your good
mood?' Connie smiled at him hopefully as she
placed a steaming cup in front of him. Recently,
and to his complete annoyance, she too had made
numerous hints about him settling down. 'Absolutely everyone was gossiping about you.'

'Gossip must be very light on the ground if a
simple conversation and one dance are being mis-
construed.' Hal was pleased he sounded sufficiently bored enough that his sister's face dropped.
When she turned back towards the sideboard to
fetch her husband's tea, he took the opportunity to
flick one plump, white mistletoe berry at Aaron
across the table cloth. His brother-in-law's eyes
narrowed further as he pocketed the damning

fruit. They both knew better than to alert Connie to their wager. She still hadn't forgiven them for causing the shocking scene at the Serpentine last summer. 'Although I believe Sullen Lizzie was quite taken with *me*.' He shot Aaron a pointed looked and stifled the bark of laughter when he saw him practically foaming at the mouth in indignation at being thwarted.

'Sullen Lizzie? What a dreadful nickname. I hope you are not the root of it, Hal. Nicknames can destroy a young woman's confidence.' She shuddered involuntarily at the memory, making her husband scowl. Thanks to Aaron, Connie had been known as the Ginger Amazonian for years on account of her unusual height and vibrant red hair. It was something his brother-in-law still felt guilty about.

'Am I never going to be forgiven for that one, stupid mistake?' Aaron said.

'Of course not, darling. You know I live only to make you miserable.' But the pair of them were staring at each other soppily again, something they did a great deal, and for once Hal found himself envious of their obvious affection rather than baffled by it. It must be wonderful to have a person look at you like that. To know you completely and understand you so well…

Something which brought him up short. What the blazes had got into him? He was not yet thirty and had far too many wild oats still to sow.

The rest of the meal was its usual chaos. His mother arrived, echoing Connie's sentiments about his current interest in Lizzie. Then his nieces made a mess and a lot of noise whilst doing it and the adults were forced to converse across the table in a volume usually reserved for the hard of hearing in order to be heard above it. Hal loved these occasions in the Berkley Square town house as they would never have been allowed in his father's time. The Stuarts and Wincantons had been at loggerheads for centuries before Aaron had married his sister despite the fact their country estates were next door to each other. But now, with Aaron's town house sold and his father festering in the ground, they all gathered here together. The once-cold house almost felt like home.

Except, there was something missing. Something untenable and ethereal which kept niggling at him. Something he kept trying to put out of his mind, yet which kept creeping back in again. His discontent was beginning to anger him, so he tried to ignore it while he ate his breakfast.

When the ladies disappeared to sort the children, Aaron launched like a cannon ball. 'You kissed her, then?'

'I did indeed.'

'I will need details.'

'A gentleman never tells.'

'The pertinent details which allow me to ascertain if the terms of the wager have been fulfilled. Where did you kiss her?'

'On the lips. They tasted like cherries and she smelled of pink summer roses.' Hal sighed for effect because bating Aaron was fun.

'Not details of the kiss, you buffoon. The location!'

'Oh, right. The terrace. I found her shivering behind a statue hiding from Ockendon. And for your information, I believe Ockendon saw us, although there was no mention of needing witnesses in our original terms. As a gentleman and a peer of the realm, you have my word the kiss occurred and I am frankly offended you would think I would lie.'

Aaron appeared disgruntled, but nodded. 'Fair enough. I cannot deny I am disappointed with Lady Elizabeth for allowing it to happen. However, I am reassured by the knowledge that stealing four more is likely to be more problematic. She will see through you in no time, if she already hasn't. Her father appeared particularly scandalised by your association and that will also work in my favour. In fact, if I am any judge of character, she will already be bitterly regretting her lapse in judgement and has already resolved never to go near you again. Mornings have a habit of reminding one of the folly of the evening's mistakes.'

Hal smiled enigmatically as he rose from the table. Aaron did not need to know about the alliance yet or the fact that Lizzie and Hal would be spending a great deal of time together for the sake of their own sanities, lest he try to sabotage it. Such things were always saved and discussed at great length during the required post mortem of a wager. It was part of their ritual, after all, and always done over a good bottle of cognac.

Chapter Six

Lady Bulphan's annual Christmas Concert was always a dull affair. For some inexplicable reason, despite having more than enough money to pay for a proper orchestra, Lady Bulphan thought it was fun to assemble a rag-tag group of musicians, and the world's worst choir, drawn from the ranks of society. At best, their musical stylings were dismal. Famously dismal and after so many years no longer funny. But because Lord Bulphan was one of Prinny's advisers, they were too well connected for anyone to dare to ignore their invitation so the affair, though no longer a crush, was always well attended. The sensible had ready-made excuses months in advance. Lord Bulphan also happened to be one of her father's oldest and dearest friends, so not only were they always in attendance, they had also come early in a show of support.

It was all right for Papa. He was ensconced at the 'secret' card table, known only to those in the inner circle and would remain so for hours and thus spared the pitiful and painful renditions of Christmas carols from the Bulphan Ensemble. They were currently murdering 'Hark! The Herald Angels Sing', or at least that was what Lizzie assumed it was meant to be. It was difficult to tell over the screeching of the ten violins. Ten violins who all appeared to be playing from completely different parts of the score.

To make matters worse, in her attempt to sit as far away from the performance as possible, she had chosen one of the most uncomfortable chairs she had ever had cause to sit upon. And her corset was too tight. In a rare flash of vanity, she had insisted her maid tighten it to allow her to wear this particular blue gown, and Lizzie now bitterly regretted it. Why had she been so determined to emphasise her eyes when she was not intending to attract anyone? At least not consciously. Subconsciously, she had been oddly nervous about this evening, or more specifically about her planned liaison with a certain handsome and charming rake this evening. It was his fault her corset pinched and her mood was foul.

'Good evening, Lady Elizabeth.' She smelled the Earl of Ockendon before she saw him and her misery was complete. 'We missed our dance the other evening.' In deference to the musicians he was speaking just above a whisper and far too close. She recalled Hal's claim the man's breath had nearly singed his eyebrows and sympathised with the comment.

'As I do not recall you either asking me to dance or heard myself accepting it, I shall have to take your word for it.' Lizzie turned her head rudely to focus her full attention on the caterwauling from the choir. Still, he sat in the next chair but one to her. What was it with men and sitting where they were not welcome of late? Maybe she was not sending out clear enough signals as to her ambivalence to all things male.

'I did not give you leave to sit, sir.'

'You have a tart mouth, madam—but I confess I like that about you. Amongst other things.' He looked pointedly at her bosom and his thin lips curved into a slimy smile. Lord save her! Another reason to regret this uncharacteristically glamourous and exposing choice of gown.

'Your good favour is wasted on me when I find I like nothing about you.'

'Your father wants you wed and I am merely putting myself forward as a candidate for your consideration.'

In horror, Lizzie faced him and allowed her rampant disgust to show in her expression. 'I have no desire to be wed and even if I did, it certainly would not be to you, *my lord*.'

He chuckled and for some reason it sent a chill through her. 'I hope to convince you otherwise.'

'Something that I can assure you will never happen.'

'Never say never, Lady Elizabeth. I am a powerful man who can be very *persuasive*. Perhaps all you need is the right *incentive* to lure you out of spinsterhood?'

There was something about the way he answered, as if there was an underlying threat which made her breath shorten, even as she stared back at him blandly. 'I can assure you I am stubbornly and happily wedded to spinsterhood.'

'And why is that, Lady Elizabeth? Is there some dreadful, deep, *dark* secret which keeps you from committing yourself to Holy Matrimony? Something you keep *hidden*, perhaps? Something that has scandalously been hidden for *years*?'

An odd thing to say, unless… Unease made her

spine stiffen. Did he know? The man moved in powerful circles, it was true. Had somebody let something slip inadvertently? Nausea threatened, but Lizzie forced herself to remain unaffected as he watched her carefully. The way his eyes narrowed slightly suggested he might suspect something, but there was enough of a hint of question to reassure her he was still unsure. She needed to speak to her father, but getting up now and rushing to do so would give the game away for certain. All Lizzie could do in the interim was sit impassively and brazen it out.

'You are astute, sir. There is a dreadful deep, *dark* scandalous secret I have been keeping *hidden*.' The knowing half-smile she offered him was borne out of the fierce desire to protect Georgie. Ignoring her acute physical disgust, she leaned closer and fought the urge to gag. 'You see, my lord, I discovered early on that I despise all men and want nothing to do with any of them. Your good self, included.'

'Really? Aside from Redbridge, I presume. You appeared quite partial to him yesterday, as I recall. And then there was that erstwhile fiancé of yours. What was his name?' He tapped his chin thoughtfully, his cold, dead eyes never leaving hers for a second. 'Ah, yes. The Marquess of Rainham. You were quite partial to *him* as well.' His eyes swept up and down her body and lingered on her bosom again. 'Quite...*partial.*'

'Yet I shall never feel partial to you, my lord. Of that I am quite certain.'

'Passion *and* a tart mouth. A splendid dowry... and of course, your *hidden* secrets. What a tantalising package you are, Lady Elizabeth' His thinly veiled threats and coded words hit too close to home for her comfort.

'Go tantalise another spinster, my lord. I am sure there must be someone desperate here who would lower themselves to consider you.'

He chuckled and stared at her bosom again while she fought the urge to dash away and bathe. 'You will make a fine wife indeed, Lady Elizabeth. A fine, young and *fertile* wife...'

'I have been looking everywhere for you.' Hal strode confidently into the fray and smiled at her. Lizzie had never been so pleased to see another person in her life.

'I am sorry I am late, Lizzie dearest. My sister had a hairdressing crisis, delaying our arrival.' Like her own personal bodyguard, he smoothly sat in the tiny chair which separated her from the odious Earl, forming a pleasant-smelling, solid buffer between them. 'Have I missed much, aside from your delightful company of course?'

The easy smile and casual manner did not hide the question in his intelligent eyes. Lizzie had no idea how much he had heard of her whispered conversation with Ockendon, but he had heard enough to be irritated on her behalf. His arms were folded stiffly across his chest, his thighs spread just wide enough to edge the old Earl away and let him know his presence was unwelcome.

Acting bored despite her unsettled nerves, Lizzie smiled at Hal in what she hoped resembled outright adoration. 'You missed an interesting rendition of "While Shepherds Watched Their Flocks by Night". Lady Bulphan pretended to be a shepherdess, complete with crook and stuffed sheep. She acted out the words.'

'Then I am sorry I missed it. Was it as tuneful as "Hark! The Herald"?' Hal had angled his body ever so slightly towards her. His broad shoulders and back shielded her from seeing Ockendon while effectively shutting him out of the conversation like the ramparts around a castle. It gave her some comfort, though not enough. Her skin suddenly felt dirty and her stomach was churning.

'Sadly, there were no violins.' Lizzie hoped her voice was not as rattled as she felt. For Georgie's sake she had to appear calm.

'None? A travesty indeed, when all ten of them sound quite splendid from the refreshment table. But then again, there is a significant amount of rum in the punch, so I suspect it deadens the ears. Come, let us avail ourselves of a cup or two so that we might enjoy the subtle nuances of the music better.' Hal was on his feet in an instant as if he had known she needed to escape. 'If you will excuse us, Ockendon.' He waved his already crooked arm in open invitation and Lizzie was only too happy to take it. The old Earl's questions and crude insinuations had frightened her and she clung to Hal's arm with slightly shaking legs and a racing mind.

What had he meant by deep, dark secret? Passionate, partial and fertile. A coincidental choice of words? She doubted it. It all felt a little too convenient, had been said so pointedly, to have happened by chance.

Hal poured them both a cup of punch, then manoeuvred her towards an alcove, away from anyone else.

'What was all that about?'

'The Earl of Ockendon has put himself forward as a potential husband.' Yet if he knew about her son, he knew she was soiled goods. It had to be the stupid dowry. His talk of being *persuasive* and offering her the right *incentive* hinted at blackmail. Or maybe she was allowing her vivid imagination and over-protectiveness of her child to weave fanciful meanings into his words which were not there. Five years of deception tended to make one paranoid.

'I didn't care for his tone or for the way he looked at you.'

Neither did she. Lizzie still felt violated from the brief episode. The way his eyes had lingered on her bosom, the way they had darkened when he spoke of passion. However, until such a time as her secret was exposed—or wasn't—Lizzie would continue to keep it hidden. 'It hardly matters. It is no secret Lord Ockendon has long wanted a wife young enough to give him heirs.' The shiver was involuntary. Ockendon terrified her. 'I should imagine I am merely one of the many lucky ladies he has approached on his quest. Or perhaps he has exhausted all other possibilities and is now scraping the bottom of the barrel to be considering me?' Those mossy-green eyes regarded her thoughtfully, unsettling her further.

'Maybe he is simply drawn to the unattainable. You present a challenge.'

'I thought you said once a gentleman knows a lady's heart is engaged elsewhere he will cease his attentions towards her. He saw you kiss me. He certainly alluded to it, yet it only appears to have spurred him on.'

'Some gentlemen have thicker skins than others. Ockendon's is clearly like leather. You have my word he will yield once he realises who he is up against.' The serious, steely tone vanished as soon as it started, replaced with the roguish devil-may-care man he usually presented, and Lizzie realised the handsome, flippant new Earl of Redbridge was not quite as superficial as he wanted the world to believe. 'With any luck, with my fortune, title and dashing good looks, he will quickly realise he has no hope for your affections against such a magnificent opponent.'

'I sincerely hope you are right. The man puts my teeth on edge.'

His hand came to rest warmly over hers. 'Do not worry, fair maiden. I shall stick to you like glue all night and if Ockendon comes within ten feet of you I will challenge him to a duel. I promise.' Something about the way he said it made her believe him.

True to his word, Hal did exactly that until her father finally surfaced. Her papa laughed off her fears about Ockendon, refusing to discuss it beyond the trivial, but granted her the excuse of pleading a headache and summoning the carriage early. Because, as he rightly stated, who wouldn't have a headache with the Bulphan Ensemble playing so enthusiastically. Clearly the card game was as lacklustre as the music because he happily accompanied her home.

'Ockendon is harmless, Lizzie, a silly old fool who is barely tolerated in the Lords. You are reading far too much into his words because you are a good mother who wants to protect her son. But let me put your mind at rest. Only Lord Bulphan knows of little Georgie's existence and he would never break my confidence. The servants are too loyal to have betrayed us and we have always been scrupulously careful about any excursions. Besides, poor Ockendon has never had a talent for being particularly charming, I doubt he has the first clue about how to go about wooing a woman.

Perhaps the fellow said what he said as an attempt to intrigue you. It's a bit of mild, and slightly pathetic, flirting, I'll wager, and nothing more. A bid to get your attention.' His lack of concern went some way to reassuring her she was imagining things and her father briskly changed the subject. He patted her hand and his demeanour changed from counselling to casual. A little too casual. 'I had the great good fortune to be seated next to Lord Hewitt at the card table and I was heartily impressed by him. He works at the Home Office and by all accounts is doing a sterling job. He is thirty. A perfectly respectable age for a young buck to take a wife and rather fortuitously he is seeking one as we speak. Now there's a catch...'

Lizzie rolled her eyes in exasperation and glared at her father across the carriage. 'I wish you would stop matchmaking, *Father*.' They both knew she only called him Father when she was angry and he bristled. 'I do not want a husband. Not now nor never. Why do you continue to refuse to accept that?'

'You might at least give Hewitt a chance. I am not suggesting you marry him, merely talk to him. You seemed to find it no great chore to chat away to that scoundrel Redbridge all night.'

'I have no interest in him either. He is not the sort to settle down into marriage, therefore conversation with him is blessedly harmless as we are both quite averse to it. That is the full extent of our attraction towards one another!'

'He does not regard you with aversion, young lady. Why, he can barely contain his pleasure at looking at you!'

Did he? Lizzie was quietly pleased with this piece of information until she caught herself. She did not want anyone looking at her covetously, whether they be Redbridge or Hewitt, or, Heaven help her, Ockendon. 'The Earl of Redbridge is a devout rake. I dare say he looks at every woman in possession of a pulse in much the same way. As I have already stated, I am quite immune to his charms.'

'That is as maybe, but can you not see while he is sniffing around you he is scaring off all of the other young men who *might* make you a suitable husband? I selected several for you to dance with the other night and because of him they were denied the opportunity to impress you.'

Thank goodness. Which was exactly the reason she needed Hal in the first place. As usual, her papa was determined to continue in the same vein he had for the last five years no matter what she said. He had promised her mother, after all, and he wasn't getting any younger. They just kept going around in ever-decreasing circles. 'It will take more than one silly dance to convince me that I need a husband, Father.'

He scowled and they both glared at each other stubbornly across the benches until he relented. 'Perhaps you are right, Lizzie. One dance will hardly change your mind.'

Chapter Seven

There was a lull in yuletide entertainments after the Bulphan Christmas Concert. After two days, Hal was practically climbing the walls with boredom. At least he hoped it was boredom, although rather alarmingly he was coming to suspect his restlessness had rather more to do with a curious desire to spend some more time with Lizzie than genuine boredom. Genuine boredom came from inactivity, and there might not be any balls or parties to go to, but he had been inordinately busy.

Estate business had occupied a great many hours, as had his speculations on the Stock Exchange. However, during each of those tasks the image of *her* had floated into his mind and made him forget what he was supposed to be doing. Hal had even dragged himself to a gaming hell in the hope it would distract him, but the card tables held no allure and the hostesses less. He'd left after less than an hour because he could not seem to stop thinking about her. Just as he was now, as he was idly strolling down High Holborn on a particular errand on this dull Thursday afternoon. It was most disconcerting.

It stood to reason he would think of her occasionally. Hal was only one kiss down and still had four more to claim in less than three weeks, but it was not the bet he kept mulling over. It was that kiss. The subtle scent of roses from her perfume. Or the way her eyes sparkled when he said something which amused her. The way she flipped between regarding him with wary hostility to forgetting she distrusted him and became entertaining with interesting, witty conversation. The peculiar sense of unease he had every time he recalled the tense exchange between her and Ockendon. The way she had been skittish afterwards. And scared. Ockendon had frightened her, yet he had no idea why such a confident and vibrant young woman would feel bothered by anything that silly old fool had to say.

Half the time Hal had absolutely no idea what was going on in her head, the other half he felt a strange kinship with her. Lady Elizabeth Wilding was a conundrum indeed and one he was intrigued to understand. To understand her, it stood to reason he would need to spend more time with her. A lot more time. To that end, he was counting the days until the Marquess of Danbury's house party at the weekend. There were exactly two of them.

Hal sighed as he came to Noah's Ark, Mr Hamley's magnificent toy emporium, annoyed with his current leaning towards unnecessary and incessant introspection. It wasn't healthy and this odd mood was not conducive to shopping for his nieces. Melancholy might lead him towards toys which were quiet and sensible and that would never do. He had come here intent on buying something noisy and entertaining for them for Christmas—something special from their naughty uncle. Something which would drive his sister and brother-in-law mad and whip the children into a state of perpetual excitement and he needed his wits about him to do it. Last year's matching, miniature soldiers' drums, complete with jaunty bright uniforms and a genuine cavalry bugle, had caused mayhem and sent Connie into one of the best temper tantrums Hal had seen in years. By hook or by crook he was duty-bound to top that. The girls were depending on him.

The bell tinkled as he pushed open the door and he took a moment to soak up all the sights and sounds. In deference to the season, shiny boughs of holly edged all the shelves and hung from red ribbons in gay balls from the ceiling. All around him were toys of every kind. Amongst all this bounty, the shop was filled with customers, no doubt all here on the same mission as he was.

Seeking out the perfect gift for Christmas morning.

A few children giggled with excitement in one corner, while their harried parents tried to prise them away from the displays, and every shop assistant was engaged in either serving or wrapping. Clearly, Hal was going to be here for some time. He didn't mind. Shopping for toys was hardly shopping in the literal sense. Literal shopping was painful. Noah's Ark was pure pleasure.

His feet instinctively took him towards the instruments, seeing as they were undoubtedly loud, and his eyes were drawn to the brass trumpets. Connie had loathed the bugle most of all, but were trumpets too similar? He would hate to become predictable. No... Not instruments again. He was turning in a slow circle, seeking inspiration, when a familiar waft of roses brought him up short and, like a dog, he began to sniff the air to locate the source just on the off chance it might be Lizzie. He followed the smell around the other side of a tall cabinet and grinned.

'Hello, fair maiden and woman of my dreams.'

She practically jumped ten feet in the air and dropped the handful of tin soldiers she had been holding.

'Hal!' She appeared horrified to see him and he tried not to be miffed. 'What are you doing here?'

'Hunting down the most unsuitable toys to give to my troublesome nieces for Christmas. So…this is the mysterious thing you do every Tuesday and Thursday when Stevens says you are *genuinely* not at home. You shop.'

She was blinking rapidly and for a moment appeared flummoxed. 'Yes… Yes… I shop. Every Tuesday and Thursday. Nothing mysterious about it at all.'

'Your terrifying butler gave the impression you were doing something far more mysterious.'

Her response was to laugh, somewhat falsely, and blink some more. Puzzled, and keen not to continue talking about a topic which had clearly made her batten down those defensive hatches and pull up the drawbridge once again, Hal crouched down to pick up the soldiers and frowned at her selection. 'You really can't give him these.'

'*Him?* What do you mean *him*?' She had stopped blinking. Now her eyes were as wide as saucers. Obviously, she was unused to being caught by surprise and he had clearly terrified her in the process. And in a toy shop of all places.

'Your brother has a young son, does he not?'

'Yes! Yes, of course… These are for Frederick… My nephew.' She smiled, although it did not quite touch her eyes as he dropped the tiny soldiers back into her palm. She stared down at them mournfully and then appeared confused as his latter comments permeated her thoughts. 'Why can't I give him these? Little boys like to play with soldiers.'

'Of course they do—but those are soldiers from the Netherlands. I am sure they are jolly nice fellows, and they are our allies, but I am certain your nephew would much prefer proper British soldiers when he sends them into battle on the carpet.' Hal reached out and plucked a tiny cavalry officer astride a charging horse from the shelf. 'Look at this fearsome chap. Proper smart crimson regimentals, that splendid black hat and his sabre poised ready to strike down any of Napoleon's army silly enough to stand in his way.'

He handed her the lead figurine and she smiled properly this time. Those beguiling cornflower-blue eyes lit up and caused Hal's throat and groin to tighten simultaneously. Lord, she was lovely. Inside and out. 'I can see you are an expert on little boys.'

'I used to be one, so I suppose that does give me a bit of an advantage.'

'Seeing as you are so knowledgeable on toy soldiers, I wonder if I might trouble you to help me select a few more.'

'It would be my pleasure.' Hal was telling the truth. Spending time with her outside their arrangement was perfectly all right by him, especially as the topic of toy soldiers had apparently done the trick and melted her impenetrable guard. 'How many do you want?'

'How many do I need?'

As he was in danger of gazing wistfully at her—goodness knew where that had come from—and had the ridiculous urge to sniff her perfume and touch her hair, he turned away to study the lead battalions stood neatly on the shelves and pretended to give the matter some serious thought. 'Are you adding to an existing collection of soldiers or starting from scratch?'

'These will be his first soldiers.'

'Music to my ears, fair maiden, and so much simpler. We should start with the basics then.'

'Which are?'

Hal was already picking up men. 'Well, you will need a Wellington. That's for sure. Somebody needs to be in charge. And a Napoleon, else who would be defeated at the end of the game?' He pressed the two toys into her outstretched palm and wished neither of them were wearing winter gloves so that his fingers could graze her soft skin. 'We will need a selection of British officers of all ranks...cavalry...infantry. A few Highlanders. Ignore the fact those soldiers are wearing skirts. They are warriors at heart and put on such a good show for us at Waterloo.' Her cupped hands were overflowing, so he began to gather the others in a pile on the shelf. 'And we are going to need cannons. Lots of cannons.'

'Isn't it all a bit extreme when we only have one Frenchman to fight?'

'You make a good point. Much as it pains me, we are going to have to buy some Frenchies.' He grabbed a handful and scowled at them, and swore he felt himself grow a few inches in height when he heard her giggle.

'You have been so particular about the British troops, shouldn't we take the same care with the French? Won't they also need officers, cavalry and the like?'

'They are the enemy, madam, and need I remind you that we beat them. Thrashed them into surrender because they are a rag-tag, disorganised and dissolute group made up of illiterate, drunken peasants and smelly cheese makers. *Of course* we will not need French officers and cavalry. We have to keep things realistic and the French guillotined all their leaders years ago.'

He really was very charming, especially when he was being irreverent, and Lizzie was grateful he had saved her from purchasing the wrong soldiers. Her son would have noticed instantly that they were wearing the wrong uniforms and it would have given her father the opportunity to point out that this was exactly why her son needed a father. Much as it pained her to admit it, it would never have occurred to her to buy officers or cavalry or an enemy army for them to fight against.

'Thank you.' She felt quite emotional, knowing she would be giving Georgie a Christmas gift he would love. Sometimes being a mother to a little boy was a challenge and getting more so now he was growing. The whole journey to and from their weekly jaunt to Richmond Park, he had talked about nothing else but how much he wanted a proper army to play with. This was what he had meant and she had potentially ruined it because she did not know the difference between the enemies or the allies. Thank goodness she had run into Hal—although he had given her quite a fright.

One minute she had been thinking about him, hardly a surprise when she had been incessantly thinking about him since his impertinent kiss on the Benfleet terrace, and then he had been stood next to her as if she had conjured him with her mind. Looking all windswept and handsome. Then he had saved her again. He had an irritating habit of being in exactly the right place at exactly the right time—something which probably had a great deal more to do with luck than the niggling suspicion that Henry Stuart, the charming and handsome Earl of Redbridge, might be someone she could depend on. 'I think it is only fair I return the favour.'

She was being nice. Towards a man who she was not related to. Whatever next? Yet as out of character as the offer had been, Lizzie did want to do something nice for Hal. He had saved her from one balding dullard, twice from Lord Ockendon and he had just saved Christmas morning. 'You say you are here to find presents for your nieces, a task I am eminently suitable for—seeing as I used to be a little girl.'

'I don't want anything sensible. Or quiet.'

'Why ever not?'

'As the naughty uncle it is my duty to purchase toys which will drive their parents to distraction. Last year it was drums and a bugle. I had to stuff handkerchiefs in each ear to drown out the cacophony and went to bed with a headache.' Hal smiled boyishly, clearly very pleased with himself. 'It was marvellous.'

'Oh, I see. You have not come here to buy gifts for your nieces at all, merely gifts for yourself.'

He appeared affronted at the suggestion. 'My nieces always love my gifts. They are the highlight of every Christmas morning.'

'And are they played with after Christmas?'

Because Lizzie had the distinct impression they miraculously disappeared, consigned to the attic with all the other inappropriate toys. His dark brows drew together and after a long pause he huffed.

'Now you come to mention it, no. They aren't.'

'Then wouldn't it be better to choose something different? Something they'll love and their parents can live with? Something truly special which can be played with all year? From their favourite naughty uncle.'

'Hardly a naughty uncle if I am giving sensible gifts. I've been training Prudence and Grace to be hellions since the day they were born. Girls saddled with such pious names should always be a handful.'

Lizzie's mouth curved into a smile at his belligerent expression. 'Although I already know I shall regret asking this question, but how does one train one's nieces to be hellions?'

Mischief twinkled in his green eyes and he leaned towards her, covertly looking both left and right, as if the information he was about to give her was of the utmost secrecy. 'It has been a three-pronged attack. Firstly, I have always actively encouraged naughtiness. Hiding just before they are due to go out, sliding down banisters, inappropriate horseplay. Lots of high-pitched noise—especially when there are guests in the house. I find a bit of quiet praise after the event or a well-placed dare works wonders.' The image of him playing with children came easily. Except, for some reason, she could not picture him playing with any other child except little Georgie. 'Secondly, to be proper hellions, I have made sure their arsenal of weapons is always well stocked. I have invested hours schooling them in the subtle art of practical jokes and taught them to be resourceful with the materials at hand. Jam, cobwebs, flour, et cetera. Creepy crawlies are always good. Connie loathes things with lots of legs and, although he would rather die than admit it, my brother-in-law Aaron does, too. Therefore, I have meticulously shown the girls where to hunt for the best specimens, how to trap them and keep them safe until exactly the right moment. Timing is everything, after all.' His voice dropped to a whisper and Lizzie found her head intimately close as she strained to listen. He smelled of fresh air. Spicy cologne and something heady, wholly him and completely unidentifiable. It was probably the aroma of sin. 'Last spring, totally unprompted, Prudence filled her mother's favourite riding boots up with frog spawn. I cannot tell you how proud it made me.'

The bubble of laughter surprised her and she covered her mouth with her hand. 'Your poor sister. I feel so sorry for her.'

'Don't you dare. It is nothing more than her just deserts. She tortured me as a child. Mercilessly. Being older, she was always so much bigger and used it to her advantage. I have lost count of how many times she overpowered me, rolled me up in the nursery rug and then sat on me. I'll have you know I spent hours incarcerated in that blasted rug. I have suffered violence at that woman's hand and as a gentleman, I could never physically retaliate and she knew it. On one occasion, she then went on to use my father's razor to shave off one of my eyebrows. It took months to grow back and made me the laughing stock of the village. Is it any wonder I now shudder at the sight of a tightly-weaved Persian?'

'Maybe I feel a little less sympathy for your sister now, but I still think you should buy something for your nieces which they will love and continue their hellion training on the sly.'

'I cannot say I am happy about it, but I shall bow down to your better judgement. You were once a little girl after all, as you say, although I doubt you were a hellion.'

'Why ever not?'

He pretended to study her, then frowned. 'You are far too—nice.'

'Good gracious! Your life must be filled with dreadful people if you think I am one of the nicer ones.'

'Actually, my mother is thoroughly nice. My sister Constance is predominantly nice but has moments when she is terrifying, and her husband Aaron is the best friend a fellow could wish for. I am surrounded by decent sorts so I know one when I spot one. You may try to hide your niceness from the world at large, but I know the truth. In fact, I am of the opinion you are really far too nice be associated with a man who is wilfully training his nieces to be hellions.' He gently took her hand and curled it about his arm and began to lead her to another part of the shop. Lizzie tried not to feel content at the closeness or the compliments.

'On the subject of your hellion-training—what, pray tell, is the third prong in your three-pronged strategy?'

'Oh, that is the easiest part.' The wolfish grin

made her pulse instantly flutter. 'I make sure I always lead by example. I am, Lady Elizabeth, a *thoroughly* naughty boy.' And Lord help her, that was exciting.

With her guidance, Hal reluctantly bought two beautiful wax dolls of the highest quality. Then he happily allowed Lizzie to select different outfits for the dolls so the girls could play dressing-up games with them. As he walked her back to her carriage, insisting on carrying all the many packages himself, it occurred to her that she had had a thoroughly enjoyable time in his company and was disappointed to be going home.

'You will be at Danbury's tiresome house party this weekend, won't you? My mother is insisting on going.'

Lizzie was trying to avoid it. 'I hope not.'

His handsome face fell. 'Oh, don't say that! I was relying on you to be there and now I am doomed for certain. Please come, Lizzie. The hordes will be there en masse and there are few places to hide at a house in the country, apart from the countryside, of course, and it is frightfully cold. I shall be for ever in your debt.'

'I don't know...' She dithered and he grabbed her hand and stared mournfully into her eyes.

'Have you any idea how dangerous a house party is for a confirmed but deliciously eligible bachelor? I would sooner run the gauntlet than attend one undefended. There will be parlour games. What if they play Hot Cockles? Everyone knows that is merely a flimsy excuse to kiss someone you've got your eye on. Without you as my partner, I will be a target. The hordes will stampede towards me and I might well end up crushed. And then there will be wassailing and there is no telling what danger I will be in once those young ladies are emboldened by alcohol. I shall have to keep my bedchamber door barricaded as I wouldn't put it past a few of the more ambitious ones to visit me in the dead of night and then claim I ruined her. This house party is the single most perilous event of the whole Christmas season because there is literally *nowhere* safe for me to hide. I will be a captive and will hold you entirely accountable if I end up compromised into marriage.'

He gripped her fingers and gave her a pitiful gaze. 'Please come. We have as good as sworn an oath of allegiance to one another. You save me and I save you.' He was sounding increasingly desperate and looking totally miserable. Adorably miserable. 'How about this? Regardless of our arrangement, if you come to the Danburys' I shall owe you a huge favour which you can demand from me any time of the course of my entire life. In the small hours if need be and in the Highlands of Scotland. Or even that desolate place they send convicts in the Antipodes. No distance is too far. I will ride through wind and rain, climb mountains... I am now literally begging you. Throw me a bone... I will be at your beck and call. Just do me this one favour, Lizzie darling.'

Her pulse fluttered at the word 'darling'. It shouldn't have, but it did. 'I'm not sure...'

'But I am at your mercy. Take pity on a poor, irresistible, terrified earl!'

It was only one weekend, she supposed, wavering, and they did have an arrangement. He had rescued her from Ockendon and smoothly extricated her from his vile company and he had just saved her from inadvertently buying the wrong soldiers for her son. 'All right.' It was just two nights away from Georgie and would please her father. 'I shall be there. But under duress.'

His green eyes brightened as his face split in the biggest grin, making him look quite boyish and even more adorable, if such a thing was possible.

'If we weren't in public, I would kiss you!' And rather bizarrely, if they weren't in public, she was sorely tempted to let him. She was still all a quiver at his throwaway use of the word 'darling'. 'Oh, to Hell with it, nobody is looking...' Before Lizzie could stop him, he had opened the carriage door to shield them from view, lifted her off the floor, spun her in a quick circle, then briefly touched his lips to hers. 'Thank you, Lizzie darling! You are a life-saver.'

It had not been anything more than boisterous exuberance brought about by his gratefulness, but regardless, being held in those strong arms for just a few seconds was quite something. Even the chaste, friendly kiss fizzed through her system till she felt it all the way down to the tips of her toes. Her nerve endings were still tingling when he stepped away. Her lips still tingled as he helped her up into the carriage. Her thoughts were jumbled; she didn't know whether to sigh or moan or laugh, his kiss had scrambled her wits so effectively. It was rather like being struck by lightning. Quick, unexpected and potentially deadly. Something which made her feel quite unsettled all the way home.

Chapter Eight

'A message just arrived for you.' Hal's sister Connie swept into his study, grinning. 'One of the Earl of Upminster's footmen hand-delivered it. Said it was *most* urgent.' She plopped her bottom resolutely on his desk before she handed it to him. A clear sign she intended to stay while he read it. Hal tried to ignore the tickle of excitement as he stared at the feminine, sloping writing on the front, or the desire to slowly trace the pad of his index finger over the pen marks. Since he had waved off her carriage this afternoon he had done nothing but mope. Whilst it had hardly been much of a kiss, ostensibly done out of opportunism to smugly press the second mistletoe berry into Aaron's hand, Hal wasn't fooling himself. At the time, he had not given the wager a thought, he had simply needed the contact. His body still hummed from the effect it had had on him and he was not entirely sure what to make of that fact. Had she felt it, too? Against all his better judgement he did hope she might say as much in her unexpected letter.

Unless it was a chastisement?

Or worse.

'Thank you. I shall read it later.' He placed it on the corner of his desk and stared back down at his ledger, hoping Lizzie was not reneging on her promise to attend the Danbury house party after all. If she was, he might have to resort to throwing himself down the stairs in order to sustain a believable injury to get out of going. Without Lizzie it would be dreadful and he was strangely excited about spending time with her.

'It might be important.'

'I sincerely doubt it.'

'It might be from *her*.'

Hal shrugged and began to add up a column of figures in a last-ditch attempt to convince his sister he was ambivalent. It was the wrong move. Connie's hand shot out and grabbed the letter, then she scampered to the other side of the study with it, giggling, just as she had when they were children, banished to the nursery because their father was at home and he found their very presence an irritant. The seal was cracked open before he could get to her and she swiftly sidestepped his attempt to lunge for it.

'That is my *private* correspondence, Connie! Give it back.'

'"Dear Hal..."' She gave him a knowing look as they circled each other like gladiators across the Persian rug. 'That's nice. You are on first-name terms.'

'I'm warning you, Connie!'

'"I have an emergency..." How exciting! And you are the first person she turns to.'

'If you don't give it back...' He lunged again and managed to grab her arm, but being a tall woman and a terminally vexing one, she simply used her other hand to hold his precious letter and read it at arm's length.

'"And you did say that if I had an emergency, no matter where or when it was, you would come and rescue me..." Be still my beating heart. I never thought I would see the day when my irritating little brother would grow up to become a knight in shining armour.'

Desperate times called for desperate measures. Hal hooked his leg around hers and grabbed her firmly around the waist, but despite his best efforts to stop her wriggling, the damn letter remained resolutely out of his reach. With no other option, he seriously considered toppling her to the floor and rolling her up in the rug. 'Give me my letter now, Connie—or so help me!' He tightened his arm around her ribs and squeezed in warning. Hardly an act of war, but what else could he do under the circumstances? She was a woman and, even though she was a termagant and often his torturer, he was morally incapable of physically harming her. Being a human corset was the best he could do.

'"I would be eternally grateful…"' *Squeeze.* '"If you could…"' *Squeeze.* '"Come to dinner tonight. I know…"' *Really big squeeze.* '"It is short notice and I apologise. We always eat promptly at eight. Lizzie."'

When only one hand and her vibrant red head poked unapologetically out of the cage he had formed around her, a breathless Hal finally snatched the note out of her frantically waving and ridiculously long arm and scanned it himself, but that was all there was. Five sentences leaving him none the wiser, but elated. Not only had she *not* retracted her promise to be at the dreadful house party as he had initially feared, she wasn't telling him off for the stolen public kiss and wanted to see him. Hal could not bring himself to care about the particular circumstances although he suspected it might be dullard related.

'Shall I inform Cook that we will be one less this evening?' There were times he wished he wasn't a gentleman so that he could strangle his smug sister. Even physically restrained, she always had something to say. Hal did not bother answering as he let her go and paced to the opposite side of the room to read the letter again to see if he could glean any more from it.

'I believe this is a first for you.'

'I have dined with women before. On numerous occasions.'

'Yes, but I assume on those occasions you dined *alone* with them.' Connie settled her bottom into his vacated chair and began to twiddle with his letter opener. '*This* will be vastly different.'

He should ignore her; he knew that from old. 'How so?'

'Well, for a start, you will be in company.'

Hal had assumed as much. Lizzie was hardly the sort of woman who would ignore propriety and there would be at least one dullard in attendance as well. 'I eat dinner in your company every day and to the best of my knowledge I haven't managed to disgrace myself once. Well, not in the last few years at least.'

'That hardly counts seeing as we are family...' His sister smiled the patronising smile she used when she thought she knew better than him. Unfortunately, damn her, she usually did. 'However, to the best of *my* knowledge, Brother dearest, this is the first dinner you have ever taken with a woman and *her* father. You are going to be on display. Scrutinised. Judged. The Earl of Upminster is a well-respected member of the Government. Only the best sort will pass muster for his daughter. From what I witnessed at the concert he heartily disapproves of you already. This dinner could be a potentially painful and dangerous affair, fraught with pitfalls. It could ruin your chances like that.' She clicked her fingers for emphasis and stared back at him seriously.

As their alliance was a mutually beneficial sham, brought about by a secret wager with Connie's husband, who was blissfully ignorant of the separate bargain he had made with Lizzie to win his wager with Aaron, it seemed prudent to respond with casual uninterest.

It hardly mattered to Hal what Upminster thought of him. It was not as if he was *really* applying for the position of the man's son-in-law. Too many wild oats, et cetera, but if he appraised his sister of his alliance with Lizzie to stop her vexing him she was bound to tell Aaron, because she told Aaron everything. And if she got wind of the Mistletoe Wager then both he and Aaron were as good as dead because they had both promised Connie faithfully they would never enter into another wager again after the unfortunate incident at the Serpentine.

Good grief! This was all becoming unnecessarily confusing. His sister watched his face carefully as he considered it all, clearly searching his reaction to try to gauge the strength of his feelings for Lizzie.

'If you make a hash of this dinner, her father could forbid Lady Elizabeth from seeing you.'

Which rather put a different spin on things and gave him more to worry about than his complicated deceptions. Lizzie would be at the mercy of Ockendon, he would be chased by the hordes and Aaron would gloat while Hal had to shovel dung.

A quick glance at the mantel clock alerted him to the fact that it was less than an hour until eight.

Instantly, he was off the floor and dashing to his bedchamber, determined to make a good impression.

Lizzie wanted to pace the floor of the drawing room or to stare expectantly through the lace curtains to see if Hal was going to come and rescue her. However, as her father's hostess, she was stuck making small talk with the insipid bunch of gentlemen he had foisted on her for the evening. She should have anticipated this scenario the moment her wily papa had conceded that *one dance* would hardly convince her to take a husband. Two paltry hours' notice was all he had given her for tonight's *impromptu*, informal little dinner, as he had sprung it on her the moment she arrived home from the toy shop.

Although it did not appear to be particularly impromptu as far as he was concerned. No, indeed! A great deal of planning had gone into this little shenanigan. Georgie had been fed and was safely ensconced in the nursery and any sign there was a child in the house had been eradicated by the servants before she had learned they were expecting company. Not including her father there were three single gentlemen in total and not one single lady apart from herself. 'This is merely a meeting of colleagues,' he had said by way of explanation. 'An informal gathering arranged in haste so we hardly need to stand on ceremony. None of the gentlemen will expect it.'

They came in all shapes and sizes, she had to give her father credit for that at least, because he had considered variety even if the gentlemen in question were all drawn from the junior ranks of the government. But each and every one was only here for either her dowry or to impress her powerful father. In reality, all three were probably here for both. Lizzie was nicely trapped and doomed to get to know these crushing bores far better than she ever wanted.

Lord Hewitt was everything she had suspected he would be. Sensible, bland and filled with an overwhelming sense of his own importance. Lord Cheshire, on the other hand, looked as though he wouldn't say boo to a goose and blushed pink to the tips of his ears every time he so much as glanced in her direction and the least said about the stick-thin Lord Roseby the better. Like a lapdog he was hanging on her every word, a little too close, a little too cloying. His pale skin had a blue hue about it which made him appear ill.

Blue, pink and bland. A fine bunch of dullards, who would be here for hours trying to *impress* her properly seeing as they had been denied the opportunity on the dance floor. If that wasn't bad enough, her papa was currently listing her virtues like a litany. Intelligent, kind-hearted, accomplished, a sensible household manager, a good hostess… Of course, he was conveniently omitting her other attributes. Ruined. Compromised. Soiled. Comes with additional baggage you will need to find room for. No doubt it would take a significant amount of palm-greasing to erase those stains.

At five minutes to eight, when their butler came in to the drawing room looking harried, Lizzie almost visibly slumped with relief. 'The Earl of Redbridge is on the doorstep, my lord, and he is most insistent he has been invited here to dine.'

'Why, that is preposter—'

'He has, Stevens. Do show him in.' Lizzie stood and smiled sweetly at her father's outraged expression. He was not the only one who could casually lie and scheme on the quiet. 'Seeing as this *impromptu* dinner is a meeting of your colleagues, I didn't think you would mind if I invited someone to converse with when the conversation inevitably turns to state matters. Besides, with the Earl of Redbridge we are now six and six diners perfectly balances the table. You know I hate odd numbers.'

'If you wanted to balance the table, you should have invited some ladies!'

'So should you. Had I been given more notice of this evening's plans I would have. At such a late stage I could only extend an invitation to one of our close neighbours. The Earl resides around the corner in Berkeley Square.'

'There must be a great many young ladies living closer, Lizzie!'

'Oh, there are, but I do so enjoy Hal's company, Papa.' Clearly she had to abandon her original plan to appear disinterested in the Earl of Redbridge's attentions in front of him. However, as her father had taken an immediate dislike to Hal he would likely be relieved when their sham courtship came to its natural conclusion in the new year, so she was hardly giving him false hope and banished the pang of guilt.

'If the gossips are to be believed, a great many women enjoy Redbridge's company, Lady Elizabeth. I am surprised you would tolerate him.'

How marvellous. Lord Hewitt was patronising as well as condescending and bland. Lizzie shot a warning glance at her papa and set her jaw stubbornly. 'If my *chosen* guest is not welcome with the present company, *Father*, then I shall take tea with him in the morning room and then eat my dinner alone in my room. On a tray.' The temptation to poke out her tongue and flounce off was enormous.

'Of course he is *welcome*, Daughter. If you have invited him as a guest, then I am sure he has a great many redeeming qualities which make him deserving of a place at *my* table and I should be glad to learn of them over the course of the evening. As I am sure *you* will make every effort to learn about the redeeming qualities of our *other* guests as well.' Lizzie loathed it when her father used his politician's voice. His mouth said one thing, but his tone and expression said quite another.

There was not time to make a pithy retort to that effect as Hal strode into the dining room confidently, clutching the most beautiful bouquet of hothouse flowers, and his eyes locked warmly on hers. A wonderful extravagance which must have cost a small fortune in December and one which nicely told the dullards he had no need of her dowry. Nestled amongst the blooms were pink roses and one single stem of prickly holly. The holly made her feel all funny because she knew he had put it there deliberately. For her.

'Lizzie, you look stunning.' He gave her the flowers and then very slowly kissed her hand, gazing up at her with questioning eyes. She supposed it was right that she should appraise him of the reason for her summons although the feel of his lips on her skin was making casual, coded conversation difficult.

'I am so glad you were able to come, on such short notice, but as you can see, my father decided at the last minute to invite some of his government colleagues and you know how *dull* I sometimes find matters of state.'

'*Ah*...yes.' People could say what they liked about Hal's dubious scandalous reputation, but there was no denying the man was as sharp as a tack. He gave her a saucy wink. 'State matters. Very dull indeed. I am glad I could come to your aid.' He squeezed her hand reassuringly before dropping it. Only then did he turn to the other men in the room. 'Thank you for having me Lord Upminster. It is a great honour to *finally* be here.'

She watched Hal's eyes wander towards Stevens before he smiled at the scowling butler triumphantly.

Her father smiled stiffly and Lizzie tried not to be openly amused at how Hal cheerfully greeted his guests and how they responded with barely disguised disdain. Lord Hewitt attempted to look down his nose at him—however, being more than several inches shorter, he had to do so looking upwards which rather spoiled the effect and drew attention to the frightening size of his flared nostrils and the profusion of hair growing within them. Pink Cheshire was clearly intimidated up against such a powerful specimen of obvious, confident manhood and did his best to blend into the wallpaper whilst Roseby began to resemble a ghost stood next to Hal, a pale, reedy apparition who would blow away like mist in a strong gust of wind.

If only they all would.

Thankfully, they were called in to dinner at the stroke of eight. In hopeful anticipation of being saved, Lizzie had arranged a sixth place setting without her father's knowledge and had also had the good sense to swap around the name tags he had placed strategically on the table hours before. Now, the pompous Lord Hewitt was seated next to her dear papa at the opposite end of the table, Hal was sat to her right and pink Cheshire was to her left. Never having spoken to any of the other men before, it was undoubtedly a stroke of luck she had accidentally placed herself next to the shy one as he was hardly going to dominate her time. That said, the uncomfortable silence around the table as they all waited for the soup was quite painful and as hostess she supposed the task of finding an initial topic of conversation fell to her.

'Are any of you attending Lord Danbury's house party this weekend?'

Both Hewitt and Cheshire nodded, but only Bland Hewitt spoke. 'Indeed I shall—but for the hunting, you understand. Nothing more. I find the typical yuletide entertainments puerile. I am of the opinion silly parlour games should be played by children, not grown men.'

'Oh, I don't know, there is something to be said for the odd parlour game. Occasionally, they can be fun.' Her papa was a great lover of charades and quite ridiculously competitive at all games involving cards. Speculation was a particular favourite because he always insisted it was played for money and tended to be a very sore loser if he lost his. This comment earned him a frown from Lord Hewitt.

'Cards are tolerable, I suppose, as long as money is not wagered, but playing the fool for the entertainment of others is not something I could ever demean myself to do. I cannot abide seeing grown men prance around the drawing room miming words, or groping around blindfolded or humiliating themselves by getting involved in silly, improper games involving women.' His gaze flicked disapprovingly towards Hal. 'I prefer to behave like an adult.'

The pompous tone made her father bristle, but as he had high hopes of his only daughter settling down with someone sensible and staid he covered it quickly. 'Yes, I do understand your reticence.' Clearly he wanted to give Hewitt another chance, but Lizzie had taken an instant dislike to him and decided to kill her father's forlorn hopes swiftly.

'You are always the first to suggest charades, Father. You always appear to heartily enjoy it.' This earned Lizzie a pointed look from the end of the table, but she was unrepentant. Papa needed to know that she and Lord Hewitt were incompatible. 'And *so* do I.'

'Me, too,' said Hal loyally, immediately getting

the gist of what was really going on, 'The sillier the better. I shall enthusiastically join in with every one of Lady Danbury's parlour games if you are playing them, too, darling Lizzie.' Whilst this was said flirtatiously for the benefit of the dullards, he used his knee to nudge hers under the table and Lizzie couldn't stop herself from beaming at him. Of course, to everyone else it appeared that she was encouraging his advances and she did not care. Having Hal here helping to thwart her father's overt matchmaking plans was certainly turning what could have been an awful evening into a passably pleasurable one.

'I might even be tempted to partner you in one or two of them if the mood strikes me.' Lizzie's eyelashes fluttered and she realised, with a start, she was genuinely flirting. Where had that come from? Panic and surprise made them bat quicker and her pulse sped up.

'You surprise me, Lady Elizabeth.' Lord Hewitt tilted his head back a little so he could look down his nose first at Hal, then her. 'I would have thought a lady who was sensible enough to shun frivolous dances or balls would baulk at the prospect of pursuits so banal.'

'Lizzie has a great sense of fun.' Hal gave her

a glance filled with complete mischief, as if they were sharing some great secret, which of course they were. 'And she does thoroughly enjoy being twirled about the floor when she is presented with a spirited, handsome and charming partner. Why, at the end of *our* waltz she could barely contain her delight at having danced it.' Thanks to Hal's magnificent public shredding of her dance card, it was highly likely Hewitt and the rest of this motley crew had been prevented from twirling her as well.

Lord Hewitt's eyes narrowed at the subtle dig, then his expression became bland again. 'Do you hunt, Redbridge?'

'I try to avoid it.'

'I suppose it is too gentlemanly a *sport* for you.' Hewitt offered a patronising smile to the table at large and Blue Roseby made no attempt to suppress his chuckle. 'Or perhaps the choice of prey is not to your taste?'

'Careful, Hewitt. There is a lady present. I doubt Redbridge would care to discuss his favourite *sporting* pursuits in front of Lady Elizabeth and her father.' Even Lord Cheshire nodded conspiratorially before he saw her expression and blushed like a beetroot.

How charming! They were all closing ranks to try to make Hal uncomfortable, intent on dredging up his past indiscretions to gain her father's, and probably her, censure in the process. Hot on the heels of her unexpected foray in to flirting with him came the overwhelming urge to defend him although, to his credit, Hal did not appear bothered by the barbs or need her help.

'I like a good gallop across the fields as much as the next man, old boy, but I have never understood the peculiar excitement which comes from stalking a defenceless animal.'

'Hunting does take a particular strength of character, I will grant you.' Lord Hewitt took a slurp of his soup and failed to notice the drop which missed his mouth and fell on to his intricately tied cravat. 'It is not for all men. Do not feel bad about not having the stomach for the *noble* sport.'

'Strength of character?' I see nothing either strong or manly, or indeed noble, in a pack of over-excited gentlemen, complete with a half-starved pack of snarling hounds, chasing after a terrified fox or deer and then revelling in seeing it being ripped apart at the end.' Hal's amused green eyes were locked on Hewitt's and did not waver.

'I suppose that is where the pair of us differ, Redbridge. I am clearly a *man's* man.'

Three male heads bobbed in agreement, although Lizzie was delighted to see her papa's nod was very half-hearted to say the least, more a twitch than an actual inclination of the head. He had never had the stomach for hunting either and was obviously having second thoughts about his most recent preferred candidate to be his son-in-law. Hal had shown Hewitt up for the stuffed shirt he was with very little effort. Hal, of course, managed to appear nonplussed and remained his usual, good-natured, charming self even though he was being grievously insulted.

'A *man's* man. Yes, Hewitt, I believe you must be. In which case, I suppose that makes me a *ladies'* man.' He looked positively delighted at the prospect.

'Or perhaps, in view of your lack of stomach and immature behaviour, you are still a child, Redbridge, in which case, I think we would all prefer it if you were seen but not heard. Even better, neither *seen* nor *heard*.' He chortled at his own tart wit, blissfully unaware that in one sentence, Lord Hewitt had effectively moved her from mild dislike to hating him with a vengeance—and her father knew it. A new tension settled over the table. One only Lizzie and her father were part of.

'Come now, Hewitt,' her father said, 'I am sure you cannot mean that and I am certain you will make a splendid father. Seen but not heard, indeed! That is funny. You sound like a stodgy, old-fashioned and staunch disciplinarian.'

Of all things, this apparently was the one which most offended. Hewitt's self-important expression became outraged. 'I believe discipline is the single most important role of a father, Lord Upminster, and one I intend to take very seriously when I have my own sons. Unruly children grow into unruly adults.' Hewitt glared at Hal as if to prove his point, then continued undaunted spewing more nonsense out of his pompous mouth. 'To avoid bad habits forming, it is imperative to raise one's offspring correctly. Obedience is one of the first lessons they must learn.'

Insufferable man! 'Oh, really, my lord, pray enlighten us to more of your thoughts on child rearing. How, for example, does one teach one's offspring obedience?' Lizzie voice came out silkily and she watched her father wince out of the corner of her eye.

'I am glad you have asked me that question,

Lady Elizabeth, for it shows you are willing to learn and that is a most excellent quality in a young lady. Strict punishments are the key. Spare the rod and spoil the child.' He smiled and nodded as if he were the unquestionable expert on the subject. 'Bed with no supper for mild indiscretions, withdrawal of all privileges…liberal use of the strap.'

'And you would use the strap on young children, too?' Pigs would have to sprout wings and soar through the clouds before she would allow this buffoon anywhere near her son.

'The younger you start, the better.'

Lizzie's father stared at her, looking completely miserable. Pleading with her silently not to lose her temper, but it was too late. Whether it caused a scene or not Lord Hewitt was going to receive a piece of—

'My father used the strap on me daily, for as long as I can remember, and look how I turned out.' Hal's timely interruption made Lizzie pause. 'I have lost count of how many times I went to bed without supper, how much of my allowance was held back or how many things he confiscated. Dear Pater was cold, dictatorial and devoid of all humour.' Hal waved his wineglass conversationally. 'Yet all that rigid discipline failed to achieve what he wanted. We did not respect him. In fact, my sister and I hated him. He had pushed us both so very far away we did not care about his good opinion and made it our life's work to grow up completely opposite to his wishes. Any father who believes sparing the rod will ultimately spoil the child is doomed for ever to be loathed by their offspring and probably blissfully ignored in the long run. However, it does beggar the question: if you wish to be estranged from them for ever, why have the poor children in the first place?' Hal smiled sweetly to the table at large. 'Would you mind passing the salt, please, Cheshire?' He let the silence stretch as he sprinkled some and stirred it into his consommé, tasted it, then smiled as if he had not just said something earth-shatteringly brilliant. 'Lord Upminster, Lizzie was telling me there are reports of Napoleon's health failing.'

'Yes, indeed…' And just like that calm descended over the dinner table again. Hewitt was po-faced and silent for much of the rest of the meal, his flaring nose plainly out of joint. Without him, pale Lord Roseby kept his comments in check and poor Lord Cheshire continued to blush at everything and did not add anything of any value to the conversation over all five of the 'impromptu' courses. A little after eleven, only Hal remained, looking quietly pleased with himself and rightly so. He had been both a subtly attentive suitor, leaving the three dullards in no doubt they did not stand a chance with her, and an intelligent and lively conversationalist who had, frankly, saved the sorry debacle of a meal.

Like her rat of a fiancé, Rainham, he had an immense talent for charming people, yet Hal was refreshingly different from Rainham on so many levels. Despite his outer layer of superficiality, he proved he had an extensive knowledge of current affairs, had a keen interest and perceptive head for business and clearly not only attended many debates in the Lords, but also paid attention. On many topics, he was more informed than the other young men around the table, who should have known better because they were part of the Government. There was so much more to him than ready charm and Lizzie found herself quietly proud of him.

Even her father appeared to have revised his poor opinion a little, although he had practically cemented his bottom on the sofa next to his only daughter and made it quite obvious that was where it would stay until Hal left as well. He had also spent the last fifteen minutes unsubtly flipping open his pocket watch and reminding them of the time.

Something her unlikely comrade found very amusing as he took an inordinate amount of time finishing his second glass of port. With a contented sigh, he placed his glass on a side table and stretched out his long limbs languidly. 'I suppose I should wend my home, too.'

'I shall show you to the door.' As soon as Lizzie stood, her father did, too, and she glared at him. 'I think I can manage seeing Hal out, Papa. I shall only be a minute.'

'I hardly think it is proper to leave you alone with—'

She held up her hand and cut him off mid-flow. 'As I recall, I saw out all three of our other guests alone without any issue. In fact, you insisted upon it.'

'Yes—but your father knew nothing untoward would happen with those fellows.' Hal unfurled his long body out of the chair and elegantly stretched out his spine, his casual and unoffended manner effectively diffusing the situation. 'I am an altogether different kettle of fish and I completely understand your father's concerns. If I had a daughter, and she was being courted by someone like me, I would be exactly the same.' He bent and placed a soft kiss on the back of her hand which made her breath hitch. 'I shall say my goodbyes to you both here. Goodnight, Lord Upminster. I look forward to seeing you again at the Danburys'.'

Her father acknowledged the statement graciously, but soon resumed his over-protective bluster. 'I would appreciate a proper conversation with you this weekend, Redbridge, concerning your *exact* intentions towards my daughter, because I shall tell you straight—I disapprove of your association. If I may speak *plainly* to you, sir, I am afraid your reputation precedes you and my Lizzie needs a sensible man in her future.'

Hal smiled wistfully at this and shrugged in his typical good-natured way. 'Perhaps. However, from what I know of your daughter, sir, with her clever mind and feisty temperament, I will tell *you* straight that Roseby, Cheshire and that pompous fool Hewitt are not in her league and, if I may speak to you *plainly*, too, sir, you do her a disservice by foisting them upon her.'

What a thoroughly splendid thing to say. The

urge to kiss him was instantaneous. Only a small fraction of that urge was born out of gratitude. The rest of her simply wanted to melt against him for being so wonderful. Her father's mouth hung slack, he was so taken aback at being so politely chastised. For a second his jaw twitched as if he were about to counter, then he clasped it shut tightly, and simply blinked. Hal was still holding her hand in both of his and brought it back to his lips again. Lingered.

'Goodnight, Lizzie darling. Sleep tight.' And in three broad strides, he was gone.

Chapter Nine

Hal had managed to glean enough of the Earl of Upminster's travel plans over their dinner to know he had important business to attend to at the Foreign Office on Friday and therefore would not be leaving for the Danbury house party until late afternoon. This allowed Hal to time his own journey to the Danbury estate to coincide his arrival within a few minutes of Lizzie's.

This did mean delaying his sister Connie, Aaron and his mother, who had wanted to leave directly after luncheon. They were particularly unimpressed with Hal's prolonged disappearance after luncheon, which in turn made the initial atmosphere in his own carriage tense, to say the least. Of course, the frostiness might also have something to do with his jaunty festive attire. The sprig of mistletoe, with its three remaining white berries pinned to the lapel of his coat, did a splendid job of making Aaron uncharacteristically belligerent. It was near eight o'clock when they rattled up the Danburys' drive. Eight o'clock and pitch black; they were all stiff, starving hungry and absolutely freezing cold.

'Had I known we would be travelling this late into the evening I would have had additional hot bricks and blankets put in the carriage.' Connie rubbed her hands together to ward off the chill of the brisk night air. 'I really cannot understand what you were thinking, Hal, to have delayed us for so many hours.'

'Oh, I think I know exactly what he was thinking,' said Aaron, glaring at the fancy coach being unloaded just in front of them, the Upminster crest barely visible in the darkness. Connie's eyes followed her husband's and a knowing smile crept up her face when Lizzie's well-turned silk-clad ankle chose that exact moment to appear out of the door. Hal allowed his own eyes to feast upon the sight, purely because he had always had a particular fondness for a good pair of legs regardless of the female they happened to be attached to, and then hastily stared elsewhere when he saw his sister's interested expression.

'Oh, yes...now I think I understand it, too. Come along. Let us not waste the opportunity my lovestruck brother created for himself. We must befriend her.' And she was off, like an arrow shot from a crossbow, dragging their mother by the arm on a determined trajectory towards Lizzie and her father.

But Aaron stood rooted to the spot, his arms folded across his chest and his dark eyes narrowed. A stance which made Hal laugh. 'Now don't be a sore loser, old chap. It is hardly my fault your wife is thrilled with my association with Lady Elizabeth. Look at them all talking. I will lay money on the fact she is already extolling my virtues.' He patted his mistletoe corsage for effect. 'I sense another one of these berries will be gracing your palm imminently.'

'My wife might be extolling your virtues, but I intend to spend the weekend appraising Lady Elizabeth of your true nature.'

Poor Aaron. Hal almost felt sorry for him. 'Do your worst. Not only do I suspect it will not make one whit of difference, I am supremely confident she will happily let me continue to court her. By the ball on Twelfth Night, you will have all five berries.'

'And then what?'

'What do you mean *and then what*? Why, you will be spending January the seventh in my stables, that ageing back of yours creaking from the exertion of an inordinate amount of shovelling.'

Aaron waved this off stony-faced. 'That aside, what are you going to do about Lady Elizabeth? It is morally wrong to trifle with a woman's affections when you have no intention of making a commitment.'

Of course, Aaron's conscience would surface now that Hal was winning the wager—however, Hal had no intentions of telling his friend the devious truth. 'Do you wish to concede the wager?'

'You should be the one to concede it, Hal.'

'I will extricate myself from the situation gently once I win.' The lie tripped easily off his tongue. Lizzie was as opposed to marriage as Hal was, thank goodness, which was the most significant part of her attraction, and their arrangement was concluded after Twelfth Night regardless. 'I have not made any declarations or promises, nor have I even alluded to the prospect of more and, for the record, neither has she. This is merely a flirtation. For both of us.'

'She invited you to sit at her father's table. That is fairly significant.'

The conversation was beginning to make Hal uncomfortable. He couldn't tell the truth, yet pretending he had no conscience over the situation did not sit right with him either. If he and Lizzie did not have a particular and mutually beneficial arrangement, he already knew he would concede the wager. She was too good to be trifled with and if anyone else tried it he would nip it in the bud swiftly and mercilessly, something he never thought he would ever hear himself think about a woman he had no family connection to. 'Lizzie knows what I am, Aaron, and doubtless sees the situation for exactly what it is. Come along. We are appearing rude by not joining the ladies.'

After the flurry of polite hellos and the taking of coats and cloaks, Lord and Lady Danbury came to meet them in the holly-decked hall. Lizzie had come to stand next to Hal as the hosts greeted each guest individually. As they were at the end of the line, the raucous sounds of laughter coming from the crowded drawing room bizarrely gave them privacy. 'I am sorry about my papa's behaviour towards you the other evening. He means well, but has a tendency towards over-protectiveness.'

'Think nothing of it. I am quite used to that sort of reaction, I can assure you. It is probably deserved.' He was lying. It was definitely deserved, although for once he felt a little ashamed of his past. Aaron's reservations were also bothering him.

'Doesn't it upset you? Having everyone judging you and dismissing you as a superficial hedonist?' It hadn't up until now. For years, he had worn the mantle of rake proudly to vex his father. The more scandal he created, the more satisfying his father's explosive reaction was. However, whilst he could not deny his past, Hal realised he did not want that to be how she judged him.

'The *ton* loves to gossip and I give them an outlet to do so. However, compared to some, I fear I am not as great a scoundrel as the gossips make out. I have hidden depths.' What had possessed him to say that? He had meant it to come out as a flippant, flirty remark, instead it had sounded too earnest, because it was true. There were many aspects of his character he kept hidden. His new conscience being one of them. Aaron would have a field day if he knew he was getting to him.

'Oh, I am well aware of your hidden depths.' She was smiling, but not in a patronising way.

'Beneath the layer of boyish charm lies a thoughtful and intelligent man. You are well informed, clearly read the newspapers and not *just* the gossip pages, have a great understanding of commerce and diplomacy...'

'Diplomacy? I wouldn't go that far.' Except Hal desperately wanted the compliments.

'A diplomat knows how to deal with all manner of people, something you manage to do very effectively without causing an argument. Look at how deftly you stopped Lord Hewitt from dominating the conversation with his own silly opinions. Or how you politely chastised my father for foisting those dullards on me the other evening. You were quite wonderful. Your comments hit home, by the way. He has been most introspective about it all since. He even apologised for springing them on me and for promoting Lord Hewitt as a potential suitor. Thanks to you, he learned quickly what sort of a pompous fellow Lord Hewitt is. A man who can achieve all that, so casually and without causing an argument, is very skilled at the art of diplomacy.'

You were quite wonderful. For some reason Hal had latched on to those words and swore his chest expanded with pride at the sound of them. At least he hoped it was pride, although pride didn't tend to make one's heart hammer excitedly or one's throat tighten with emotion. And why was it he was suddenly unable to look away from her?

'Oh, look! Our two lovebirds are under the mistletoe.' Lady Danbury's excited voice brought him sharply out of his daze and simultaneously he and Lizzie both glanced up. Suspended from the chandelier on a long piece of scarlet ribbon was a huge ball of mistletoe. 'You must kiss her. It's bad luck to ignore it!'

'Yes, Hal—kiss her!' Connie joined in the call and every eye in the hall was suddenly locked on them expectantly. Apart from the Earl of Upminster, who appeared most aggrieved at the suggestion, and Aaron, of course, who was glaring with barely concealed disbelief at the fickle hand of fate. It was probably that glare which cut through the sudden and inexplicable nerves and convinced Hal to go for it. Another berry would soon be plucked and poor Aaron would be there to witness it all. Although, he doubted that had much bearing on the giant butterflies which were now flapping away in his stomach.

He looked down at Lizzie, who was a little wide-eyed and clearly waiting to follow his lead, watched her lick her lips nervously and felt his own warm in readiness. 'We wouldn't want to court bad luck, would we, fair maiden?' His voice came out deeper. Softer. Hopeful.

She shook her head imperceptibly and he watched the tip of her tongue dart out to moisten her lips as her face tilted up a little. An invitation? He hoped so. Hal would rather they did not have an audience, although usually something like that would not bother him, but he was damned if he would let such a sterling opportunity slip. His hand came up to touch her cheek of its own accord before his mouth came down to lightly touch hers and, in that instant, everybody else disappeared.

She tasted of home.

Those were the first thoughts which permeated his brain after his body rejoiced at the contact. Warm and comforting, yet at the same time incendiary. The second her lips had touched his, his body had needed more—however, his heart appeared very content to simply savour the peculiarly intimate moment. He felt no desire to hurry nor could he deepen the kiss in public, so he simply stayed exactly where he was, grateful she did not step back either.

'That's quite enough of that!' Lizzie's father

tugged her away and shot daggers at Hal through eyes narrowed to slits and the beautiful, sensual spell was broken. 'Come along, Lizzie, we have dawdled in this hall long enough and we both need to change for dinner. We do not want to hold the meal up.'

Her cornflower eyes slanted briefly to his in apology and Hal did his best approximation of a roguish smile to fluster her already flustered father some more, and saw the delicate blush staining her cheeks at being made a spectacle. Then she dutifully followed her father and a footman up the stairs.

She moved with such grace, he noticed, her trim hips undulating slightly in a very pleasing, feminine fashion with each step. At the top she turned and their gazes locked once again, except there was no apology in them this time, more bemusement, making him wonder if their very short, very chaste kiss had had the same effect on her as it had on him. Hal's head was spinning. His pulse a notch too fast. His cravat suddenly far too tight and his body desperate for more.

Of her.

The urge to bolt up the stairs and simply take was extremely unsettling.

All this time he had wondered where his missing vigour had gone and it had chosen this precise moment, when he was on full display in a crowded hall, to suddenly reappear with a vengeance.

He wanted Lizzie.

Good gracious!

Properly wanted her. It had nothing whatsoever to do with his wager with Aaron and he was quite certain this new feeling of actual desire for Lizzie was certainly contrary to the terms of their alliance. Nor did it resemble any of the multiple ways he had wanted women before. Those had been solely about passion. Whilst he most definitely felt that for her, there was also something else lurking inside, something dangerously bordering on affection and emotional need rather than the purely physical.

Good grief! His heart was engaged.

A new startling and unexpected development Hal needed to think about.

Alone.

His suddenly weak knees nearly buckled at the revelation. How the devil had that happened?

'Oh, look!' Lady Danbury decided to clap her hands together at the same time to achieve maximum impact. 'They cannot bear to take their eyes off each other. Look at the pair of them gazing at each other over the banisters! When they are wed, I shall proudly tell everyone the romance blossomed under my very roof!'

The word *wed* made him feel decidedly queasy, but Hal managed a weak smile while he gathered his wits together and tried not to feel guilty to see both his sister and mother beaming at him in excitement as they began to follow another footman upstairs. The only person not beaming was Aaron, whose expression was best described as total incredulity mixed with disgust.

'It staggers me that luck continues to favour you when you really don't deserve it.'

'Don't be a poor sport, Aaron.' Hal took the stairs two at a time with his heart thumping, hoping he appeared nonplussed. 'I did not even see that fortuitous ball of mistletoe and neither did you.'

'Aha! So you admit it was a fluke? Therefore, it doesn't count towards the five.'

'There was no stipulation that fluke kisses were not included, old boy, and well you know it. I am three down and have only two left to go. You are just peeved you did not spot the mistletoe first.'

'If I had, I would have stood beneath it myself and refused to move.'

'It is Christmas, and at Christmas one has to expect mistletoe to crop up somewhere, and thus I am now hopeful a few more stray sprigs will be conveniently dotted around this estate—in entirely different locations, of course, as stipulated in the terms of the wager—although we both know I won't need the aid of mistletoe. I am irresistible to the ladies. I doubt you remember what that feels like now you are past your prime, old boy.'

'I am blissfully married to your sister, not past my prime.'

'If you say so. I am blissfully thrilled that you could be there to witness that kiss. Your face was an absolute picture. Who knew your jaw could fall open that wide? Seeing it has made the inevitable victory significantly sweeter.'

'What are you two whispering about?' Connie was stood looking down at them suspiciously.

'I was just commenting on how splendid the Danburys' mouldings are, my darling. Why, the craftsmanship on the ceiling is positively exquisite.' His friend smiled innocently up at his wife although it was plain she did not believe her husband one bit.

'Oh, really? Miraculously, after five years of marriage, you have a sudden interest in mouldings?'

Aaron threaded her arm through his. 'Five *blissful* years of marriage, Constance. You keep forgetting the word *blissful*. Ah, look! Our bags have arrived.'

His wife suitably distracted, Aaron made a very rude hand gesture to Hal below, then they went left on the landing while another footman waited to escort him and his baggage to the right, explaining Lady Danbury had ensured the single ladies were placed alongside the married couples whilst the bachelors were to be housed at the furthest end of the west wing for the sake of propriety. Although that kept him firmly and gratefully away from the clutches of the hordes, it also neatly separated him from Lizzie which was probably just as well now that his missing vigour had crawled out of its hiding place and still lingered in his breeches.

Hal watched his brother-in-law's retreating back and could not resist a final dig. 'Oh, Aaron, aren't you forgetting something?'

He sent the third white berry whizzing through the air with such perfect timing, it hit its intended, and supremely irritated, target smack in the middle of the forehead.

Chapter Ten

Lizzie closed her bedchamber door and gratefully sank on to her mattress, feeling more than a little overwhelmed. A silly, innocent kiss under the mistletoe should not have turned her insides into mush and given her body ideas it had no right having. There should be a warning note pinned to Hal, letting all ladies know never to let his lips anywhere near their person as it scrambled the brain. Hours later and she was still flushed from the experience. Hot all over and thankful they had been in company all night and that her father had brought the kiss to an end swiftly, else she probably would have quickly lost all sense of reason, wound her arms around his neck and happily dissolved into a puddle at the man's feet.

And if she was brutally honest with herself, it was not only the intoxicating nature of his kiss which was worrying. The moment she had seen him standing on the drive, six feet and some of glorious, handsome male, a rakish smile on his face and a knowing glint in his eye, Lizzie had been ridiculously happy to see him and more than a little excited at the prospect of spending the entire weekend in his company. Why she was having these thoughts, when he was a charming rake like Rainham, who by his own admission was wholly against marrying any time this decade, and when she was a confirmed spinster who had sworn off men for ever, was a mystery. However, there was no point denying the odd frisson she felt whenever she was near Hal was attraction and perhaps there was a little affection in the mix. Henry Stewart, Earl of Redbridge, for all his faults, was very easy to love.

Not love! Lizzie hastily corrected with alarm, sitting bolt upright again...*like*. He was very easy to *like* and, truth be told, she was in grave danger of liking him a great deal.

Fortunately, their hostess had seated them at completely opposite ends of the dinner table because Lizzie had needed the distance. Unfortunately, the pair of them kept locking eyes during the meal and what was worse was that a great many of the other diners noticed. Hal's sister was one of them and clearly delighted at their interest in one another. When the interminable dinner was over, Lizzie initially avoided him. A situation which he complied with, as if he sensed her reluctance or perhaps felt the need for some distance himself. A sobering thought indeed, especially as the idea he was attracted to her, too, and similarly avoiding her hurt. Which was, of course, ridiculous. For an hour, they were across the room from one another, yet at all times Lizzie was painfully aware of exactly where he was and exactly what he was doing.

When two young ladies commandeered him, practically backing him into a corner of the room, Lizzie realised she was being unfair. Her odd mood was hardly Hal's fault and she had agreed to keep the hordes at bay. Thanks to his well-chosen words to her father, for the first time in years, he was not openly trying to matchmake at a social function. A whole weekend of peace stretched before her and Hal had been entirely responsible for that. Just because she was no longer suffering did not mean the need for an alliance was at an end. That would be unforgivably selfish. Fair was fair and she owed him. Taking a deep breath,

Lizzie had straightened her spine and set a course to rescue her Earl.

'Oh, there you are, Hal, *darling*.' She had pushed her way through the barricade of persistent silk and wove her hand possessively around his elbow. 'I am sorry to interrupt, ladies, but I must steal him away. Your sister has been searching for you.'

His warm palm came to rest atop hers and had squeezed gratefully. Once again, her body seemed to stand to attention at his touch. 'Is she indeed? Then you had best take me to her. Quickly.'

'I shall *expect* you back presently my lord,' said Lady Arabella Farlow, a statuesque blonde with far too much of her décolleté on show and a permanent and well-practised pout which she obviously thought was attractive. 'Lady Elizabeth has monopolised you quite enough this yuletide and I am *dying* to get to know you better.' She punctuated this with a little wiggle of her shoulders which made the parts of her spilling out of her dress wobble.

Lizzie had blatantly stared at the younger girl's chest, mimicking the disapproving face her mother had used to such great effect. 'My dear Lady Arabella, I do believe you have misplaced your fichu. It might be prudent to retrace your steps to go find it.'

As intended, Lady Arabella coloured with embarrassment and Lizzie whisked Hal away before the vixen found her bold voice again.

'You might want to give Lady Arabella a wide berth.'

He sighed and squeezed her hand again. 'I have been trying to give that chit a wide berth for months, but she is outrageously persistent. Just before you saved me, she was quizzing me about the exact directions to my bedchamber.'

'I hope you did not give them to her. She's the type to visit.' Lizzie tried, and failed, to ignore the knot of irrational jealousy that clawed in the pit of her stomach, reasoning she was merely being protective of her friend. Hal *was* her friend now. Odd feelings aside, she genuinely liked him and enjoyed his company. They looked out for one another. Who'd have thought she would have befriended a notorious rake? Not her. A month ago, the very idea would have sent her into a rage.

'Oh! I gave her directions all right. The third room to the right as you go into the west wing.' Lizzie paused and stared at him in disbelief, only to watch him throw his dark head back and laugh.

'The third room to the right is not mine, you nod-cock. I am not that stupid. It's Lord Hewitt's.'

Lizzie tried to maintain her outrage, but her lips were already twitching at the thought of the pompous Hewitt being awoken by the predatory and pouting Arabella. 'You shouldn't have done that either.'

Hal laughed heartily and once again her insides did a funny little wiggle and she found herself staring hungrily at his lips. 'Nonsense. Of course I should. Besides, I couldn't resist a bit of revenge on Hewitt, and who knows? They both might thank me one day. What an interesting couple they would make. I am so delighted with myself, I might stay awake all night and wait for the screams. Which one will scream louder, do you think? My money is on Hewitt.'

For the rest of the evening, they remained together wherever possible, drinking far more wassail than was sensible and laughing conspiratorially at one inappropriate comment after the next. He partnered her in charades and spillikins, and then sat, with her father sandwiched unsubtly in between them, for a long and raucous game of speculation, which he won with very little effort and to her father's complete and utter disgust. And just now, he had stared deeply into her eyes as he had bid her goodnight and then he had kissed her hand, in that slow and sensual way of his, so she practically floated up the stairs thinking a stream of silly thoughts which were most unlike her.

There should definitely be a warning pinned to his coat. Tomorrow, perhaps a brisk, solitary walk across the cold, hilly parkland was in order? The exercise might help to unscramble her wits. This alliance was not quite working out the way she had expected, because she had certainly never expected to develop any feelings for the man. Or for any man for that matter. Especially charming, handsome men with tarnished reputations and a way with women. Yet with each passing hour, a little bit of her resolve was steadily chipped away. If he hadn't been a rake, and if she was in the market for a husband, Lizzie would be sorely tempted.

And now she was lying to herself, because she was sorely tempted. Hal had reawakened a part of the girl she had been. The effervescent, witty, social young woman who enjoyed laughing and had wanted to marry her prince, then live happily ever after. Worse still, her hardened, shredded, battered heart was beating again, except it had chosen to beat for another man like Rainham. Infinitely more handsome and charming. Undoubtedly more noble, but still very, very dangerous. Twelfth Night really could not come soon enough.

After a fitful night's sleep, Lizzie arrived to breakfast deliberately late only to find the dining room filled with people, including a very dashing-looking Hal. The moment he spotted her he waved, a look of panic on his face, and numerous young ladies sat around him in the most predatory fashion. 'There you are, Lizzie *darling*! I saved you a seat.' He patted the chair next to him and she realised, in that instant, any chance of a restorative solitary walk had just flown out of the window. As he had feared, poor Hal was at the mercy of his baying hordes. This morning she would be his personal bodyguard, although pasting a lovestruck expression on her face did not prove to be as difficult as it usually did. Nor did looking jealous. She pierced Lady Arabella with such a fearsome glare that the younger woman blushed and her fingers flapped nervously at the lacy fichu she was clearly not used to wearing.

The seat Hal had managed to save was far too

close to him. The baying hordes had barely left her enough space to wriggle into and, once seated, Lizzie's hip was pressed intimately against his.

'Did you sleep well?'

'Like a log.' She hoped the dark circles under her eyes were not too evident. 'You?'

'Surprisingly soundly.' His voice dipped to a whisper which warmed her neck. 'I barricaded the door with the dressing table.'

'Very wise.'

'You missed the show this morning. Lord Hewitt turned quite an impressive shade of crimson when he collided with Lady Arabella.' Perhaps that explained the fichu and the flush, yet the girl was obviously intent on still stalking Hal, as she brazenly interrupted their hushed conversation by calling across the table.

'A few of us are going riding, Lord Redbridge, and would be delighted if *you* would accompany us.' Talons back in place, she shot Lizzie a look which told her that she was most assuredly not invited.

'Lord Redbridge is otherwise engaged this morning.' Lizzie smiled tightly and took a sip of the tea which had just been placed in front of her.

'Oh, really? Doing what? Because if it is more interesting than riding then perhaps I could join you?'

'We are going into the village to shop for ribbons.'

She felt Hal instantly stiffen at the suggestion and hoped, for both their sakes, that ribbon shopping was a poor alternative to all the entertainments on the Danbury estate. There was a beat of silence, then Lady Arabella beamed. 'Perfect. I need new ribbons and I dare say you and the Earl of Redbridge are desirous of a chaperon.'

'We already have a chaperon. The Earl's sister is accompanying us and...' Surely there must be something dreadfully dull and unappealing she could think of to dislodge the barnacle-like Lady Arabella, although Lizzie's mind had gone quite blank. Then it came to her. 'And I have arranged to meet Lord Hewitt in the hall. Did I mention *he* was accompanying us as well?'

Despite the fact Hal had to walk to the village for the sake of authenticity, dragging his delighted sister and less delighted brother-in-law along, too, he had a thoroughly pleasant morning. His sister monopolised Lizzie all the way there and back, leaving him to chat to Aaron as they trailed in their wake and, aside from the distinct lack of baying hordes, it was nice to see her getting on well with his family. Especially Connie. His sister had never suffered fools gladly and her good opinion mattered to him more than anyone else's. Not that he wanted her good opinion in this case, of course, but it comforted him none the less to know that he had it.

The afternoon wafted by without incident, although he had scarcely had two minutes alone with Lizzie all day. Largely because Aaron had decided to attach himself like a leech in case Hal succeeded in stealing another kiss from her. Even the outrageous stories he kept telling about Hal's exploits, all sadly true, were directly intended to ward her off and the poor fellow was getting increasingly frustrated by her cheerful, laughing acceptance of it all.

'Surely you have heard about Hal's scandalous exhibition at the Serpentine, Lady Elizabeth?'

'My father mentioned something, but I must confess I have no idea what occurred.'

'I am not sure we need to discuss that, Aaron,

darling. Not when I am still furious at *you* for your part in it.' Connie's voice dripped venom which her irascible husband ignored.

'It was a warm summer's day and we decided to have a race. A lap of vigorous swimming around the lake and then a sprint to Hyde Park Corner.'

'Aaron dearest, do you want to sleep in Lady Danbury's stable tonight? Because if you do, you are going the right way about it.'

Undeterred and encouraged by Lizzie's obvious interest, Aaron took her arm. 'We found a secluded end of the Serpentine and stripped down to our drawers...'

'Aaron James Wincanton, this is hardly a proper conversation for a pleasant walk in the countryside.'

'Oh, let him have his fun, Connie.' Hal took his sister's arm, grinning cheerfully. 'The incident is hardly a secret.' At least a hundred people had witnessed it and it had made the papers and, more importantly, poor Aaron had no idea it would not make the slightest bit of difference to his alliance with Lizzie.

Aaron went on to recall, in great detail, how when they had concluded their neck-and-neck swim around the enormous lake and then heaved themselves out of the water to dress, ready for the gruelling next leg of the race, they had discovered that all their clothes had been stolen. Like the gentleman he was, Aaron had hidden in the bushes to spare the blushes of the many people in the park. Hal, on the other hand, had refused to concede and had sprinted across the grass in his soggy drawers and claimed victory.

'You ran from the Serpentine to Hyde Park Corner in just your underthings?' Lizzie stared at him dumbfounded. 'Hal, you really are incorrigible.'

'But that is not the best of it, Lady Elizabeth.'

'It gets worse?'

Aaron paused for effect. 'The water had rendered his drawers transparent. Everybody who saw him fly past could see his unmentionables!'

Lizzie giggled and Aaron's face fell. 'As shocking as the incident was, it made him a great deal more popular with the ladies… Oomph!'

His sister's elbow rammed into her husband's ribs with some force. 'It is not too late to have our marriage annulled. Husband.'

'*Blissful* marriage, my dear. You keep missing out the word blissful.'

They arrived back at the Danbury residence just as the sun was beginning to set. Lizzie was more relaxed and contented than he had ever seen her. His sister, on the other hand, appeared ready to skewer her husband. To that end, Connie had practically dragged Aaron upstairs to 'dress for dinner', a euphemism for 'I am going to give you a sound tongue lashing', if ever there was one, and at last Hal had her to himself for the first time that day.

'Ribbon shopping? That was the best deterrent you could come up with?'

She slanted a cheeky smile up at him and something peculiar happened in the vicinity of his heart. It felt like a twang. As if some imaginary string had been plucked. 'I saved you from Lady Arabella, didn't I?'

'I cannot fathom why she is being so persistent.'

'You are an earl with a reasonably good face.'

'A good face? Am I starting to grow on you, Lizzie, darling?'

'I'm afraid your scandalous behaviour at the Serpentine has quite put me off.'

'You wouldn't be saying that if you had seen me. I look quite spectacular in my birthday suit.' Flirting was second nature to him, but flirting with her was dangerous. Probably best avoided. 'Come upstairs and I'll show you.' His voice instinctively deepened and what was meant as a naughty retort intended to shock and make her giggle sounded a lot like an invitation. His long-lost but recently found vigour was urging him on, as was his heart. 'My bedchamber is the third room to the *left* as you go into the west wing should you feel the urge to visit me in the night. Shall I leave the dressing table in its correct place—just in case?'

'You are shameless.' But she was still smiling and that twanging happened again, accompanied by his suddenly racing heart as she lent closer. Desire had never felt quite so...personal before. 'I certainly hope somebody is within earshot to hear all this outrageous flirting. I would hate for your efforts to be wasted.'

The easy smile Hal gave her was false and not easy to achieve. She assumed he was acting, as per the terms of their agreement, when he hadn't meant to be at all. Forgetting the remaining two berries, he wanted to kiss her. Badly. Kiss her until they were both senseless and then carry her to his bed. Make love to her, then talk to her all night...

Talking? Good grief! The sudden and visceral need to know her on a deeper level was unsettling.

A footman went past, carrying steaming cups

of wassail, and Hal grabbed some to stop himself from touching her. She sipped hers slowly and gazed around the room. 'Lord Hewitt has not so much as looked at me all day, so I hope he has decided I am no longer potential marriage material—however, he has been casting longing glances in Lady Arabella's direction, although she still looks at you.'

Was she? Hal hadn't noticed. He was developing a worrying habit of not noticing anything but Lizzie whenever he was with her. 'Poor Lord Hewitt. I am inclined to feel sorry for him. To covet something you cannot have is torture.' Never were truer words spoken. Her lack of reciprocal romantic interest in him was painful.

'I cannot bring myself to feel sorry for him at all. Although I am encouraged to see my father has avoided him, too, so clearly the bloom is off that rose. Dear Papa has also, thus far at least, avoided trying to foist any new dullards on me.'

'Your father strikes me a good man, Lizzie. However, I fail to understand why he believes you would be happy with a fellow like Hewitt.' The more he considered it, the more improbable it all was. Lizzie was beautiful, intelligent and positively ripe for the picking. Why was Upminster determined to sell her so short when any man would be over the moon to have her?

'After so many years sitting happily on the shelf, my father despairs of me. I believe he is now getting quite desperate as the calibre of gentleman he parades under my nose has significantly declined. He has given up hope of my snaring a prince or a duke. Now we are trawling the depths of the lesser peers and sirs. Although even by those standards, Lord Hewitt was a dud.'

Hal had skilfully manoeuvred them to a quiet alcove to watch the proceedings from a distance, and—if he was being brutally honest with himself—so he could have her all to himself for a little while longer.

'Talking of duds, I see Ockendon has just arrived.'

To begin with, she merely stiffened, but then colour quickly drained out of her face. The cup of wassail tilted, spilled and Hal instinctively took it from her as he followed her gaze. But it was not Ockendon who had caused the odd reaction. It was his companion. Another man Hal could not place. Whoever the fellow was, Lady Danbury did not look at all pleased to see him, because she was smiling tightly as a hovering footman took his coat. A smile so brittle it appeared likely to shatter at any moment.

'Do you know him?'

Lizzie stood like a marble statue, frozen on the spot for several seconds, her gaze never leaving the latecomer. When Ockendon began to lead his companion into the room, she backed further into the alcove, clearly distressed.

'Lizzie! What is the matter?'

Only then did she look up at him, those cornflower eyes swimming with frightened tears. 'I have to go!' Quick as a flash, she spun around and stumbled towards the French doors. Before Hal could deposit the two cups on a table to reach for her, she had wrestled open the handle and bolted out into the dark garden beyond. It was so unexpected, so out of character, her reaction made him panic, too. Something was very wrong.

Chapter Eleven

A quick glance around the secluded alcove told him nobody had noticed her frantic escape and Hal knew she would hate to be the cause of a scene, so on stealthy feet he followed her outside and quietly closed the door behind him. There was no sign of her on the terrace and, because it was close to freezing outside, no lights had been lit in the garden. Obviously, the Danburys had assumed nobody would be mad enough to go outside.

'Lizzie?' Although barely above a whisper, his voice sounded loud in the silence. She did not answer, forcing Hal to strain his ears for sounds of movement. There were none. The silhouetted shapes of clipped bushes and trees were shrouded in mist as he plunged into the garden.

Ten minutes later and his fingers were frozen and his stomach was in knots. He had kept a close eye back on the house and he was certain she had not returned there, and without a coat or shawl she must be chilled to the bone. The further into the grounds he walked, the less the pale crescent moon illuminated his surroundings; looking for Lizzie in this was like searching for a needle in a haystack. Hal doubled back, skirting around the edge of the lawn towards the stables to fetch a lantern and wanted to cheer in relief when he spied her, sat all alone and hunched on a bench.

His feet crunched on the frosty grass as he hurried towards her, alerting her to his presence. She looked up, her lovely face totally wretched, and visibly sagged when she saw it was him rather than someone else. She had been crying. Her face was wan and drawn, her eyes and nose slightly swollen. Her slim shoulders still trembled and her fingers were twisting a crumpled handkerchief nervously. Wordlessly, Hal sat down and wrapped his arm around her, pulling her closer beneath his coat to share the heat from his body. She didn't pull away. Instead she burrowed into the crook of his neck gratefully.

'I've been worried sick.'

'I'm sorry. Seeing him after all these years gave me quite a start.' Despite their close and intimate position, she was staring out into nothingness. The old, guarded expression painted on to her pale face. Pretending all was well when it clearly wasn't.

'Seeing who?' Whoever he was, Ockendon's companion was at the root of all this.

'The Marquess of Rainham... We were engaged...once upon a time.'

'Ah.' Recognition dawned at the same moment intense jealousy sliced through him and left a bitter, unfamiliar taste in his mouth. The Rainham Hal remembered had been a handsome fellow who enjoyed his pleasures. The years had not been kind. The man with Ockendon had the pallor of a man who lived hard. Imagining her shackled to a wastrel like Rainham made the bile rise in his throat. 'You had a lucky escape all those years ago, I think.'

'I thought so...' Her voice trailed off and she stared mournfully at the twisted handkerchief in her lap. 'But now he is back.' Her voice caught and she covered her face with her hands, burrowing closer into his chest as fresh sobs racked her body.

Instantly protective and desperate to ease her pain, Hal smoothed his hands over her back and hair. The bitter taste of jealousy made him frown involuntarily and he was glad she could not see his face. 'You loved him?'

'At the time I did. I was head over heels in love with him. Charles was as charming as he was handsome.' And Hal hated him with a passion. He sincerely doubted he had ever hated anyone more than he did *that* man at *that* moment. Even the loathing he had for his own father paled in comparison to this new and potentially violent hatred which burned inside. 'Everyone warned me he was trouble, but I was too besotted to listen to them.'

'But you came to your senses.' At least he hoped she had. If she still carried a torch for the man Hal might have to commit murder. 'Do you still…love him?' His hands ached to clench into fists while he waited for her answer, fists he would enjoy pummelling in to Rainham's unworthy, pale face.

He felt her head shake against his throat. 'I loathe him. And I loathe myself more for my foolishness all those years ago. I hate how trusting and besotted I was right to the last minute.'

Hal let out the tense breath he had been holding unconsciously, thankful that her feelings for her former fiancé were dead and buried. 'We all make mistakes, Lizzie. Thank goodness you realised he was no good and terminated your engagement, even if it was at the very last minute.'

She stiffened in his arms and he swore he felt her inwardly go to war with herself. On a ragged sigh, she eventually laughed with no humour whatsoever. A bitter, harsh sound which was difficult to hear and filled with raw pain. 'I didn't terminate the engagement.' She sat up straight, pulled away from him, her eyes downcast. Guarded. Then she huffed out a sigh which sounded like defeat. 'You might as well know the truth... That day... I was actually at the church. In the vestry. Waiting for him...like the silliest and most trusting of fools.' The next noise was a cross between a laugh and a sob. 'But my devoted fiancé...he never bothered turning up.'

Her words took a few moments to sink in, she could tell. When they did he sounded incredulous. 'You were jilted?'

Lizzie shrugged and stared off into space, knowing he would see the truth if she dared to look in those intelligent green eyes. Thanks to her blind panic and foolhardy decision to run, he would be able to piece together a great deal. It was obvious there was unfinished business between her and the Marquess of Rainham. Obvious her foolish heart had been shredded into tiny pieces. The very last thing she ever wanted anyone to see her as was an object of pity. Least of all Hal, when he saw her as someone else. Someone courageous and bold and pithy and fun. She should have stayed. She knew that now. Stood proudly. Looked the scoundrel dead in the eye and feigned uninterest at seeing him again.

The trickle of unease had begun the moment Ockendon had arrived. His wily old eyes had scanned the room, searching for her. She had known it emphatically when they had briefly locked with hers. She had seen him smile maliciously, then slowly turn towards his companion in introduction. The satisfied, knowing smile he wore was unsettling. At first, she had not known who it was. His back had been to her as he removed his greatcoat; the coat finally gone, Ockendon's companion turned around and nausea slammed into her. Lizzie literally couldn't breathe. All the air had rushed out of her in a stinging swoosh the moment she saw Rainham, tight bands of panic wrapped around her ribs prevented her from sucking any more in and, like a frightened deer, she had bolted towards the French doors.

The dire implications did not need to be spelled out because she had feared them for five long years. Ockendon knew she had secrets. Perhaps not all of them, but enough ammunition to force his suit. Aside from her secret, her poor papa had been through so much already. Her debacle, his wife's untimely death soon after—he did not deserve to see his life's work and good name ruined, too, because of her mistake.

If only she had had the courage to put her escape plan in to action sooner. The little house was waiting for her and Georgie in the north. Had been waiting for two months now. She had wanted to give her dear papa one last Christmas, putting off the dreadful day when she had to tell him she was leaving and taking his beloved grandson with her—she knew how much this would upset her father. Suddenly, that upset seemed kinder than what was about to happen. Her carefully constructed façade, the façade her father had worked hard to create on her behalf, was on the brink of collapsing like a house of cards. Unravelling into the mother of all scandals.

Hal was still in a state of complete incredulity. 'But everyone believes *you* called off the wedding.'

'No. My fiancé had found another, richer prospect. A duke's daughter. They were bound for Gretna Green—but intercepted before her life was ruined, too. Two silly young ladies had a lucky escape that day, I think.' His hand came up to rest on her cheek and she saw the pity. The need to understand. To help. To fix. As if he could, by some miracle, make the tangled web of lies and secrets disappear. Why did he keep doing things that made her heart melt?

Lizzie turned her head away from his touch. Much as she wanted his comfort, and she *did* want his comfort, she dared not confess all. There was too much at stake to risk baring her hand completely. Even to Hal. Not yet. Not when there still might be a chance to avoid it. 'My father used his government connections to get it all hushed up.'

She also suspected he had paid a fortune and pulled all manner of high-placed strings to completely ruin Rainham and have him banished from society. Her father was not a cruel man, but as a parent herself she understood he would have done whatever was necessary to protect his offspring. She would happily murder anyone who tried to hurt Georgie. Murder them and then happily hide the corpse. She sincerely doubted her father would feel any different. He was fiercely

loyal and devoted to his family. It was no coinci-
dence that her fiancé, normally a stalwart at all
society functions, had disappeared so completely.
He would not have disappeared without some serious persuading. Or some serious threats. Threats
which would end her papa's career in disgrace
if the world suddenly found out he had abused
his power in such a self-serving way. Lizzie had
been so content knowing she would never see the
wretch again, she had never asked her father to
explain. Now she wished she had, although she
doubted he would have told her even then. In her
papa's mind, women needed protecting from the
world. Even fallen women.

Why had Charles surfaced here? Why now? To
see him with the slimy Ockendon, hot on the heels
of the odious old Earl's unexpected and creepy
proposal, set alarm bells ringing. And the way
Ockendon had looked at her—mentally undress-
ing her, making no attempt at even trying to
charm her. Behaving as if a union between them
was little more than a formality.

Inevitable.

It was all *too* coincidental.

Her mind was racing, trying to understand what
the pair of them were up to and what, if anything,

she could do about it. Lizzie needed to choose her next words very carefully. 'I haven't seen him since the day before the wedding.' Blithely climbing down the wisteria, his passion spent in her willing body, his traitorous lips still lying to the end as he had blown her a final kiss goodbye.

Was he now in cahoots with Ockendon?

Probably. After what he had done, she would put nothing past Charles. He was the lowest of the low. Lower. If he was in league with Ockendon, then the old Earl knew he had lain with her. What else did he know? Her mind was spinning with questions. Had she slipped up somewhere? Had Georgie been seen? Had a servant talked? One glance at the sorry excuse for a man she had nearly married confirmed categorically what she had always suspected. Her son was the image of his father. The same dark hair. The same dark eyes. It would not take a genius to put two and two together.

Lizzie needed to speak to her father.

Hal took one look at her, saw the acute sadness, the distress and the fear, and instantly went on the offensive.

'He broke your heart!' She had never seen him so furious. 'How dare he jilt you!' He shot upright and she saw his hands fist, apparently ready to avenge her for the slight and she loved him for that. 'I think that snake and I need to have words!'

'No, Hal. The last thing I want is for him to ever know he mattered.' She reached for his hand. Squeezed it. And because she wanted to hold it tight, lace her fingers with his and rest her head on his shoulder again and stay there for ever, she dropped it and went back to worrying the handkerchief she had ruined. 'Or for the world to learn of the truth.' At least that was the truth. There were more reputations at stake here than her own. Her father's. Perhaps Lord Bulphan's, too. Other good men who had helped her father erase Rainham from her life. Even the lovely, furious Earl stood quaking with rage in front of her. Earls could be rakes. In youth, it was practically expected. But regardless of his youthful indiscretions, he did not deserve to be pulled into this scandal when all he was guilty of was protecting her from her father's matchmaking attempts. She had to distance herself from him, too. Now. Before it was too late.

'I still want to kill him. But I won't—if you don't want me to.' Hal was clearly still furious, but loyally bowed to her logic.

'Seeing him was a shock. I simply needed a few minutes to gather myself together. When I greet him, I want to be dispassionate, not...not like this.'

'Then you will greet him with me. On *my* arm. I want him to know I will skewer him if he so much as mentions anything to embarrass you.'

'Agreed.' Hal would act as a shield one last time until she knew what was at play. She also needed his strength and his presence more than she cared to acknowledge. 'Just give me a few more minutes to compose myself.' Her enemies would not see her with puffy eyes, her nose red from crying. They would see only the formidable and detached Lady Elizabeth Wilding. The one the world still believed had a pristine reputation.

Hal nodded, snapped a fresh handkerchief out of his pocket and waited for her to fix her face. As she did so, he began pacing back and forth in front of the bench like a caged tiger. His angry breath sawing in and out in frozen, white puffs, his powerful long legs tearing up the ground. Gone was the erudite and charming face he presented to the world. The man who lacked both substance and purpose was nowhere to be seen. Stripped of that mask, Hal was formidable. His height and strong build had never been more apparent. There was so much more to him than the dashing rake. If anyone could intimidate her would-be fiancé and her former fiancé, it was Hal.

When she finally stood, it was on shaky legs. Her knight in shining armour smiled, although there was ice in his eyes and a hardness about his jaw she had never seen before. Physically he appeared to have grown. Devoid of his veneer of charm, he was huge. Menacing. Ready to charge into battle like one of the lead soldiers he had picked out for her little boy. 'Are you ready to step into the lion's den, fair maiden?' The charming smile was false this time. Pasted on for her benefit to make her feel better. Beneath it his temper was tangible.

'As ready as I will ever be.' At least she had a tiger on her side as she ventured forth into the lion's den. For the time being anyway. Their liaison was only ever meant to be a convenient sham, yet he was once again going above and beyond the parameters of their bargain. Ockendon and Rainham were a completely different kettle of fish to the dullards he had agreed to keep at bay. But, of course, when they had made the arrangement, she had no inkling her secrets were on the cusp of being exposed. A way to enjoy a month of peace before she began a new life.

Far away.

From everyone and everything she held dear.

With a jolt, she realised she would miss Hal, too. When this was all over, if she emerged from it all unscathed, she would still see her papa on high days and holidays when she moved north. If the scandal erupted, her dear papa would probably be forced to withdraw permanently to his estate in Cheshire, and if Georgie's existence became public knowledge, Lizzie supposed she could at least retire there, too. Either way, she would never see Hal again. The realisation rooted her to the spot for a moment as she gazed at him, pathetically trying to sear his image in her mind. Exactly as he was now. Solid. Strong. Loyal to a fault. Ready to defend her even though he did not know the half of what it was he was offering to defend.

He saw her hesitation as further evidence of her fear and wrapped her chilled hand about his arm. 'Come on then, Lizzie darling. Let's show the snake you are unfazed.'

An eerie calm settled over her as she stepped back into the Danburys' enormous drawing room. Hiding or running would not put off the inevitable. The guests had thinned out this close to dinner, all gone to change or rest or whatever people did when there was a gap in the proceedings. Her father was missing, probably frantically searching for her, and so were their hosts. The Earl of Ockendon and the Marquess of Rainham were not. In fact, their strategic position in the very centre of the room could only mean one thing. They wanted her to see them. It was why they were here, after all.

Beneath her palm she felt the corded muscles in Hal's forearm stiffen. Aside from that he was the very picture of casual male confidence as he led her on a path directly towards them. His strength prevented her step from faltering when her former lover turned to look at her for the first time. Smiled nervously, then eagerly stood when Ockendon nudged him, just in case she tried to avoid conversing with him.

'Lizzie. You look wonderful.' There was a tremor in his voice. Fear? Guilt? 'The years have been kind to you.'

She could not say the same. He appeared to have aged far more than five years. Still handsome, he was paler. The dark hollows under his eyes suggested he was a creature of the night or did not sleep well. She hoped for the latter although suspected he was too shallow to have a conscience. Although it was plain to see he was not comfortable to be in this room. There was a jerkiness about his posture—as if he was on the cusp of running away. His breathing was uneven. His face sweating. His dark eyes, so like Georgie's, watched her carefully. It was strange that one could unconditionally love and despise the same set of eyes at the same time.

Regally she inclined her head. 'You are too kind, my lord.' Lizzie feared she would snarl if she said his actual name. It reminded her that he knew her far too well. All of her. She flicked her eyes to Ockendon who, she noted, had failed to stand in her presence. There was no sign of discomfort in his demeanour. He was enjoying this. 'My Lord Ockendon.' Another polite nod, although she made sure he saw her true feelings by turning her face up partially in disgust. He would not see how much he frightened her. Not now. Not ever.

'Gentlemen.' Hal, too, nodded and then smiled lazily at her. It was the sort of secret smile that couples shared. One which warned the two men she was his. To her it said something else entirely.

It said *I've got you. Don't worry.* It buoyed her to be bold. After all, there was no point beating about the bush. They were here for a purpose and one which likely included blackmail.

'Lady Danbury had assumed you were not coming, Lord Ockendon.' Lizzie was baiting him, as she feared his purpose. She also knew she could not fight against whatever he had planned unless she was appraised of the plan beforehand. If scandal was inevitable, she would meet it head on and then decide how to play it, if indeed she could. She had already decided she would do practically anything to protect her son—or her father. With a shiver, she realised, that might have to include marrying Ockendon.

He eyed her up and down somewhat lasciviously, his rheumy eyes lingering too long on her bosom again. 'Oh, I always intended on coming, lovely Lizzie. You knew that, though. Didn't you? After our last little chat, I believe I left you in no doubt of my intentions.'

She felt Hal tense and squeezed his arm to stop him replying. 'I have still not given you leave to call me by my first name, sir. Nor will I ever.'

The Earl smiled smugly. 'Oh, I think you will. One day soon.'

Hal's thumb began to slowly caress the back of her hand.

Obviously.

It drew both men's' eyes very effectively, as he had intended. 'There is something pathetic about an older man chasing a young woman, don't you think? Especially when it is blatantly obvious her affections are directed elsewhere.'

His gaze pulled her in and she was powerless to do anything except stare up into his hypnotic mossy-green eyes. Hal would think it was for show. Self-preservation in front of her two tormentors, and in part that was true, however, Lizzie also knew she was branding him into her memory. Squirrelling away the possessive gleam in his expression, wishing for once that it was more than just pretend. Wishing circumstances were so very different.

'As far as I see things, Redbridge, nothing is set in stone until a lady walks back up the aisle with a ring on her finger.' A blatant dig which told her he knew she had been left at the altar. He grinned at his companion. 'Isn't that right, Rainham?'

True to form, Charles appeared devoid of any guilt for what he had done to her. He nodded at his odious friend, too eagerly, and then vainly avoided looking back towards her. Gone was the confident rake she had fallen for and in its place was a subservient lapdog; Ockendon was undoubtedly his master. 'The absence of a ring means a lady is still fair game.'

Chapter Twelve

Hal sensed there was more going on here than he knew—however, he knew enough to intervene. As much as he wanted to feel Rainham's nose shatter against his fist, his first duty was to help Lizzie save face and get through this uncomfortable and unexpected ordeal with her head held high. He forced the corners of his mouth to curve upwards. Forced himself to stick out his hand. Tried not to allow the revulsion show on his face as he shook Rainham's heartily and took some comfort from the slightly bewildered and obviously terrified expression on the bounder's face. Rainham was here under duress. Ockendon had some hold on him too.

'We are all adults here…this nasty undercurrent is completely unnecessary. If anything, I should thank you, Rainham. Had you not been such a thoughtless, money-grabbing scoundrel, then I would have been denied the opportunity to have my darling Lizzie now.'

He watched Ockendon's eyes narrow and forced himself to pat the man on the back jovially, too. 'I know Rainham here jilted her, old boy. Lizzie and I have no secrets from each other.' Or they wouldn't once he had got to the bottom of whatever was going on behind those guarded cornflower eyes. And he would get to the bottom of it. Of that he was determined.

Ockendon knew something about her, something dreadful if Hal was any judge, and was going to use it to snag himself an heiress. His father had been as mercenary whenever money was concerned so he recognised the signs. Locate the weakness, put pressure on that point mercilessly until it gave way, then reap the ill-gotten rewards. Whatever Ockendon had planned would not come to fruition. As soon as he got back to town, Hal was going to thoroughly investigate the man's business affairs and any other affairs while he was about it. Rainham's, too. He would dig and dig until he found dirt he could use. Their weaknesses. As much as he hated his father's methods, Hal had been well schooled in the art of forcing the hands of others from the moment he could talk. He might not usually have the stomach to sink to such dastardly depths, but Ockendon had made himself fair game. He needed to speak to Lizzie. 'If you will excuse us, gentlemen. We need to change for dinner.'

'If I might have a word with Lady Elizabeth in private...'

Hal's face came within inches of the Earl's. 'You may not.'

'I believe that is for the lady to decide.'

As she was still holding on to his arm as if her life depended on it, Hal had felt her body stiffen at the request. 'She has already decided she does not want you. Therefore, keep your inappropriate comments and filthy, impertinent looks to yourself. Tell the world your little friend here left her standing at the altar. It is in the past and she has me now. Try to frighten her or leer at her again and I will hunt you down and *destroy* you for it. Better yet, take this sorry excuse for a man back to whatever debauched and debased hellhole you found him in. *Tonight.* If either of you has the audacity to be seated at the table at dinner, then I will not be held accountable for my actions.'

Rainham, like the snivelling toad he was, was

visibly shaken by the threat. His eyes widened; his nostrils flared. Instinctively his gaze flicked towards the exit. Ockendon was fuming, but held his tongue. Just as well. Hal was praying for any excuse to punch him. They stared silently at each other for several moments, before Ockendon finally stood and stalked towards the door with the snake scurrying beside him as if his breeches were on fire. As an afterthought, Ockendon turned, walked slowly back towards them and made a great show of pretending Hal did not exist. 'I am a powerful man. It is in your *family's* best interests to talk to me, Lady Elizabeth. Make it sooner rather than later.'

He turned and marched towards the door Rainham had already disappeared out of. Hal started after him, only to be stayed by Lizzie's tight grip on his arm. 'Please, Hal, leave it.'

'Leave it? The audacity of the man makes my blood boil.'

'They have gone. Just as you asked them to. Thank you for saving me.'

Except she did not look like a woman who had been rescued. 'Is there a possibility that Ockendon knows something else about you?'

Her mouth moved to answer, then clamped

firmly shut. In the end, she ignored his question and unwound her arm from his. 'I need to speak with my father.'

'I would prefer you speak to me first. What's going on, Lizzie?'

The shutters went down. 'You saw for yourself what is going on. Clearly Lord Ockendon wants to use Rainham's treachery and the threat of a scandal to press his suit. Let him. Enough years have passed and I no longer care if the truth comes out.'

She was a dreadful liar. Her eyelids fluttered like butterfly's wings as she tried to hold his gaze. What wasn't she telling him? For the sake of privacy, he tugged her into a dark corner under the stairs. 'Is there something else? Only I get the distinct impression *there is* something else.'

Her eyes widened. Her tongue flicked out to moisten her top lip. 'Of course there is nothing else.' She was lying. He knew it in the same way he knew she was petrified. 'I am merely a little shaken at seeing Rainham again. I shall be my usual self over dinner. You'll see.'

A typical Lizzie-like pithy response, but her eyes were so troubled, awash with unshed tears, and it undid him. His fingers came up to brush her cheek and she leaned into his palm. Closed her eyes. Sighed softly. A single, fat tear trickled down her cheek, betraying her. Gut-wrenching proof that his suspicions were correct. He gently brushed it away with the pad of his thumb. When she began to pull away Hal brought his other hand up to cup her other cheek, then allowed it to slide down the delicate column of her neck. Her skin was like velvet, but her pulse beat a rapid tattoo beneath his fingers. The outer shell she was trying to portray was as much of a sham as their public *romance*. 'Please tell me what's wrong. I want to help you.'

She stared deeply into his eyes, as if she was searching the inner depths of his soul to see if she could trust him and he recognised the exact moment she decided she couldn't. He recognised it as it came with a sharp slash of pain, like a knife to the chest. Utter disappointment at not being considered worthy enough. His hands dropped ineffectually back to his sides when she took a decisive step backwards. She did not want either his help or his touch. 'Please stop worrying about me. There really is no need. My broken heart mended a long time ago.' Another lie. Another pain jabbed close to his heart.

'Rainham was a blasted fool to jilt you! Had I

been in his shoes, I would have counted the seconds till I put the ring on your finger.' Where had that come from? His aching heart began to hammer erratically against his ribs. Wherever it had come from it was true.

Good grief.

'Maybe you *should* marry me, Lizzie.'

'W-what?' Her mouth hung open.

Hal's head began to spin. He had just proposed. Very badly and out of the blue. Hopefully she would turn him down. He had always avoided commitment and hardly knew this woman yet, horror of horrors, right at this moment this felt right. Even the appeal of sowing his wild oats was apparently waning. A voice in his head was making him question it. *Why would you waste time with other women when the only one your heart wants is currently stood right in front of you?* Looking at him as if he had just gone completely stark, staring mad. Which clearly he had. Perhaps Lady Danbury's wassail was off.

'You are very kind, but—'

'I am not being kind!' The annoying voice in his head told him he had to convince her it was the right course of action. 'We could announce our engagement tonight over dinner. With a special licence, we can be married by Christmas. Then you will no longer have to fear Ockendon or Rainham or the scandal of being jilted because everyone will be gossiping about our wedding.' Oh, Lord! Nonsense kept spilling willy-nilly from his mouth. He did not want to be shackled to a wife just yet. It was too soon… Far too soon. Thank goodness he hadn't given her any enticing or romantic sets of reasons to make her want to marry him.

But, the voice said, *they are sound and pragmatic ones. Lizzie might respond better to logic than the fact that your heart seems to think you were meant to be together.*

The walls tilted. Good grief! What the hell was going on? Soppy romantic ideas about two people who were meant to be together, especially when one of them was him, were ridiculous. He couldn't possibly think the pair of them were meant to be together.

Could he?

He certainly liked her and desired her. She was fun. Entertaining. Lovely to behold. So what if he had a sudden urge to wake up with her every morning? Spend his days with her. Grow old with her…

Dizziness swamped him. There had to be something in the wassail which did not agree with him, that could be the only explanation. To keep himself upright he grabbed the wall for support and hoped he did not look as blindsided as he felt. If he *hadn't* been poisoned, his current behaviour was very worrying.

'I can't marry you.'

His knees went then and he sat down shakily on an oak chest. He should be rejoicing the fact she had turned him down. His proposal had been rash to say the least and had literally come out of the blue. Instead, he was crushed. His breathing became laboured because of an acute pain in his chest. 'At least give it some thought. It's not really such a terrible idea when you consider the benefits.' And now, to top it all, apparently, he was not averse to begging.

'The benefits?' He saw bemusement and pity on her face. Both made him panic.

'We rub along well together.'

There is this odd feeling in my heart every time I am with you. It sort of swells and feels content.

'We are both cynical in nature and find the expectations of society tiresome.'

I want to spend every minute in your company.

'I do believe we have a mutual attraction to

one another, which I doubt most married couples could claim, and it would save us both from the dullards and the hordes.'

Be mine for ever, Lizzie. I have a sneaking suspicion I'm a little bit in love with you.

Good grief!

Was he? How had that happened? He needed to stop speaking. Clamp his wayward jaws shut.

'I can't marry you.'

'Why not?'

'It would be totally wrong… For so many reasons.' To soften her words, her fingers came up to rest on his face and she gently brushed back his hair. He wanted to haul her into his arms, beg her to reconsider, but his pride was battered quite enough already and he was so confused by what he had just done he couldn't think of anything remotely sensible to say. If Hal was being completely honest with himself, he could not think of anything sensible to think either. He watched, as she lowered her body to kneel before him, rejoiced when she closed the distance between them and pressed her lips to his.

Home.

Those were his first thoughts before his body burst into flames and he did haul her into his arms. He wasn't sure which one of them deepened the kiss, but all the urgency, all the despair and all the longing he felt came tumbling out as he clung to her. At some point he tugged her on to his lap, let his greedy hands explore the curves of her body while his mouth worshipped her and his heart burst with joy. She wanted him, too. She *would* marry him.

It was Lizzie who tore herself away and stared up into his face for the longest time. Her fingers began to trace his features. 'You are sweet, Hal. I never thought I would ever hear myself say such a thing about a man with your reputation, but it is true nevertheless.' He could hear sympathy in her voice, feel her withdrawing back into herself. Withdrawing from him. From them!

When she stood up, stepped away, putting both physical and emotional distance between them, her expression was inscrutable. That damn drawbridge had been reeled in and she was hiding behind row upon row of battlements again, shutting him out. She did not believe in him enough. Or feel the same way. His poor heart twisted painfully in his chest and he could hear the damn voice in his head howling in protest. Hal jumped up, but before he could move towards her she stayed him with her hand. Shook her head definitively.

She smiled sadly and started towards the stairs, then hesitated and stopped. When she turned around her expression was wistful. 'Thank you for being there, Hal, and for offering to sacrifice yourself for me. It means the world. Thank you also for all you have done in the last few weeks. You have been a good friend to me and bizarrely at a time when I needed a friend the most. This silly Christmas season has been a pleasure. I will always remember it fondly.'

Chapter Thirteen

Alone in his bedchamber, still reeling from both the earth-shattering surprise of proposing and the despair at being swiftly turned down, Hal paced the floor. Perhaps the wassail had been tainted. With some sort of drug which rendered one stupid and prone to folly. His proposal had certainly been foolhardy. It was undoubtedly ill timed. The poor girl had suddenly been confronted with a man who had broken her heart, another who wanted to use that information against her and Hal had gone and sprung a proposal on her.

A pretty lacklustre and, now he came to think upon it, unconvincing proposal. *We rub along well together.* As if an intelligent and vivacious woman like Lizzie, who was plagued with dullards and wary of marriage, would be tempted by a declaration quite so bland? For a man renowned for his way with both words and the ladies, that was frankly pathetic. It was a blessing she had turned him down and an even bigger blessing she had thought his proposal was a noble, selfless gesture. It allowed him to save face even though he was feeling quite wretched at the rejection whilst still reeling from his bizarre reaction to their kiss.

Home.

That word kept haunting him. How the blazes could a woman be home? It made no sense, yet it made perfect sense. Perhaps he was going down with something? A fever, perhaps? Fevers made people delirious. That had to be what was wrong. A decent dinner, a soothing draught and a good night's sleep were probably in order. Tomorrow he would endeavour to get to the bottom of whatever was going on with Ockendon and see if that made a difference to his odd mood. Only then, if the silly voice in his addled head was still plaguing him, would he give the matter of his romantic feelings towards Lizzie some more thought and decide how to proceed with them. The sprig of mistletoe sat on his nightstand and he picked it up. This was meant to be a bit of fun. A harmless wager. Nothing serious. But that kiss had been serious. It had been significant. He plucked off another berry and tossed it into the fire.

Good grief! He was seriously considering a proper romance. What was that if not a Christmas miracle? If he hadn't been feeling so miserable, he would laugh at the cruel irony. A fortnight ago his vigour was missing and his life lacked something. Now he had plenty of vigour and his addled mind had decided what was lacking. It was Lizzie. She was home. And she didn't want him. Something he would doubtless get over as soon as he stopped feeling the urge to rescue her. He hoped, at least, that was all that was wrong. With that in mind, he probably should rescue her swiftly.

Hal quickly dressed for dinner and then headed back downstairs in search of Aaron. His friend was holding court at the refreshment table, but quickly excused himself when Hal motioned to him. 'You don't look particularly happy. Something I am going to take as a very good sign. I take it you have not made any more progress with the berries.'

'Forget the berries.' Hal had. The very last thing on his mind was the Mistletoe Wager when he suspected his heart was a little bit broken. 'What do you know about the Earl of Ockendon?'

'I know he smells.' Aaron's face wrinkled. 'And I know I've never liked him. Why do you ask?'

'I think he is trying to blackmail Lizzie.'

'That's a pretty serious accusation.'

They might be overly competitive with one another, but aside from his sister Hal trusted no one more. 'There is a scandal in her past. Rainham jilted *her*. Ockendon knows it and has brought the snake here to flaunt it under her nose.'

Aaron was silent for a moment, taking the news in in the calm measured way he did when something was important. 'At best, that news is a minor scandal now. Their engagement was years ago. The gossip will be harsh, as it always is with a titbit so juicy, but quickly forgotten.'

'That's what I would have said, but…' Hal raked his hand through his hair and shook his head. 'But my gut says there is something more to it. Something much worse. She was frightened. Ockendon was so…certain of his power over her.'

'Did you ask her?'

'Of course I asked her. She denied it.' But Hal had seen her. She had been broken. Had remained broken even as she had climbed the stairs less than an hour ago. The more he thought about it, the more it all bothered him. Which probably accounted for his ridiculous *'marry me'* outburst. 'I think she's in trouble, Aaron.'

'Then all you can do is keep a close eye on the situation and hope it either comes to naught or she confides in you.' Not what Hal wanted to hear. Whatever was troubling Lizzie he wanted to fix *now* and banish the fraught look which tugged on his heartstrings and made him make lacklustre but genuine marriage proposals on the spur of the moment. 'Unless, of course, she is embroiled in a truly awful scandal…in which case it might be prudent to distance yourself from her.'

'How can you say that!' The very thought was preposterous. 'Would you abandon Connie at the first sign of trouble?'

His friend watched him thoughtfully for several seconds. 'The last time I checked, Connie was my wife and Lizzie was a wager.' Hal felt his expression harden, then saw Aaron's change, too.

Awe and wonder.

Amusement.

An irritating grin crept over his face. 'Good Lord! I never thought I'd see the day! You're developing *feelings* for her?'

Denying it was pointless, because he was. He wasn't entirely sure what sort of feelings they were, labelling them as anything quantifiable terrified him. Hell—his hasty proposal had terrified him, although not quite as much as her refusal had. And frankly that terrified him more. Hal was starting to think they were meant to be together one day. Not yet, of course, he had far too many wild oats still left to sow. But one day he could see himself quite content with Lizzie, in the not-so-distant future… And there it went again. His addled mind was wandering down paths it had no right wandering down. Like a besotted idiot, he still hadn't answered his brother-in-law's question.

By the look on Aaron's face, any sort of response would be tantamount to an admission of guilt and Hal was certainly not ready for that either. Not when his head was all over the place and his heart hurt. 'I *like* her, Aaron. Lizzie is a good sort and I would hate to see her wronged by Ockendon. You have to admit, her former fiancé turning up here with him, after being absent from society for years, is a bit contrived.'

'It is. That I will grant you. And if Ockendon needs money, your lady-love has a temptingly huge dowry to entice him. I concede that, too. Her father has certainly made her an obvious target for fortune hunters.' Without telling him of his suspicions, Aaron's line of thinking was along the same lines as Hal's. In his head, he could hear his father's voice repeating his usual mantra. *'The world runs on coin, Henry. Nothing else matters.'*

'I will do some subtle digging on your behalf tonight, Hal, over dinner. I suggest you concentrate your efforts towards the young lady in question. Use some of that devilish charm to see if you can wheedle any more details out of her.'

With no better plan, Hal would do exactly that.

Fate, or rather Lizzie, denied him the opportunity. When she and her father failed to materialise, he went off to look for her, only to be informed by Lady Danbury's butler that the Earl of Upminster's carriage had left well over an hour before. Standing alone and confused at the bottom of the very staircase he had last seen her on, it dawned on him. Lizzie's final words to him had not been words of pity or thanks at all.

They had been a goodbye.

The journey home had been an emotional one. In view of the Earl of Ockendon's thinly veiled threats and the sudden reappearance of her treacherous fiancé, her father waved away her concerns.

Ockendon, he assured her, was all bluster. So what if he knew she had been jilted? There was no way he knew about little Georgie when the boy's father had no idea he existed. At best, all Ockendon could do was enlighten the *ton* to gossip now so old it was not worth repeating. Besides, he had argued, he had friends in high places and no newspaper would dare print the story of how she had been abandoned at the altar. He would sort it all out. She wasn't to concern herself with it. Lizzie had fervently pressed him for details about how he had banished her former fiancé from society and he had patted her hand and said that, too, did not matter. His troubled eyes gave him away even as he denied it. As always, he was excluding her from decisions which would directly affect her in the name of protecting her!

He was delaying the inevitable. Being jilted was not the worst of what had happened. She had been very thoroughly, and quite compliantly, ravished by Rainham. One day the truth was bound to leak out. And aside from the fact her pristine reputation would be left in tatters, her father's good name dragged through the mud in the process, her little boy was growing up fast, and it was not fair on him to keep him cooped up in the Grosvenor Square house for ever. If anything, Lord Ockendon's behaviour highlighted how tenuous her situation had become.

'If you had chosen a husband, Lizzie, if you were now married as I have always wanted, then Ockendon would not be able to use the past to threaten you.'

'If you had not insisted we maintain appearances and forced me back into society, then he would have forgotten me. I have said for some time now that I should set up a household of my own and disappear from society for ever.'

'And how would you find a husband then?'

She wanted to scream, instead everything came tumbling out in an angry, frustrated rant. It was not the best way to inform him of her plans to leave in the New Year. Her papa's temper had exploded when she confessed she had already purchased a house with her own money behind his back.

'I will not allow it, Lizzie!'

'You cannot stop me. My mind is made up. I have to think of my son and his best interests. It is not fair to continue to curtail his movements in the way we do. Soon he will grow to resent his lack of freedom and will feel like a prisoner. Is that how you want him to grow up? It is certainly not the life I want for him.'

'But you will be all alone up there, Daughter. Who will protect you?'

From then on, the discussion had deteriorated in its usual fashion. They were like two angry rams, their horns locked, battling to see which one of them had a thicker skull. He would not listen to reason and accept Lizzie was long past the age when she could look after herself. Had he not faithfully promised her mother, on her death bed, that he would see her married to a good man? In desperation, he had even suggested he would allow her to marry the Earl of Redbridge, if that is what her heart wanted, which in turn led to her confessing the truth about her unlikely alliance with Hal and her frustration with the near-constant parade of dullards and her father had hit the roof. She had not seen him so angry since the day Rainham had abandoned her in a church full of lilacs and a child in her belly.

The final hour in the carriage had been spent in stony silence. Neither spoke. What else was there to say? She had done things her dear papa's way for five long years, and now, despite all the hiding, all the keeping up of appearances and his fervent quest to see her wed, what did she have to show for it? A spiteful old earl trying to blackmail her into marriage and another broken heart! What a roaring success. If the honest truth had succeeded in anything, it had succeeded in making relations between father and daughter worse than they had ever been.

Several hours later, and by tacit agreement, they were still avoiding each other. Her papa was holed up in his study, no doubt plotting how best to salvage the situation whilst still keeping his daughter in the dark, and Lizzie was sat with her son in the morning room, trying not to let him see her turbulent mood. Intense fear mixed with anger, frustration, and the unexpected sadness at having to sever her relationship with Hal. Despondent and completely broken and so very tired. Even her bones ached. Georgie was spread-eagled on the carpet, thoroughly engrossed in drawing a picture, and showed no sign of having noticed.

'What are you drawing?'

He paused, then turned to her, grinning. 'I am making you a present. Nanny said I should give you a gift for Christmas and I know how much you love my pictures. This one is going to be extra special. It is a picture of us.'

Love filled her heart. Gave her the strength she needed to do what was necessary when the time came. 'You are exactly right. I will adore it. How did you know I wanted a picture of us for Christmas?'

'Grandpapa told me. He said that I was the most important thing in the world to you, therefore you would much prefer a picture of me than the stag beetle I drew for you last week. You can have that one for your birthday instead.'

The guilt was instant and painful. Doing what was necessary did not make the doing of it any easier. 'Grandpapa is a very wise man.' Tears prickled her eyes at the thought of separating him from his grandson. The two most important men in her life were devoted to one another. They had been since the day Georgie came squalling into the world. From the first moment he had held her baby, her papa had loved him unconditionally and without judgement—just as he had always loved his daughter. The circumstances of Georgie's birth had been irrelevant. If only there was another way to keep them both safe without having to separate them.

Georgie's little tongue poked out as he returned to concentrate on his masterpiece, his chubby fingers clutching the coloured chalk too tightly, and she took a moment to watch him work whilst reminding herself she *was* doing the right thing. Society was unforgiving of babes born on the wrong side of the blanket. Had she been a man, a titled man, then things might have been different. The Regent acknowledged his bastards and they were tolerated by the *ton*. Many of the children born to the mistresses of powerful men lived openly within their ranks. People turned a blind eye. The circumstance of their birth was frowned upon, but only to an extent. Such toleration only extended so far. Men were expected to sow their wild oats. Young ladies were certainly not. Lizzie would be branded a fallen woman and cast out of their ranks without a backward glance, her innocent little boy destined for a life tainted by her shame. Her father disgraced…

The quiet appearance of the butler brought her back down to earth with a start.

'Sorry to disturb you, my lady, but the Earl of Redbridge is outside. He refuses to believe you are not at home and is currently sitting on the front step. He claims he will remain there until you grant him an audience.'

At the mere mention of his name, her heart began to yearn. She still could not believe he had offered to marry her in an attempt to save her. How sweet. How endearing. How utterly selfless and romantic. In that moment, she had realised he was nothing like the rake she had once planned to marry. Hal was noble. Too noble for his own good. One day, he would make some lucky woman a wonderful husband, but it couldn't be her. When she had turned him down he had appeared genuinely wounded rather than relieved. She had hurt his feelings and that saddened her. At the time, she had wanted to tell him the truth. He deserved to know why she had said no, yet a part of her hadn't wanted to see if his nobleness would extend that far. Would he miraculously see past her youthful indiscretions? The realist in her knew she was clutching at straws and certainly not being fair to him.

In truth, once he learned of Georgie she knew he would bitterly regret proposing in the first place, then she would have had to suffer seeing him distance himself from her. Who could blame him? He was a handsome, rich and charming earl who could have anyone. Why would he settle for some other man's second-hand, soiled goods or take on the unwelcome responsibility of a scoundrel's by-blow? Severing their acquaintance was the sensible and kindest thing to do. It protected him, at least, from the scandal which was about to erupt. Her attempt at being equally as noble.

Knowing he was but a few feet away was torture, but her mind was made up. Now that her father knew about their alliance, her too-brief relationship with the handsome, charming, all-too-lovable and heartbreakingly noble Earl had reached its natural conclusion.

'Could you give him this, Stevens?' Lizzie had written the letter as soon as she had arrived home in the small hours when sleep had evaded her. It was a cheerful missive, purposely so, because she wanted him to remember her fondly and did not want him to continue to worry about her. She thanked him for acting as her deterrent, expressed her regret that she was unable to fulfil their bargain for the entire month, but had decided to leave town for her father's estate imminently to spend the rest of Christmas and New Year with her brother. She wasn't sure when she would be coming back. She also made light of her dealings with the Earl of Ockendon and of Hal's generous offer of marriage as a consequence, reminding him that they had made a bargain to keep him *from* the parson's trap—not to snare him in it. Oh, the irony! How amusing…

She did not see any point in warning him that she might well about to be in the centre of a scandal of significant proportions. Whatever his reputation, he was her friend and did not deserve to be caught in the crossfire. Some distance now would allow him to escape largely unscathed if the truth could be kept until New Year's. Enough lives would be damaged as it was without having Hal's on her conscience as well. It did not matter that tears had been dripping down her cheeks as she had written it, or that her heart ached to know she had seen him for the very last time or that a part of her would bitterly regret not knowing him sooner, or Heaven help her, meeting him before she had met Rainham. She did not see any need to tell him she was fond of him. Very fond of him. Perhaps more than fond. There was no point.

'And if he refuses to leave?'

'Tell him I am not at home, Stevens.' Allowing Henry Stuart to get close to her in the first place had been a mistake. Allowing anyone to get too close to her was foolhardy in the extreme. She had lived by that edict for five long years—until him. Already he knew more about her than anyone outside of her family. Perhaps more. Hal seemed to understand her far better than her father. They were kindred spirits on so many levels. She felt it in her heart. There had been an honesty between them which had mattered a great deal. Growing affection. Undeniable attraction. 'Tell him…' Her voice caught with regret for all that could not be. 'Tell him I will never be at home to him again, Stevens—but I wish him all the best with the hordes.'

'The hordes?'

'He will know what I mean, Stevens.' Hopefully he would understand. Lizzie wasn't entirely sure she understood anything any more. Not when everything in her life had been tossed up into the air and had thus far failed to land. A few weeks ago, she would never have believed it if someone had told her she would have feelings for a man again, romantic and affectionate feelings, especially for a self-confessed and charming rake. Yet here she was, more than a little bit in love with the one currently sat on her doorstep.

The butler regarded her with sympathy. 'As you wish, my lady.'

A few minutes later he returned. 'He has gone, my lady.'

Of course he had. Lizzie should have felt relief. Instead, waves of pain and disappointment washed over her, when she had not thought she could feel any worse. 'Did he leave me any message?' A little something she could cling to in the dark days ahead.

'He did not, my lady. Should he have?'

Yes! Yes, he should have. Underneath the brave face she was struggling to maintain, a tiny part of her had hoped he would fight for whatever it was they had, even if it was doomed to be futile. Lizzie selfishly needed to know he would mourn the end of their association as keenly. That he felt the same pull. The same need. The same heady connection. She shook her head and gazed down at her son again. She had no right to be selfish and expect more from Hal than he had already given freely. 'No, Stevens. I was not expecting him to reply to my message.'

'I could fetch him if you wanted. His house is a short walk from here.'

Another reason why it was prudent to leave

Mayfair as soon as possible, not that she needed another one. Being so close to him would drive her mad with longing. 'There is no need. That will be all, Stevens.' The little man sat contentedly at her feet, diligently colouring his mother's hair purple, was the only man she could ever permit to matter henceforth.

Chapter Fourteen

Hal had never been much good at loitering. His huge build and short attention span had made hanging about and waiting for things to happen anathema to him. However, in view of the unusual circumstances, and his current foul mood, needs dictated he must. To that end, he had been loitering in Grosvenor Square for the better part of two hours waiting for all the lights to go out in the Earl of Upminster's Mayfair fortress. Technically, he wasn't actually in the Square. An hour ago, when the stable lad on guard had briefly disappeared to answer the call of nature, Hal had sneaked around the back of the garden and scaled the ridiculously high walls. He was currently lurking amidst the shrubbery closest to the house. A rose bed, he assumed, judging by the amount of nicks he now had in his breeches. Thank heavens he had the good sense to wear his sturdiest boots and a robust pair of leather gloves. A solid suit of armour might have been more appropriate.

His hour in the cold, frigid December air had not been completely wasted because he had caught several glimpses of Lizzie—at least the silhouette was shaped like Lizzie—and was fairly certain he knew which of the many bedchambers was hers. Unfortunately, her window was firmly closed. Shouting up in anything above a whisper would likely alert the servants to the presence of an intruder and Hal did not fancy his chances up against the Wildings' giant butler. There was a solid-looking ancient wisteria climbing up the back of the house and, as he was determined to get to the bottom of whatever nonsense was going on and she had refused to see him, Hal had little choice other than to climb it.

Frankly, if it gave her a fright it would damn well serve the wench right, because he had been in a perpetual state of worry since she had bolted out of Lady Danbury's French doors. And he had proposed. Having never had cause to propose before, the occasion was momentous and the more he recalled her horrified reaction at his offer, the more upset and offended he became. He had wanted to help her. Begged her to let him help her and she had cut him out as if he did not matter at all. That stung. Thanks to her heartfelt and ground-shaking kiss closely followed by her swift and silent exit from the house party, Hal had suffered several hours being stalked by a very determined Lady Arabella, then a sleepless night worrying.

Some time in the small hours his temper kicked in and he decided enough was enough. He had been an attentive fake suitor, suffered through a painful dinner with Lord Hewitt and rescued her from the Earl of Ockendon twice. Then sent the man packing with her toad of a former fiancé so that she was spared the sight of them for the rest of the weekend! And he'd proposed, something which still caused his head to spin, because he suspected he had meant it. He deserved the truth. Not a letter! To that end he had ridden for hours across the countryside, alone, and had damn well nearly frozen to death in the process. How dare she send him a letter after all that? Especially one which told him next to nothing.

Fuelled with righteous indignation, he began to heave himself up the knotted branches. The blasted woman was going to talk to him, and if it took him all night, he was not damn well leaving without some proper answers. Why was she terrified of Ockendon? What secret did the man know about her and why had he dragged her wastrel of a fiancé into it? More importantly, why wouldn't she see him? They were supposed to be friends, looking out for one another, contractually obliged to be a deterrent until the Christmas season was over. The last time Hal checked, that was Twelfth Night.

Twelfth Night! And they were still only a few days from Christmas Eve. She owed him another fortnight. Another fortnight and some jolly good reasons why she had curtly refused his proposal without giving the matter some serious and proper thought. It was not as if he was a rancid, money-grabbing specimen like Ockendon. Hal had all his own teeth, was financially secure and was widely regarded as a catch amongst the sea of hordes who were stalking him incessantly. Lady Arabella would not have said no! No, indeed, she would have jumped at the chance. The sorry-looking sprig of mistletoe sat limply in his pocket would have been missing all five of its berries well before now, if the wager had been about Arabella, and certainly not still sporting one. Perhaps that was the answer. He and Lizzie seemed to lose their heads whenever their lips touched, so perhaps he should simply kiss her into submission and be done with it.

His frozen fingers finally gripped the deep, stone window ledge and he pulled his face level with the glass. Heavy curtains prevented him from seeing anything other than the reflected blackness of the midnight sky, and even though there was the distinct possibility he was dangling outside the wrong window, he was not going to give the minx beyond the opportunity of raising the alarm and having him forcibly removed from the trellis before he had said his piece. Surprise was the only immediate weapon in his poorly stocked arsenal. The only others were dashing good looks and bucketloads of charm, neither of which apparently held any appeal whatsoever to the confusing vixen who had kept him awake for the better part of two days.

Silently, he tested the frame. It was a sash window and to his utter delight was blessedly unlocked. Somebody was on his side. Somebody or something. Out of respect for the miracle he glanced heavenwards and quietly thanked the Almighty for giving him the means to break in, then pulled the window upwards and threw himself blindly through the aperture.

He landed on the floor with a thud and untangled himself from the curtains. 'Now listen here, Lizzie…' The room was empty. It was undoubtedly a feminine room. An abundance of lace and delicate furniture gave that away. There was a single candle burning on the nightstand, the bed was turned down in readiness and her perfume wafted in the air. Wherever Lizzie was, it wasn't far away. It was also just as well she had not been there to witness his arrival—aside from the fact it had hardly been graceful, she probably would have screamed the place down and woken the whole house. This way was much better. It gave him time to collect himself.

Feeling a touch self-righteous, Hal stripped off his gloves and greatcoat and tossed them on to a ridiculously spindly-looking chair. He did not dare sit on it. The legs were so thin his immense bulk would likely shatter it into matchsticks. As there were no other chairs in the bedchamber, he eased his big body down on to the mattress to wait. Ten minutes later and still no sign of her, Hal plumped up a pile of pillows to rest against and made himself comfortable.

The object of his frustration eventually came in, clutching a book and wearing a gossamer nightgown which made his throat constrict with sudden lust before she shrieked a little too loudly for comfort and lunged at him, brandishing the book like a club.

'Shh! It's just me… Hal.' He placed one finger to his lips and held his other hand up in surrender. She skidded to a halt inches away, looking delightfully confused, the book still raised like a shield.

'Hal?' Shock quickly turned to anger. 'Hal! What are you doing here?'

'Try to whisper, Lizzie darling. I would rather we did not alert the household to my presence.'

Her eyes turned swiftly to the door before fixing on him. The candlelight made them appear darker, like the sky before a thunderstorm. Judging from the thunderous expression hovering around the edges of her confusion, it was an apt description. 'How did you get in?'

'Seeing as your henchman Stevens refused me entry earlier—repeatedly, I might add—I had to resort to covert methods to gain entry.' Feeling pretty pleased with himself for circumventing the many layers of security and certain he could soften her tense mood with his charm, he shot her his best naughty grin and settled back against the pillows smugly. 'I scrambled up the wisteria.'

She became instantly furious. All signs of delightful bewilderment vanished and she glowered down at him with her hands fisted at her sides. 'How dare you! How dare you sneak into my house. My bedchamber! And what the hell do you think you are doing on my bed?'

'So much for whispering.' At this volume, it was only a matter of seconds before the alarm was raised and Stevens would eject him bodily. 'Could you try to lower your voice an octave or two? Take a couple of deep breaths...try to remain calm.'

'Calm!' Her finger prodded sharply into his breastbone. 'You expect me to remain calm when you have broken into my house?'

'I needed to talk you.'

'I wrote you a letter!'

'Which said next to nothing!'

'So you thought the best course of action was burglary?'

The accusation made him smile. 'Er... I think you will find that a burglar enters a property with the intention of removing items from it.' He held his palms up for effect. 'Not guilty, your honour. Now please sit down...'

'Get out.' The finger jabbed again, repeatedly, firing his temper again. He was the one trying to be reasonable, yet she appeared oblivious to the fact her recent behaviour had been anything but.

'Not until I get what I came here for.'

She recoiled then, seemed to remember she was dressed in only her nightgown and snatched the eiderdown to wrap around her like a shield. 'How dare you!' Her jabbing finger flapped ineffectually near his face. 'You are a scoundrel, Henry Stuart. How dare you assume that I would climb into bed with you just because I allowed you to kiss me?'

'Oh, for goodness sake!' He stood up then and took some enjoyment in looming over her. She took a panicked step backwards and he closed the distance, then watched her eyes widen with indignation.

'Keep your hands to yourself, sir!'

Furiously, he waved both of them in front of her face. 'You have got completely the wrong end of the stick and, frankly, I am insulted. I have *never* had to force myself on a woman and I resent the accusation. What the blazes has got into you? I came here to *talk* to you. To get some answers. To hear the damn truth rather than the pack of lies you have fed me!'

'You were on my bed!'

This was really not turning out as he had intended, although he supposed reclining on her bed with his feet crossed and his elbows thrown above his head might be construed as a seductive position, and he supposed he had just scared the living daylights out of the girl. 'In case it has escaped your notice, I am still wearing my boots and everything else for that matter. And need I remind you that it was *you* who kissed *me*!' She had the good grace to look guilty, but still clutched the eiderdown about her as if he were some pillaging Viking intent on ravishing her. Hal sighed and plopped his bottom back down on the edge of the bed. 'I was merely waiting for you. Just to talk. That doll's house chair at your dressing table didn't look like it could hold my weight.'

Her eyes flicked to the chair, then back to him before he watched her shoulders drop and her combative stance disappear. 'You still should not have come here. Not like this.'

'Did you give me any other choice?' Hal stared directly into her lovely blue eyes and she dipped her head. It was all the acknowledgment he needed. 'I called several times today. You knew that. You had your henchman give me this letter.' He tossed the missive on to the mattress and sighed. He wanted her guard down, not up. 'When it became apparent you had no intention of honouring me with a proper explanation for your odd behaviour, and because I have genuinely been frantic with worry, I had to resort to sneaking in. And I would like it noted that sneaking in was no mean feat. Thanks to you and your uncharitable butler I had to stand in the cold for hours waiting for the opportune moment.'

'A gentleman doesn't climb up a lady's wisteria uninvited.'

'A lady doesn't send a letter to a gentleman terminating their acquaintance, especially if the said gentleman has selflessly proposed to the lady hours before and then ridden across two counties in the small hours to check she was well. What the blazes is going on, Lizzie? I think I deserve to know.'

'Please don't make this any more difficult than it already is, Hal. I had reasons…good reasons for leaving Lady Danbury's.' Once again she could not hold his gaze.

'Which are?'

'Things I would prefer to keep to myself.' Her arms came around to hug herself, an unconscious action which spoke volumes. Hall reached out and tugged at the eiderdown, forcing her to sit beside him.

'You might as well know I am not leaving until you tell me. You'll have to get that menacing butler of yours to tear me limb from limb first.' He could sense her indecision, so wrapped his arm around her shoulders and whispered into her hair, 'I am your friend, Lizzie. Whatever is going on, I want to help.'

She was still for a long time and he gave her the space to decide what her next move would be. When she eventually spoke, it was in a small voice. He heard the defeat and the fear. The deep well of sadness. 'You cannot help me, Hal. I fear Lord Ockendon has learned something which will explode into a huge scandal if he shares it with the world.'

'Take it from someone who had been embroiled in many a scandal, they all blow over eventually and I doubt yours is anywhere near as bad as you think it is. I bet you have never dashed across Hyde Park flashing your nakedness to all and sundry.' He had wanted to make her smile, but the attempt fell flat.

'Oh, it's bad, Hal. So bad that it is enough to blackmail both me *and* my father with if Ockendon is of a mind to, which I am in no doubt he is. What I need to decide is whether I want to unleash the scandal, knowing full well it will ruin a great many lives, or whether I can bring myself to agree to the Earl's demands.'

Now she was making him very worried. 'Surely you cannot seriously be contemplating marrying *him*?' Something which beggared belief when she had readily turned down Hal's proposal.

'I hope it will not come to that. Lord Ockendon is yet to bare his hand so I am hoping there is a way out of the mess.'

'There is. Marry *me*.' This proposal did not make him feel as nauseous as the first had. A worrying turn of events in itself, although like the first time, his heart told him it was right. His hand came up to touch her cheek and he traced the pad of his thumb over her lips. 'I think there is more than friendship between us, Lizzie. Don't you?' Of its own volition, his face moved towards hers. Her chin tilted up and her eyes travelled to his lips. She felt the pull of attraction, too. Her body had instinctively turned to press against his. 'We will weather the scandal together.' The tips of their noses touched. It was a strangely intimate and compelling moment which he did not feel the urge to rush. Their mouths were a whisper apart. He could feel the steady, rapid beat of her heart against his own pounding one. Their shallow breathing in perfect tandem. The warm and comforting sense of rightness. She pulled away before he could kiss her.

'I can't marry you, Hal.'

'But you can marry *him*? A man you hate and who terrifies you?'

'I won't marry him either. I shall disappear. It is not as if I am unused to hiding.'

'Hiding?' Lizzie was talking in riddles. Hal still had no idea what sort of a mess she was involved in and was downright angry at the rejection of yet another proposal without any sound reasons as to why. The woman was infuriating. He took a deep breath to prevent himself from shouting. He reached for her again, a little desperately. 'Just tell me what the blazes is…' The bedchamber door opened and the angry, frustrated outburst died in his throat.

'Mama… I had a bad dream.'

A dark-haired little boy came in, rubbing his eyes with one chubby hand and clutching a tatty stuffed toy. Lost for words, Hal watched Lizzie stand, the heavy eiderdown she had wrapped around her falling to the floor as she scurried to the child. Bent down. Lifted him into her arms. 'My poor darling.' She ruffled his hair and kissed the top of his head. 'It was only a dream, Georgie. It cannot harm you.' Her eyes sought Hal's with what looked like regret.

'Mama?' The word came out strangled. Incredulous. Hal scrambled to assimilate this new and totally unexpected information.

She turned towards him proudly then, clutching the child to her protectively. 'Yes. Mama.'

'Who is he?' The boy stared at Hal, clearly only just registering his presence.

'A friend.' She watched him defiantly. 'He is leaving. He won't be coming back.'

'I don't understand…' Although he was beginning to, good grief he was beginning to, and she watched his face dispassionately as all manner of emotions skidded haphazardly across it unchecked. Shock. Disbelief. Disappointment.

Horror.

Her cornflower eyes hardened at that. 'I am sure

you can let yourself out in much the same manner you let yourself in.' A brittle tone, like jagged glass. 'I am going to sleep with *my son* in the nursery. We are leaving in the morning. Goodbye, Hal.'

In a billowing cloud of linen, she turned and went.

For the first time in their short acquaintance, Hal felt no desire to go after her.

Chapter Fifteen

The snow started some time in the middle of the night. She knew this as she had watched every second of the interminable darkness tick by, worrying. About hers and Georgie's future, Ockendon's threats and the potential damage to her father's reputation and career from the impending scandal. As awful as those things were to consider, they were less painful than recalling the expression on Hal's handsome face when he had realised she had a child. All her procrastinating and avoidance in appraising him of the truth had, she realised, been as much about protecting herself from his inevitable reaction as it had been about protecting her family. She could have confided in him sooner, from the outset, in fact, and in all probability he would have still helped her and kept her secret. He was that noble beneath all the swagger. But a part of her had enjoyed the frisson of attraction between them. It had made her feel young, unburdened and gloriously alive again, even though she had known it was not something which she could ever consider acting upon. Until she *had* acted upon it and now wished she hadn't. Being held by him, feeling his passion and losing herself in his kiss had made her yearn again for all the things she could not have as a mother of another man's baby. A wastrel's son.

Watching him recoil the second after he had proposed again had cut like a knife. Lizzie had been so hideously disappointed in him then, even though she had no right to expect otherwise. Hideously disappointed in him and ashamed of herself. The guilt at feeling shame for the innocent child in her arms galvanised her. Georgie was her everything and she was tired of fearing the judgement of others. Her final words to Hal had been curt and proud. How dare he judge her by a different set of standards to those in which he had lived his own life? Hal had likely lain with more women than he could remember. She had only been with one man and had paid the ultimate price. So she had called him on it when her son had asked, inwardly daring him to contradict her.

He won't be coming back.

Hal had not denied the assertion. He had left swiftly afterwards. She knew because she had been compelled to check, just in case some miracle had occurred and he had dithered. They had shared a poignant and special moment before Georgie had burst through the door, so she hoped perhaps he would linger. What for or what she wanted beyond that was not something she allowed herself to consider. But her bedchamber was chilly and empty, much like her bruised and battered heart, so she supposed she had an answer even though it turned out not to be the one she wanted.

By the time Lizzie dragged herself exhausted into the breakfast room a little past dawn, there was a foot of fresh snow covering the ground and, by the looks of the pewter sky, it was in no mood to stop any time soon. The head coachman had already sent word he believed the three-day journey to Cheshire was foolhardy in the extreme until the weather cleared and she had to bow to his judgement. The larger roads would be difficult, the smaller ones and the narrow lanes which ran through the Peaks in the north would be too dangerous. Even the elements were conspiring against her.

To his credit, her papa did not gloat at the news she was staying, albeit temporarily. He simply nodded and patted her hand. 'I will sort all of this out, Lizzie. I promise you.' Then he had bundled himself into a heavy coat and trudged out of the front door. She had no idea where he was going and there was no point in asking him. If he was hellbent on protecting her and Georgie, he was notoriously tight-lipped about how he intended to go about it and would tell her no more than he thought she should know. For five years, he had done much the same and would continue in the same vein unless she put a stop to it all once and for all. But she had seen the tight lines of worry which pulled at his face, the heavy, burdened gait and wished he would include her in his ongoing attempts at protecting her. Being kept in the dark was soul destroying.

Sat in the drawing room impotently staring at the walls, Lizzie decided to tackle the problem head on. She went to her mother's old escritoire and put pen to paper. Her note to the Earl of Ockendon was short and to the point. She was tired of his pointed comments and veiled threats and demanded he explain himself, asking him to meet her in St James's Park this very afternoon or, failing that, to leave her alone.

As much as she dreaded the meeting, it was necessary. The young footman she sent with the note came back directly with the reply. It was shorter than Lizzie's, missive and menacing.

I am glad you have come to your senses. Two o'clock. Come alone.

In five hours she would know her fate. Until then, she would force herself to enjoy a blissful couple of hours with her son. Perhaps the last blissful hours they would be able to spend in quite some time.

Stevens appeared out of nowhere and coughed politely. 'There is a caller at the door, Lady Elizabeth. The Earl of Redbridge.'

The pang of longing and pain caught her unexpectedly and she winced. 'Tell him I am not at home, Stevens. We have been through this.'

The butler frowned, clearly uncomfortable. 'He is not here to see you, Lady Elizabeth. Or your father. He says he has come to visit Master George.' He whispered this as Georgie was in earshot, drawing another insect on the floor near her feet contentedly. 'Under the circumstances, I ushered him inside. Just in case any passers-by overheard.'

Lizzie fought to keep her nerves under control. She hadn't expected to hear from Hal again and could not imagine why he had called asking to see her son. 'Where is he now, Stevens?'

'I put him in the green drawing room, Lady Elizabeth.'

'And I decided not to stay in it.' Hal's dark head popped around the doorframe and he eyed the now outraged butler warily. 'Please don't kill me, Stevens. I am not worth going to gaol over.'

Stevens looked to Lizzie for guidance and would, no doubt, cheerfully pummel Hal into a soggy mess at her instruction. He had been recruited specifically to protect her and her little boy, and took the responsibility seriously. Too seriously if his expression was to be believed. 'You can leave us, Stevens. I shall call if I need you.'

Hal edged into the room as her bodyguard glared at him murderously. 'I will be just outside the door. *Just* outside the door.'

'Message received and understood, Stevens. Whilst you are out there, I don't suppose you could rustle up some tea?' Hal grinned cheekily and she quite admired his bravado. 'Only it's dashed cold outside and I could do with something to warm me up.'

Stevens grunted and stalked out, slamming the door behind him in an obvious display of superior masculine strength. 'I don't think your butler likes me. It's most upsetting when one considers all of the cheerful little chats we have had every time I've come to call and he's merrily sent me packing.'

She would not be charmed by him, although the charm did not completely cover his discomfort. There was an awkwardness about him she had never seen before. An air of trepidation. 'Why are you here, Hal?'

His gaze travelled to Georgie, who had stopped colouring to stare back at him. She had no idea what her son was thinking. He had never been in the company of anyone other than the immediate family or the highly paid and fiercely loyal servants in their employ. This was the second time he had seen Hal in a few hours and the first had been in her bedchamber last night. Something which had hardly been appropriate, yet he had been too tired and too distressed from his bad dream at the time to question her flimsy explanation.

'I came to introduce myself to your little boy. I thought it only right and proper after…' He looked away then, clearly embarrassed. Those splendid broad shoulders of his rose, then fell on a ragged sigh. 'I realised he must be curious. Little boys are curious about most things. I certainly was. And last night was a little out of the ordinary. For all of us.'

At a loss at what to say, and more than a little overwhelmed at both his thoughtfulness and his presence, Lizzie shrugged and watched transfixed as Hal crouched down on the carpet a few feet away from her son. 'Good day to you, Master George. My name is Hal. I am a very good friend of your mother's and am very pleased to make your acquaintance.' He stuck out his big hand and gently shook Georgie's little one. A bit bewildered but accepting of the extraordinary, as children are prone to be, Georgie cheerfully gripped the strange man's palm and smiled up at him. The sight made her throat clog with emotion. Under a different set of circumstances…

No! She could not think like that. It served no purpose.

'I see you are an artist, Master George. What is that you are drawing?' As if he conversed with children every day, Hal lowered himself on to the carpet and mirrored her son's cross-legged pose.

'It is a common wood louse, sir. Did you know they have fourteen legs?' Her little boy was always delighted to have a conversation about insects.

'Fourteen! Good gracious, that is a lot of pairs of boots to polish.'

Georgie peered at him sceptically until he saw Hal smiling and realised one of his two legs was being pulled. He grinned back. 'Do you like insects, sir?'

'What's with all this sir business? My name is Hal, not sir.' He ruffled her son's hair and her heart clenched. 'And, yes—I do like insects. I am a huge fan of all creepy-crawlies. I find they are the most perfect things to scare girls with. My sister hates them and it is enormous fun to watch her run around the room screaming at the sight of something with a profusion of hairy legs. I have never hidden any woodlice in her small things—though now that I know they have fourteen spindly legs apiece I shall do so at the first opportunity.'

Always keen to help, Georgie frowned. 'I don't think you will be able to gather any till spring.

Woodlice tend to hide away in winter. It's too cold for them. But once the weather gets warmer I shall help you find some. They live under stones and things. We have a big urn in the garden and when Grandpapa lifts it up for me there are hundreds of woodlice there.'

'Well, that is just grand. My sister will have an apoplexy.' Hal leaned closer and dropped his voice to a conspiratorial whisper. 'Perhaps we can hide some and scare your mother, too.'

Georgie giggled, already charmed, and playfully nudged Hal as if they had known each other for ever. 'It wouldn't work. Mama is not scared of bugs.'

'Your mama is a very brave woman indeed.' His eyes drifted up to rest on hers intensely. They were troubled. Apologetic. Lizzie had no idea what that meant and helplessly stared back. Just as it had the night before, the atmosphere became charged; the air heavy with things unsaid and emotions not acknowledged.

'Your tea!' Stevens practically kicked the door open, snapping Lizzie out of the spell, and slammed a laden tray down on the table. He shot Hal a menacing look and curled one meaty paw into a fist. 'I will be *just* outside the door!' He stomped out, leaving the door ajar this time.

'Stevens means well.'

'You do not need to explain. I might not be the most scholastic of fellows, but I think I have the gist of what is going on.' Hal offered her a half-smile. 'We need to talk, I think. When we are alone.'

She nodded, grateful that he understood what needed to be said was not for little boys' ears. Hal turned back to her son and picked up some coloured chalk and began to help Georgie colour in his woodlouse. For some inexplicable reason, her little boy wanted it all colours of the rainbow, something Hal apparently understood. Lizzie poured tea and watched them. When the masterpiece was finished, Hal joined her on the sofa and drank the cup she had poured him, maintaining a cheerful stream of childish conversation with Georgie all the while.

'Can you draw me a ladybird, Mama?'

A piece of paper and some chalk was thrust into her hand and she felt self-conscious as she sketched out the outline of the bug. This was the first time anyone outside of the household had ever witnessed her be a mother and it was disconcerting, especially as he was watching her closely. She wished she knew what Hal was thinking. What did he see? Did he see a fallen woman? A victim? A doting parent? She sincerely doubted he saw her as an attractive young woman who roused his passions any more...or a potential wife.

'I see your mama is an artist, too, Georgie.' The familiar pet name tripped off his tongue unconsciously, but then again, Hal had also casually pulled her son to sit on his lap. He appeared extremely comfortable there.

'Mama always draws the best insects. She says it is one of her greatest talents.'

'Can she build snowmen?'

'She tries, but they always end up a bit lopsided. We are going outside to build one soon.'

'Soon? When all the snow in the garden is fresh and calling to us? I think we should all go and build one now. If I do say so myself, I build excellent snowmen. It is one of *my* greatest talents. And he will be as straight as a die. Fetch your coat, Georgie boy! And gloves.'

Hal had said the magic words as far as her son was concerned. He wiggled off his lap and dashed out of the room, squealing with excitement, leaving them both alone. Lizzie was suddenly awkward, dreading the inevitable. To hide it she continued to sketch the ladybird.

'He is Rainham's?'

She nodded.

'He jilted you because you were with child?' Hal could not disguise the anger in his tone. Outrage on her behalf. Always so noble.

'No. He does not know Georgie exists—or I hope he doesn't. He jilted me before I had a chance to tell him and afterwards I never wanted him to know I was expecting his child.'

'But Ockendon knows?'

'I don't know. He has alluded to it. My *deep, dark secret* which I keep *hidden*. That's a little too coincidental, don't you think?' His silence was deafening. 'Thanks to my father's ridiculous hope that he could still find a man who would deign to marry me and the amount of money he has thrown into my dowry to practically purchase one—not that he sees that, of course—I believe Lord Ockendon intends to use the information as collateral to force me to accept his proposal.'

'Call his bluff. Your father is a powerful man.'

How to tell him what she suspected, but didn't know? 'I fear my father would be ruined by the scandal, too, else I would not think twice, but...'

Lizzie stood to give her jumpy nerves something to do and began to pace. 'He had Rainham removed from society. I do not know how and for years I did not care, I was simply grateful I never had to clap eyes on the man.'

'But you suspect your father is guilty of some sort of foul play.'

'Yes. More collateral. Don't you remember what he said at the Danburys'? It is in your *family's* best interests to talk to me. Not mine. My family's. And he dragged Rainham with him to make sure I understood.' Now she thought upon it, her former fiancé had been uncomfortable. Frightened, even. He had looked ready to flee when Hal had threatened him, genuine fear on his dissolute face. If only she knew what her dear papa had done, this would all be so much simpler. 'My father is a good man, Hal. He would have done whatever was necessary to protect his family.'

Further conversation was prevented by the reappearance of Georgie, who had been swaddled in layers of warm clothes and began bouncing on the spot as she and Hal donned their own. Once outside, Lizzie toyed with the idea of telling Hal she was meeting Ockendon this afternoon, certain he would know how to best play the situation without giving too much away. However, deep down she knew he would never allow her to talk to the Earl alone and would insist on accompanying her. Ockendon would hardly bare his cards with a witness present. Instead she kept tight-lipped and tried to enjoy playing in the snow, watching her son laughing with Hal. Watching Hal patiently teach him how to build a proper snowman, then lift him giggling to push in the carrot nose and coal eyes before sacrificing his own hat and placing it at a jaunty angle on their creation's head. It was such a pretty picture. Hal had a natural way with children and would doubtless make an excellent father one day.

To his own children.

Born in wedlock.

Because he was an earl and such things were expected and she was a fallen woman on the cusp of complete ruination.

Chapter Sixteen

Hal left the Wilding house on a mission. It made no difference that he had not enjoyed a wink of sleep in three days, or that his body was drooping with fatigue. His mind was racing. It had been racing around in circles since the moment that little boy had burst into his mother's bedchamber.

At that moment, not only the rug but the entire floor had been pulled from under Hal's feet. She had a child. A child! One that nobody knew about. Something which was as unforeseen as it was scandalous. In that awful moment Hal had been instantly grateful she had turned down his proposal. Hell, the urge to run had been instinctive. He had no memory of climbing down the wisteria or of racing across the garden. His wits returned as the first flakes of snow melted against his face and he found himself stood in the middle of the Earl of Upminster's lawn, his breath sawing in and out and the pain in his heart so acute he was clutching at his ribs.

Anger, disbelief, disappointment, and shame at his own cowardly, yet perfectly understandable, disgust were like physical blows to his body. He stumbled to a stone bench and sucked in several lungsful of the frigid midnight air and began to count his lucky stars at his narrow escape. Except…

After a few minutes, he did not feel particularly lucky or proud of his reaction. Images of the moment flashed through his mind. Her lovely face. The defiance. The way she had protectively hugged her son.

Rainham's son.

The by-blow of a wastrel and a scoundrel.

A huge scandal.

He had watched her spine stiffen and her body turn instinctively to shield her child from whatever poisoned darts were about to be thrown, yet she had made no excuses or apologies for the truth.

The little boy's frightened eyes.

He knew what it felt like to be a frightened little

boy. Knew, too, what it felt like to be the son of a bad and selfish man. Hardly a little boy's fault.

From somewhere, Hal found the strength to move his heavy limbs. Climbed back over the high wall into the mews; dragged himself across Mayfair to home. He drank more than a few glasses of brandy which did nothing to numb the thoughts warring in his head or the confused emotions cluttering his mind. As dawn broke, he realised it all boiled down to three things.

Lizzie was his friend.

She was in trouble.

An innocent little boy was in trouble, too.

Hasty, ill-conceived proposals and unexplainable and irrational feelings aside—as her friend, he was damn well going to help her. Whatever secrets she had kept were hers to keep. Ockendon had no right to use them for his own financial gain no matter how scandalous they might happen to be. Not if Hal could prevent it. They had made a pact to protect one another from the unwanted attentions of would-be spouses and it was one which he intended to honour because...

Because.

Hal was not ready to justify what his heart and soul wanted him to do. To quantify or analyse it any further would likely terrify him and his poor head could not take any more confusion. All he was prepared to acknowledge was that he had a burning desire to protect her. Now that marriage was out of the question, he needed to give some serious thought to how he could best do that.

If his awful father had taught him anything, he had taught him people could be manipulated into bending to your will if the incentive was right.

'The world runs on coin, Henry. Nothing else matters.'

Hal might not subscribe to the principle, but he could not deny the science behind it. His father had built up a huge business empire by using whatever means were at his disposal. To the best of Hal's knowledge, that hadn't included anything illegal, but he had sailed fairly close to the wind. Veiled threats and the right kind of incentive had been his father's stock in trade, whether that be regarding business or his dealings with his own family. As much as Hal loathed behaving in any way like his father, all he needed to do was find just the right incentive to stop Ockendon.

Of course, he could have started on his quest first thing. Probably should have. But something pulled him towards Lizzie. Perhaps it was his conscience. All he knew was he had to see her. Let her know he was on her side. That he was on her innocent little boy's side, too. It was not as if the child had any say in who his father was. So he had called on them and stayed far longer than he should have, while all the time his mind had been racing. Plotting. Trying to untangle the mess. However, to accomplish that he needed to know exactly what Ockendon had over her father.

His own father had a favourite analogy for removing obstacles. In days of yore, when an army besieged a castle, they had two choices. Surround the fortress and starve the occupants out or find the most vulnerable part of the structure and ruthlessly mine under it, then stand back and watch the impregnable stone towers collapse under their own weight. Whilst both techniques had merit, he doubted they had time to wait it out, so Hal needed to find the weakest link. In this case, his gut told him it was Rainham.

As soon as he had bid Georgie a cheery goodbye and squeezed Lizzie's hand in reassurance, Hal trudged through the snow-lined streets towards the Earl of Ockendon's house. He tempered his initial and violent need to tackle the man face to face in favour of reconnaissance. Until he understood the situation fully, Hal would keep his powder dry.

From a distance, he watched a servant wrap the knocker on the front door. Clearly his odiousness was leaving town today—or had already left—as so many did this close to Christmas. He wanted to ask the butler if his master was bound for his country estate, but didn't dare. Even though he had never had reason to call upon the Earl, Hal was too well known and preferred to not enlighten his enemy to his quest. Instead he circumvented the house and headed towards the mews.

The stable was virtually empty, save the still-stalled team of greys and one solitary groom. The fellow looked thoroughly fed up as he forked old straw into a pile, totally oblivious of the fact he was not alone. When he bent to pick up a hand brush Hal spied a significant hole in the sole of the man's boots.

Interesting.

'Good morning, my good fellow!' Hal grinned as the groom's head turned. 'I wonder if you would be inclined to help me.' He idly transferred a few silver coins from one gloved hand to another and then back again in case the lad was not too bright. He needn't have worried. The groom eyed the coins hungrily.

'What sort of help?' Not the response of a man who couldn't be bribed.

'Information. About your lord and master.' Hal watched the man's face unconsciously scowl and pressed his advantage, certain there was no love lost between master and servant. 'I am happy to pay you for your discretion.'

He propped the fork in front of him and rested his wrists on the handle. 'What do you want to know?'

'I am looking for Lord Ockendon's guest. The Marquess of Rainham. Where might I find him?'

The groom waited for Hal to toss him a coin before he answered. 'He ain't got no guest. He brought a gent back with him last night, but they went out late and only his lordship returned. Haven't seen the other fella since—and, before you ask, I have no idea where he went.'

Not what Hal wanted to hear. Rainham could be anywhere, although his gut told him Ockendon would not leave his minion left to his own devices. He was too valuable. Wherever he had gone, he would be staying away from prying eyes. 'Is it possible he has gone to your master's estate?'

The groom shrugged. 'It's possible, I suppose, but as his lordship is travelling there late this afternoon in the carriage, I'd have thought they would have travelled together. A carriage is safer than horseback and the road to Norfolk is popular with footpads and the like.'

A valid point, yet Ockendon could have hired another carriage to hide his guest quickly. 'How long is his lordship expected to stay in Norfolk?'

'One week. Two. Who knows? All I know is there'll be no wages for me again until he returns.' The groom was angry. Hal saw it in the flat line of his mouth and the hot intensity of his stare.

'He doesn't pay you when he is not in residence?' Perhaps Ockendon did have money worries?

'He barely pays us when he is, but since the mistress died he employs most of us on a casual basis when he's in town, then turfs us out on our ears when he goes off again. Which he does a lot nowadays. I don't know why he don't stay in blasted Norfolk and put us all out of our misery.'

Lizzie was the only person in Mayfair mad enough to be in St James's Park in the middle of a snow storm. The frozen wasteland before her matched the numbness of her own emotions. Hours of fear, worry and heartbreak had taken too much of a toll and now her mind had shut down to allow her to function while she had trudged past all the houses like a woman condemned. The festive door wreaths and spicy scents of Christmas mocked her. There was no joy in this season. Only fear and misery. Both emotions had left her wrung out like a dish rag hanging limply from the sink. She had arrived here a few minutes before two and had now stood so long the chill was making her bones ache, but was not surprised the Earl of Ockendon was making her wait. It added to the drama and heightened the sense of tension. He would like that.

When he finally strode out of the cover of trees, she simply stared back impassively and waited for him to come alongside. He tipped his hat in greeting, the permanent smug smirk curling up the corners of his mouth, went to take her gloved hand to kiss it and she snatched it away. 'I am tired of the games. Talk.'

'I know you gave birth to Rainham's bastard. A son.'

The news was hardly a surprise. Lizzie had been braced to hear it. 'What makes you think he is

Rainham's?' Only her family had ever been apprised of that detail, although the servants probably suspected as much. Many of them had been in her father's employ at the time of her engagement and were paid well for their silence.

'His age and colouring lend themselves towards him as the sire. He has Rainham's eyes.'

He had seen Georgie? He had to have to have made such an observation. Pieced together the truth. 'Really? And how, pray tell, would you know that?'

'I will grant you, getting a decent sighting of the lad has proved challenging. Your father's house is well protected and the servants very tight-lipped. However, you, Lady Elizabeth, are a creature of habit. Every Tuesday and Thursday your carriage leaves Mayfair unfashionably early.' He chuckled at her expression, enjoying the knowledge it was her mistake which had caused her downfall. 'I confess, I stumbled across the pair of you quite by accident a month ago when I had the good fortune to be riding through Richmond Park. I was some distance away, but you are a striking woman.' His eyes strayed to her chest. 'When one is as advanced in years as I am, one recalls a great deal of gossip. I was sat in the church when the congregation were informed you had called off your wedding. It was quite the scandal at the time and the source of much speculation. I remember it clearly. Five years ago. The boy's somewhere between four and five years old, and five years is the same amount of time your erstwhile fiancé had been absent from society. Such a unique set of coincidences set my mind wondering.'

'So I have a son. Tell the world. I will still not marry you.'

Ockendon acknowledged her comment with another chuckle. 'Yes, indeed, a bastard child is a *scandal* to be sure, yet I had already anticipated it would not be enough to bring you around to my way of thinking. I had the devil of a job tracking down poor Rainham. For a little while I was certain he had disappeared off the face of the earth, then I recalled his family seat was in Cornwall.' He appeared delighted at his own industry. 'A shockingly run-down and miserable place and still no sign of your Marquess—fortuitously, he had left his usual trail of bad debt across the county and there were a great many tradesmen who were disgruntled with the fellow since his...return...but more of that later. I traced him to Bodmin Gaol and discovered he had been festering there for well over a year. He was in a dreadful state. The stress of bankruptcy had addled his mind and he was most accommodating when I offered to pay to secure his release. Told me all manner of *interesting* titbits. Titbits far more scandalous than your secret son, my lady.'

He laughed again and her temper snapped. 'Spit it out, man. Lay your cards flat on the table. If it is as bad as you are suggesting, then you already know you have won.'

'Indeed, it is bad. *Deliciously* bad. I suppose you already know your beloved had absconded with another woman rather than marry you. But do you also know the Duke of Aylesbury sought retribution? He had him tied up and dragged back to London. He wanted him dead and was happy to toss his remains in the Thames for the fish to eat. Your lily-livered father refused to consider cold-blooded murder. He was always so upright and proper. So full of his own importance. Instead, he arranged for Rainham to be chained and smuggled on board a prison boat bound for Australia.'

The gasp escaped her lips before Lizzie could stop it. 'You're lying!' Oh, God! She hoped he was lying. The Earl watched her reaction with barely contained glee.

'Isn't it marvellous? No trial, not even trumped-up charges, just the straight and highly *illegal* kidnap and transportation of a peer of the realm to Botany Bay. I wonder what the penalty for such a crime is, Lizzie?'

Her stomach plummeted to her feet. Ruination was the least she had to worry about. If this version of events were true, then her father could be facing worse than ruination. Perhaps even the scaffold. Oh, Papa! Her stomach lurched at the thought and her knees buckled momentarily until she forced herself to stand proudly. Forced her eyes to meet Ockendon's with futile defiance.

Ockendon's gloved hand came up to touch her cheek and this time Lizzie did not dare pull away. This man held her papa's life in that hand. 'The story gets better. About a year later, your father must have got cold feet. The fool had Rainham brought back without Aylesbury's knowledge, threatened him with it. Warned the poor chap that he was now an outcast in London and, if he escaped death by Aylesbury's hand, would be thrown in debtors' prison if he dared return. Ironic, really, when *that* is where I found him. For a man who is as weak-willed and self-centred as your former beau, a life in virtual and impoverished exile in Cornwall was a more attractive option than death. And, of course, I will be eternally grateful to your father for his spinelessness, because it left me a trail of crumbs to follow. Had he listened to Aylesbury and let Rainham's sorry carcase become fish food, I wouldn't stand a chance with you. Isn't fate wonderful?'

Lizzie's mind was whirring. She had steeled herself to hear something bad, dreadful even, and was prepared for an epic scandal to erupt. At her worst imaginings, both she and Papa would have to flee to obscurity thoroughly ruined. But if the authorities were to arrest her papa, if he faced criminal charges—gaol or worse—there was no way she could stand by and allow such a travesty to happen when she had the power to prevent it.

'What is it you want?'

'I want a wife. One with powerful connections. One with a significant dowry who can give me the son my barren first marriage could not. I already know you are fertile, lovely Lizzie, although I will not condone your by-blow in my house.'

A tiny part of her died. 'I will never marry you if Georgie is sent away. I will not leave the care of my son to strangers.'

'Georgie—so that is his name?' He waved a

gloved hand dismissively as if the cruel wrenching apart of mother and child was of no consequence. 'I am sure your overprotective father will see to his needs and I am not a monster. You will be allowed to visit once or twice a year.'

'And if I refuse?' Her voice came out ragged, choked with sadness. Once a year! Death would be sweeter.

'Then I will hand your father over to the authorities and feed your family's secrets to the newspapers as fodder for the gossips. But we both know it will not come to that. I hold *all* the power now.' He took her gloved hand and tugged the soft leather barrier slowly off. 'You are a *good* daughter and would never condemn your father.' Her skin now bared, he placed his lips against the exposed flesh and tasted the back of her hand with his tongue, his eyes never leaving hers as he did so. 'And I know you will be a very *good* and very *dutiful* wife. Enjoy your last Christmas as a spinster, Lizzie. I shall be attending the Earl of Redbridge's Christmas Ball on Twelfth Night. That strikes me as the perfect venue to announce our engagement, seeing as everyone will be there—including Redbridge. In the meantime, I shall have my solicitors contact your father regarding the settlements. Do tell him I will expect the dowry sweetened, won't you? Will not settle for less than double what it is now…as a starting figure, of course. And it goes without saying he will do his utmost to bring me into those illustrious circles he moves in, seeing as I will imminently become his son-in-law. A government position in the Foreign Office or Home Office will suffice.'

He released her hand, a hand which would now need to be washed in lye to remove the stain of him from her skin, and stepped back. 'I shall also procure a special licence so we can be married immediately after, so you should begin your preparations, too. A wedding in St George's in Hanover Square might be fitting—and at least this time around you can be certain your groom will turn up.' He smiled again. A cold, malicious smile. 'And as I know how much you loathe society, you will be moving permanently to my estate. Away from…mischief.'

And everyone she loved. Georgie. Papa. Hal. The numbness which had cossetted her before she stepped into the park was gone, replaced by agonising pain. Utter devastation. Ockendon saw it and his wrinkly face split into an ugly grin.

'I believe I shall enjoy our marriage bed, Lizzie.'

His eyes dropped to her bosom again, leering as if he could see through the thick layers of clothes to her nakedness beneath, leaving her feeling violated. 'Not as much as I shall enjoy spending your father's money, or utilising his powerful government connections. I am looking forward to *that* part of our nuptials a great deal.'

Chapter Seventeen

Hal had found his feet heading down Holborn the next morning as soon as the shops were open. They led him back to Hamley's Noah's Ark. A quick scan of the shelves and an even quicker purchase later, he bounded into Grosvenor Square eager to share the information he had already gathered. If his suspicions were correct, then he was certain he could find a way to rescue her.

He rapped on Lizzie's front door with peculiar butterflies flapping in his tummy and tried not to think about what they meant. Stevens opened it and his mighty shoulders slumped. 'Good morning, Stevens. Are we going to enact our usual tiresome rigmarole or are you going to let me in?'

The giant butler stood aside and gestured him into the hall whilst simultaneously threatening murder with his eyes. 'I shall see if Lady Elizabeth is at home. Stay. Here.' One meaty finger pointed to a spot on the carpet and Hal made a great show of shuffling to stand upon it.

'I shan't move, Stevens. I promise.'

The butler stalked down the hall towards the same drawing room Hal had visited the day before and, to vex the butler as much as anything, he tiptoed in his wake.

'Lady Elizabeth, the Earl of Redbridge...'

'Is here!' Hal pushed passed the fuming servant and strode with a smile into the room.

'Hal!' Georgie scrambled off the floor in a scattering of coloured chalks and barrelled towards him. His small body crashed into Hal's at speed. Hal hoisted him up and balanced him on his hip.

'How is our snowman doing?'

'He is still standing.'

'Excellent news. How about we go and make him a lady-friend later? If this snow is here for the duration the poor fellow will get very lonely all on his own. Every upright snowman deserves a snow lady to make coal eyes at.'

With the child bouncing in his arms with excitement, Hal finally turned towards the sofa to greet Lizzie and her appearance shocked him. Dark circles ringed her red, swollen eyes. Face pale and drawn. Spirit battered—or perhaps broken. Something had happened. Something dreadful. He lowered Georgie to the ground and ruffled his hair. 'I need ten minutes alone with your mama first, young man.' He handed him the wrapped package he was carrying. 'Go and see if Stevens wants to play with these with you out in the hall.'

'Wooden swords! Yippee!'

Hal waited until the child had disappeared, then softly closed the door and came to sit beside her. 'What's wrong?'

'I met Ockendon y-yesterday.' She crumpled next to him, her hands covering her face and her slim shoulders racked by the force of her distress. At a loss what else to do, he enveloped her in his arms and hugged her close.

For an age, she couldn't speak, so Hal smoothed his hand over her hair, kissed the top of her blonde head and promised himself he would flay Ockendon at the first opportunity. 'It's going to be all right, Lizzie. I promise. The rancid Earl is in debt up to his eyeballs.'

'Y-y-you d-don't understand, Hal… My f-f-f-father…' She collapsed against him again, inconsolable for several minutes.

When she finally lifted her face from the now-sodden front of his shirt, the pain in her eyes broke his heart. He knew in that moment she was about to tell him something terrible.

'My father has broken the law, Hal... He kidnapped Rainham and had him smuggled on to a prison ship under a false name. Within a few days of my being jilted he had my fiancé transported to the Antipodes as a common criminal. He left him there to rot.'

'W-what?' His mouth struggled to form words. Kidnapped. Transportation. He had not expected to hear either word.

'It was a gross abuse of his government position.' An understatement. The kidnap of a peer of the realm was a capital offence. Even assuming the Government would not wish to throw one of their own to the wolves, or suffer the embarrassment of a public trial, Lizzie's father was potentially in serious trouble. 'Papa must have had second thoughts, as he had him returned a year later...but Charles still spent a year as a prisoner in that terrible place and suffered many more months in atrocious conditions at sea.' She was shaking, Hal realised, and not with cold. 'I have no choice, Hal. I have to marry him.'

'Over my dead body!'

'I will not see my father arrested. He meant w-well…he was trying to protect m-me… It is my fault Ockendon knows. M-my carelessness that put my family in d-danger.' She told him about her visits to Richmond, weeping profusely and quivering like a leaf in a storm. In her distraught state, it took a while to piece together the whole sorry tale. At the end of it, Hal realised the existence of a bastard child was merely the tip of the iceberg. It would have been better if the Duke of Aylesbury had had the snake murdered in cold blood. Now that Aylesbury was dead, the only witness to the whole affair was the man who had wronged Lizzie so grievously. The Marquess of Rainham, despoiler of innocent young women, libertine and jilter, was now the victim.

'I will find him, Lizzie!' Hal had to find him. One life and the happiness of a great many people, himself included, were riding on it. She allowed him to tug her close again and he buried his nose in her hair. 'Without his witness, Ockendon has no case.'

She burrowed against his chest gratefully, her voice small. Matter of fact. 'There will be other witnesses. The crew of the prison ship might be dredged up to talk. There will doubtless be plenty of others in Cornwall. His creditors, gaolers.' She sighed and pulled away and he wished she were not as intelligent as she obviously was. 'He wants to announce our engagement on Twelfth Night.'

'You cannot marry him, Lizzie. Your father is a respected and powerful man. It will take more than circumstantial evidence to see him sentenced. If I can find Rainham, I am confident I can buy his silence.' Or at least he hoped he could. He had never actually tried. This was all so tenuous and needed to be more than wishful thinking. 'We need to be one step ahead of the game. Anticipate what Ockendon intends to do. Cut him off at the knees... We have a fortnight. A great deal can happen in a fortnight.' If this last two weeks was anything to go by, then anything was possible. And wasn't that the truth. A fortnight ago, the only complication in Hal's life had been his missing vigour and the eager hordes. Now he had a terrified woman, an innocent boy, a man's reputation and perhaps even his life on the line and the most persistent and worrying pain in his own heart to consider. 'Ockendon is in debt. I do not know to what extent as yet, but I will. I promise. I will find his weaknesses and exploit them. Once I am done, he will have no case to bring before the authorities. You have my word.' And he had a sneaking suspicion part of his heart, too, as it was still aching at the prospect of losing her. A horrible, hollow feeling which made him nauseous.

The thought of her miles and miles away brought a lump to his throat, yet Hal had no earthly idea how to save her. Although he had to. Somehow, by hook or by crook, he had to stop Ockendon and seal his spiteful, blackmailing mouth shut for ever. That was the only outcome he could bear. 'I am going to need to speak to your father. He will need to be involved if we are going to avert catastrophe.' She nodded. The first signs of hope had begun to glimmer in her lovely eyes and his heart swelled. He had put that there and he could not let her down. 'And I am going to need to bring in some reinforcements. With your permission, I would like to tell my family. My brother-in-law Aaron will be an asset in our quest.'

She appeared appalled at this. Ashamed, even. Her sad eyes dropped to her hands. 'I suppose the whole *ton* will learn I am a fallen woman soon enough, Hal, so I doubt it will make much difference.'

Fallen woman? She wasn't a fallen woman. She was a brave and loyal one. A wronged one. 'Men like Rainham are practised seducers. You were young and trusting. Engaged. You had no idea you would end up an unwed mother. My family will not judge you for that.' Or at least he hoped they wouldn't. If they did, he might have to have the mother of all arguments with them until they saw things his way. Punches might be thrown, Persian carpets ruthlessly rolled. 'Between us, we will find a way.'

She nodded and attempted a smile but Hal could see she did not hold out much hope. When she bravely pulled her shoulders back as her son dashed back into the room, wielding both the wooden swords Hal had bought him aloft, her gazed fixed on Georgie and her voice came out as barely a whisper. 'This might be my last ever Christmas with my son. Whatever happens I want him to enjoy it.'

Georgie was having a whale of a time with Hal, who was attempting to teach her son the rudiments of fencing when her father came in. The sight brought him up short. As he stared at them, Lizzie noticed how old and tired he suddenly appeared. He was suffering, too, yet they had barely exchanged a single word since they returned from the ill-fated Danbury house party.

She walked towards him and threaded her arm through his and his hand instantly came to rest on hers tightly. They were both apologising without words, yet both knew there were many things still to say. None of them was likely to be pleasant, not when their secrets were about to implode.

'Stevens informed me he visited yesterday, asking to speak to Master George. Your son seems to like him a great deal, Lizzie.'

'Hal is easy to like, Papa. He wants to help us.'

'I can sort this all out, there is no need to trouble yourself or…' Stubborn to a fault. Always trying to protect her.

'I met with Ockendon yesterday.'

The air left his body in a whoosh. 'You shouldn't have done that.'

'He knows about Georgie, too—and how you and Aylesbury had Rainham dispatched to Botany Bay.'

'I see.' She felt him wobble and guided him to a seat. He sat heavily, looking every inch his sixty-two years. 'At the time…well…'

'I do not judge you for it. If somebody tried to hurt Georgie I would happily do the same. However, as I am sure you have already worked out, he is threatening to turn you over to the authorities unless I agree to marry him.'

'Let him. I would rather that than—' She held up her hand before he could protest.

'I would rather not have to see you go to gaol or, Heaven forbid, hanged because of me. If it comes to it, I *will* marry Ockendon.' Her dear papa appeared suddenly so bereft. 'Hal is of the opinion we can stop Ockendon and I would never forgive myself if I did not at least try to prevent that man from destroying my life. You need to tell us the truth. All of it.'

His eyes flicked to the fencing match and Hal met his stare head on. He smiled, then went back to entertaining Georgie to give them some privacy. 'Do you trust him, Lizzie?'

A silly question when her heart was positively bursting with affection and gratitude for the man. 'Implicitly.'

Her son jabbed the point of his sword in Hal's belly. He clutched the imaginary wound, staggered left, then right and then proceeded to die noisily on the carpet. When Georgie giggled, he jumped up again, hoisted him into the air, flipped him upside down and marched him dangling by his feet towards them. The sight made her yearn for such a heart-warming picture every day. Her son's laughter. A happy home. One which Hal shared. If only her circumstances had been different.

'Are we making my snowman's lady-friend now, Hal?'

'We shall make her this afternoon. I have to speak to your grandpapa first.'

'What about?'

Hal tapped the side of his nose conspiratorially. 'Christmas surprises, young man. Secret Christmas surprises for nasty little boys who love bugs. Now, off with you. Go and pester your nanny, or, even better, Stevens. I will wager good money the man is loitering *just* outside the door.'

Lizzie took his chubby hand and led him out. Conscious that her days with him were limited, she did not hurry to settle him with his nanny. These moments were now too precious and she would not squander one no matter how dire things were for her. By the time she returned to the drawing room, her father and Hal were sat, heads together, in deep conversation. They had been joined by Viscount Ardleigh, who appeared a little stunned at what he was hearing, but no less engaged. They paused as she entered and for the briefest of moments she could tell her father was on the brink of dismissing her in his usual over-protective way. Hal patted the space next to him on the sofa. 'I have brought Aaron up to speed with your situation, Lizzie.'

'This is all my fault.' Her papa's voice was choked with guilt. 'I should have let the Duke of Aylesbury have him killed or left him to rot in Botany Bay.'

'Why did you bring him back?' Although Lizzie suspected she already knew the answer. Her father did not have a mean bone in his body.

'I don't know.' He sighed and shook his head. 'When I packed him off, I was careful. Nobody knew his true identity. The ship's captain believed him to be a fraudster, a man who had a reputation for impersonating people to defraud them. That way, I assumed nobody would listen to him ranting about being a peer of the realm. But of course, then I had no idea you were carrying the man's child. Once I learned that, and after Georgie was born, the guilt ate away at me. I couldn't stomach the thought of my grandson asking about his father and knowing that I had sent him to hell to die. I used my connections to have him brought back—but knew I never wanted him near you both. I threatened him with Aylesbury, his creditors…whatever I could to keep him away, and like a fool I let him go back to his estate, certain he would never darken our doors again. I shouldn't have done that. I put you in harm's way.'

'I put myself in harm's way, Papa. Ockendon saw me with Georgie in Richmond Park, then followed me repeatedly to be sure. As he said, I am a creature of habit. Every Tuesday and Thursday…'

Hal turned towards her and took her hand. As usual her pulse stepped up a notch at his touch. 'We need to know word for word what he said to you yesterday. What do you remember?'

Lizzie remembered it all. How could she not? It had been the singularly most important and terrifying conversation of her life. She had spent the entire night recalling Ockendon's chilling words and mourning her own stupidity. Realising you had been instrumental in your own downfall was devastating. Her outings to Richmond had given Ockendon everything he had needed. Step by step, she repeated the conversation, pausing to answer the numerous questions Hal or his brother-in-law threw at her. How did he look when he said that? Did he stipulate why he needed a wife with a large dowry? Like the most thorough lawyers they cross-examined every word, every nuance in Ockendon's behaviour, searching for clues to help. She briefly considered withholding some of the disgusting insinuations the old Earl had made about her fertility and their marriage bed, but decided against it. The information might be pertinent and if there was the slimmest chance of escaping her fate, Lizzie intended to grasp it and so did Hal. Therefore, only the truth would suffice.

At the end of her testimony, Hal stood and began to pace, royally furious on her behalf. 'We need to work swiftly if we are going to silence Ockendon. Let's find his weak spot. I shall use my contacts in the city to see if our Earl has made any foolhardy investments of late or taken out any loans.' It was obvious he was keen to get started. He was in danger of wearing a hole in the carpet.

'And I shall do some digging in Whitehall.' The old fire had relit in her papa's eyes. Yet another thing she owed to Hal. 'If he has got himself into trouble somewhere, somebody there is bound to know something. You are right—the more dirt we can find on that old fool the better. He will rue the day he threatened my daughter!'

'We could probably do with some extra help finding his accomplice. I shall head to Bow Street and engage some Runners. Rainham has to be somewhere close. The weather turned nasty the night he parted company with Ockendon and the best place to hide a wastrel is London.' Lord Ardleigh stood, too, and took her hand. 'Ockendon is nowhere near as clever as he thinks himself to be. He will have slipped up somewhere. Try not to worry.' Shocked at his kindness, Lizzie merely nodded. She barely knew this man, yet he was here, loyally supporting her because of Hal.

'What can I do?' Suddenly doing nothing felt like the worst sort of punishment. She would go quite mad with worry.

'Georgie needs you.' Hal's voice was soft. Sympathetic. 'And I think you need him, too.'

It dawned on her then that this very well could be her last ever Christmas with her son. The last stretch of uninterrupted time she might ever be allowed to have with him again and the sudden tears filled her eyes and threatened to spill down her cheeks. Stoically, Lizzie turned her face towards the window, hoping for some composure.

Now was not the time for either tears or panic. She had some hope and she would cling resolutely to it until it died. If it died.

'If you do not mind me saying, Lady Elizabeth, you shouldn't be alone.' Lord Ardleigh pressed a clean handkerchief into her hand. 'You need to keep occupied. I have a wonderful wife who will be more than happy to keep you company and two equally wonderful daughters who are about the same age as your son and would love another playmate. I have already sent word to Berkeley Square and expect them here presently. I'll wager they will help to take your mind off things.'

Hal stalked to the door, impatient to get started and ready to do battle again on Lizzie's behalf. His mossy eyes locked on hers as his hand hovered on the handle. 'Can you apologise to Georgie for me? Tell him I will be back to build the snow lady as I promised.'

He remembered her son.

Lizzie nodded and stared stunned at the now-closed door. Amidst all the panic and the plotting and the impending threat of scandal, he remembered he had made a promise to her little boy. The tears fell from her eyes so she closed them, lest her father or Lord Ardleigh see the tell-tale

emotion swirling in them. The gratitude, the wonder, the trust, the yearning, the absolute certainty
which only came from one thing.

Love.

Chapter Eighteen

The next few days passed in a blur. The men were on a quest to save her from Ockendon, so she saw her father rarely and Hal not at all. She had no idea where he had gone. All she knew was he had left London unexpectedly on her behalf and she was now worried sick about him, too. Hal had departed in such a haste that he had neglected to appraise either her papa or Aaron of his destination, except to say that he was following a rumour.

A rumour!

Did the man seriously think that was explanation enough at a time like this? However, thanks to Connie and Hal's mother, Lizzie was never left alone with her thoughts, something which was just as well as they kept turning very dark very quickly when she finally collapsed exhausted in her bed at night. The days, however, despite her inner turmoil, were filled with Christmas and the wonderful sounds of children laughing as Georgie had the time of his life with the hellions-in-training Prudence and Grace.

The Christmas part was wholly unexpected and strangely therapeutic. Every year her father closed up his Mayfair house for a week and the family travelled to Cheshire for Christmas, so aside from a holly wreath on the door Lizzie had never bothered doing anything else to honour the season whilst in town. This year, thanks to the drama she was embroiled in, the Wildings were staying put and the Stuart family had adopted them all into their own festivities.

Hal's sister Connie had been a godsend. The first time she had visited, she had come alone, insisted on Lizzie eating something, then had sat and listened quietly to the whole sorry tale without judgement. Everything had poured out, from the first moment her fiancé had scrambled up the wisteria to the dreadful ultimatum she had received from the Earl of Ockendon. The only bits Lizzie kept private were the personal and intimate details involving Hal. Although Connie was being lovely, it was unlikely she would want to hear that a totally unsuitable woman had fallen head over heels for her noble brother, or that Hal had proposed before he had known about Georgie and undoubtedly regretted it now. Lizzie's feelings hardly mattered. To her credit, Hal's sister was nothing but supportive.

The next time Connie had visited, she had brought her daughters and her mother, and the children played boisterously while the ladies chatted. Once Connie learned that there were no Christmas plans in place, she had galvanised the whole house into action, pointing out, quite rightly, that her son deserved to have a wonderful, magical time, and certainly did not need to see his mother fretting while the menfolk sorted out the 'other nonsense'.

So that was what Ockendon's threats became. The other nonsense. Nonsense which would all come to naught because Aaron and Hal would fix it. Connie and her mother were so certain of this fact, it gave Lizzie lingering hope they might be right. Even if they weren't, she wanted to believe it. Just for a few days. Just in case this truly was her last ever Christmas with her son and her father. The fear and stress was still there, but instead of mulling over it, Lizzie allowed the Stuart family to take over her life and force her to bring

Christmas kicking and screaming into Grosvenor Square.

Now, if she said so herself, the finished article was very festive. She had never seen so much holly. Shiny sprigs decorated every nook and cranny, winter greenery was woven through chandeliers, framed every fireplace and doorway and the poor kitchen was working overtime to bake every cinnamon- and spice-infused delight known to man. With the snow, and with two playmates close to his own age, Georgie was in his element, a smile of perpetual childish ecstasy permanently glued to his face. He was having a positively marvellous Christmas Eve.

'Stevens—we need more carrots.' The flame-haired Prudence issued this order as if she was the lady of the house and the soft-hearted butler stopped pushing the giant snowball he had been instructed to roll and brushed the sticky, fresh snow from his gloved hands.

'I shall enquire in the kitchens, my lady, although cook was complaining only yesterday about the amount of carrots which have recently been procured by the three of you.' He cast his eyes pointedly over the battalions of carrot-nosed snowmen now littering the lawn. All snow*men*.

Georgie stubbornly refused to have any ladies because his new hero Hal had promised they would build one together.

'If it helps the kitchen, we could make do with parsnips.' Prudence gave the butler a regal nod. 'And we shall use Georgie's chalks to colour them orange.'

Despite the weight of the world on her shoulders, the peculiar exchange made Lizzie smile as she remembered how Hal had bragged he encouraged his nieces to be resourceful with the materials at hand. The idea of them all colouring parsnips in the snow was as ridiculous as it was charming. Oh, to be a child and have such a simplistic view of the world. If only all problems could be solved with some coloured chalks!

'Is that my daughter issuing orders?'

'Papa!'

Aaron strode across the garden in his greatcoat, grinning, and his two girls squealed simultaneously and flew at him. He picked them both up boisterously, then went to kiss his wife with a wriggling daughter tucked under each arm. The public show of family affection made her envious, so she looked away, only to see her son watching the reunion intently. She walked towards him and began to assist him in slapping snow on to the body of the lopsided snowman currently under construction.

'Where is my papa?'

That knot of guilt she always carried was worse than usual. 'Far, far away, my darling.' At one point, she now knew, Australia—and by her father's hand—now back to haunt her again. Lizzie adjusted her son's woollen hat so that it covered his ears and tried to distract him. 'I think we need more snow for his head.'

'Is Hal my papa?'

Lizzie's chest tightened. 'No.'

'Are you sure? Only he is far, far away at the moment, isn't he? And we do have the same dark hair...just like Prudence and Grace have their mother's red hair. Your hair is blonde so I must follow my father. I think Hal and I look similar, don't you? And he carries me like Lord Ardleigh carries Grace and Prudence. Better, in fact, because he carries me upside down.'

With a catch in her voice, Lizzie smiled, completely flummoxed as how to answer him and yet reluctant to crush his childish dreams—or hers—just yet. 'As it's Christmas Eve, have you made a wish?'

As she'd hoped, her little boy turned to her quizzically. 'I have to make a wish? How do I do that?'

'When you go to bed tonight, you have to close your eyes and concentrate hard on whatever it is you want the most.'

'What sort of things can I wish for?'

'Well…' She began to pat more snow on to the snowman's body, absurdly grateful Georgie was distracted by the thought of wishes. She wasn't ready to talk about his father yet and would put it off for as long as was humanly possible. For ever, maybe. 'At Christmas time, people usually wish for something they do not have. A new toy, perhaps? Wooden tops, building bricks…an entire army of lead soldiers…'

His eyes lit up. 'If I wish for it, will I get it?'

'That depends on how hard you wish for it.'

'Then I shall go to bed early and wish all night.' In view of her desperate situation, Lizzie decided to do exactly the same.

It was two in the morning by the time Hal's horse trotted wearily into Mayfair. Fortunately, the skies had remained clear for his entire journey home from Norfolk, and although thick snow showed no signs of melting it had been crisp and easy to navigate. Perhaps riding through the night had been foolhardy, but he had wanted to be able to tell Lizzie his news as soon as possible, knowing she must still be worried sick. The last time he had seen her she had been so demoralised and broken, and like her knight errant he had been determined to avenge her.

He contemplated knocking on the front door, but that would mean waking the house and he selfishly wanted her all to himself first. She probably wouldn't like it, but for a myriad of complicated reasons which he did not want to have to analyse in case he thought better of it, he was going to climb the wisteria again.

Bone weary and frozen stiff, the ascent took more out of him than it had the first fateful time, and the sash window was very definitely now locked. Hal rapped on the glass and hung on for grim death. Immediately, the heavy curtains were torn apart and Lizzie's startled face appeared in the window. She was a sight for sore eyes. Her golden hair loosely plaited. The frothy nightgown an explosion of feminine lace. Her rosebud lips slightly parted in shock. At some point in the very near future, he fully intended to kiss them as he had thought of them constantly for days, although he needed to be able to feel his own lips first. The two icy strips of flesh that framed his mouth were probably unattractively blue and completely numb. He wanted to be able to feel her when he briefly succumbed to the temptation. Feel her and taste her properly because she was like a drug he craved and had gone far too long without, so it stood to reason he needed to thaw out sufficiently first. Hal gave his best approximation of a grin, which under the circumstances was less than half-hearted, and she fumbled with the catch and slid the window upwards.

'Hal.'

This time, he heard only soft relief in her voice and he tried not to hope she had been worrying about him. She gripped his arm and helped to haul him over the sill. The second he was in she began to fuss in a very encouraging manner. The window was slammed shut, she stripped him out of his damp, heavy greatcoat and gloves and ushered him towards the tiny fireplace. For the time being, her dainty chair appeared to take his weight, although he did not dare fidget just in case it swiftly surrendered under his bulk and allowed her to wrap him in the cosy eiderdown she hastily stripped off her bed.

'You need something warm to drink. I shall call for some tea.'

She most certainly would not. Rousing just one servant would negate his decision to climb the wisteria and mean he would have to behave decently, when he was really not in any mood to although knew he must. Things were very different now. She was a mother. She was in trouble and distraught. Hal had no right to want her with the fierce, possessive passion he was struggling to fight. 'I wanted to talk to you alone first...although I wouldn't mind if you went and smuggled me a generous snifter of brandy from somewhere.'

She disappeared, barefoot, in a voluminous cloud of white linen, leaving Hal to enjoy the aroma of her perfume in private. After a few moments, he realised that all the lamps were lit in her bedchamber, suggesting he had not rudely awoken her at all and he felt guilty that she had been alone and worrying for so many days and was clearly struggling to sleep. He should have sent word about where he was or what he was doing, but up until a few hours ago he had not had anything truly positive to report. Even now, all he could really give her was more hope than she had yesterday, but at least that was something.

Yet he was quietly confident his efforts would come to fruition. As much as he hated to make his blasted father right about anything, the world, it turned out, really did run on coin. Not entirely, of course, yet the liberal distribution of it in the last twenty-four hours had yielded some splendid results. There was still over a week to locate the elusive Lord Rainham and Hal still had pots of the stuff.

Lizzie dashed back in, clutching a full decanter of brandy and one glass. 'I have brought you Papa's good stuff...from his study.'

She practically filled the balloon to the top and thrust it at him. Hal took a few grateful sips and sighed contentedly as it trickled warmly down his throat and settled to heat his empty stomach. He should probably eat something, too, he realised, as nothing solid had passed his frozen lips since luncheon because he had been in such a hurry to get back to her. Hard liquor on an empty stomach might cause him to do something rash and very definitely inappropriate.

Lizzie stood nervously in front of him, her hands in a near-constant state of animation for a few seconds until she sank to the floor to sit in a cross-legged puddle at his feet. 'Please put me out of my misery, Hal. Am I doomed?'

'I don't think so.'

'That doesn't sound particularly reassuring.'

'Then let me rephrase it. I believe I have enough information to make Ockendon think twice and shortly I hope to have enough to silence him for ever.' Hal saw the light of hope begin to flicker in her eyes and gave in to the temptation to reach out and run the tip of his finger along her cheek.

'Did you find Rainham?'

'No.' The excited glimmer in her lovely eyes dimmed. 'I met a banker who had heard a rumour Lord Ockendon's house in Mayfair was heavily mortgaged, but I could find no evidence of that in any of the London banks.'

'Would the banks impart that sort of confidential information?'

'When you invest in the city, they have a certain amount of loyalty towards you.'

'And I suppose you invest in the city?'

'A great deal more than my over-cautious father ever did. I am owed a few favours.' And Hal had called every single one in. 'It appears the rancid Earl has a habit of upsetting people. His former solicitor was very disgruntled at still being owed money for his services after twenty years of loyal service. He was very happy to tell me all manner of interesting things.'

'Such as?'

Hal wasn't meaning to be mysterious, but his thoughts kept being distracted by the silken feel of the loose tendril of her hair he had wound around his hand. Good grief, he was pleased to see her. Just sitting in her presence was lovely. Comforting. *Home*. Either he was overtired or she had bewitched him. Funny how he didn't seem to mind the latter any more. He dropped the curl reluctantly and sat forward. She had waited long enough and deserved to know it all. There would be plenty of time to ponder his odd feelings later, after he had climbed back down the wisteria and trudged through the snow again towards his own bed.

'Like the fact that he used to receive three thousand pounds per annum from his wife's family, a sum which had been agreed as a part of the marriage settlement and which would continue to be paid to her children upon the event of her death. But as you already know, the poor woman died without issue and the lady's brother refused to continue the arrangement after her demise. The solicitor was instructed to find legal arguments to force the fellow to continue his payments, but failed. Ockendon refused to pay him for his services and sought new counsel—and I now know he desperately depended on that three thousand a year. It funded his lavish lifestyle while here in town. A lifestyle he is equally as desperate to maintain—seeing as he is obsessed with the idea of being powerful and when one simply cannot wield any power from the wilds of one's country estate.' Hal took another quick sip of the brandy and watched fascinated as she took the glass from his hand and took a healthy swig of it herself. He felt guilty for sincerely hoping she was also drinking it on an empty stomach and might be inclined towards rashness.

'Then it would seem your suspicions about his money worries were correct. I assume you have learned more than that whilst you have been on your mysterious mission to God knows where? A place, by all accounts, where messengers are unheard of and letters cannot be sent.'

A chastisement, yet one which told him she cared about him. That thought warmed him more effectively than her eiderdown or the brandy. 'I've been to Norfolk.'

'Ockendon is in Norfolk!'

'Yes, he is, but his minion is not. Of that I am certain. I was careful not to alert him to my presence. I don't want the scoundrel knowing I am spying on him and would much prefer to take the wind out of his sails callously and to his face. On Twelfth Night, before I summarily have him thrown out of my house, that is.' If he could find Rainham and convince him to switch his allegiance as well as plugging every leak which might cause her harm. At this stage, that was a problematic 'if'. 'The solicitor said he was spending more and more time at his estate. The mounting cost of staying in London and maintaining two staffs was crippling him, hence he hires the majority of his Mayfair servants on a casual basis. My investigations in the city were turning up nothing tangible, yet I could not shake the feeling he would try to hide his situation from the *ton* and what better place to do that than sleepy old Norfolk? I thought it best to travel there directly and it's only a day's ride.'

Once again, Hal's gut instinct had proved to be right. 'A year ago he *did* mortgage his Mayfair town house. To the hilt. The debt is owed to a bank based in Norwich. According to his steward, a man whose tongue becomes far too loose with the lubrication of ale, his estate has also had some financial problems of late. A large flood last year destroyed most of his grain crop. A number of staff were let go.'

'Is he on the cusp of bankruptcy?'

'Yes.' Hal watched the hope return and grinned. 'His situation is dire enough for me to know he recently negotiated a reduction in his mortgage repayments with the bank. A significant reduction in his repayments for six months only. That is all the leeway they would grant him.'

She stood then, agitated and began to pace. 'All the more reason why he needs to marry an heiress—but hardly enough evidence for us to stop him from exposing my father and Georgie to the world. If anything, it merely makes his situation more desperate and ours more tenuous. Speed is of the essence if the banks have only given him six months to...' Then she stopped and her eyes narrowed. 'Wait...how would you know what terms he has negotiated with a provincial bank in Norwich?' He adored her intelligence.

'Because, as of yesterday afternoon, I became the majority shareholder in the bank and thus privy to all of its dealings.'

'You bought shares in a bank?' Her jaw dropped. 'To help me?'

Suddenly uncomfortable, and determined not to ever tell her how much of a premium he had had to pay to secure the shares, Hal simply shrugged. 'It was a good investment, regardless of the particular circumstances. The Norwich Municipal Bank now dances to my tune. One of my first tasks will be to call in Ockendon's loan unless he agrees to maintain his silence.' Hal's fingers were drawn to her hair again. 'I won't let you marry him.'

'I will not allow him to ruin my father.'

'Neither will I—but if it comes to it, your father would sooner have his reputation sullied than see you condemned to a life of misery with that extortionist.' She went to argue. He could see the fiery determination in the sudden set of her jaw and her instantly stiffened posture. She was so loyal. So selfless. So irritatingly stubborn and independent. So much like her proud and noble father. Always ready to do the exact right thing by others even to the detriment of herself. It was frightening how much he had missed her these last few days. How much he had thought about her. About them. Hal couldn't help but smile. 'Wouldn't you? If it were Georgie you would sacrifice your reputation in a heartbeat. Because that is what we are talking about here. Nothing but your father's reputation. I could ruin Ockendon with a single stroke of my pen. I doubt he will continue with his quest to blackmail you once he realises how dire his financial straits now are. And I shall buy Rainham's silence, as much as it galls me to do business with such a snivelling, spineless, self-preserving...' Hal stopped himself mid-flow to wince. 'I'm sorry... He is still Georgie's father and I shouldn't bad-mouth him.'

To his surprise, she rolled her eyes. 'Please do not try to spare my sensibilities regarding *that* man. He is a snivelling, spineless, self-preserving toad. I wish every single day I had chosen a better man—*any* man—to have fathered my son. But let us not waste another breath talking about him when I am more concerned about my father. What if we cannot find Rainham? Or worse, what if we do and then Lord Ockendon still exposes what my father did?'

Hal had mulled this problem over a great deal in the last few days and intermittently on his interminable ride back to London when he forced himself not to think about her. 'I doubt his Majesty's government would condone the scandal of one of their longest-serving and most respected advisors standing trial. Despite the greatest provocation, he did not kill anyone. In fact, a good lawyer would argue quite the opposite. He did what he did to stop the Duke of Aylesbury having the blighter killed. Even your cowardly fiancé would testify to that. Aylesbury is dead, so cannot be punished either way. The whole case will stand on Ockendon's word and testimony obtained under duress. Rainham was out of his wits, if you remember, after having spent an eternity incarcerated in Bodmin Gaol. A sentence he earned fair and square because he is a wastrel who cannot pay his own debts. He was desperate. Is *still* desperate. Without Ockendon's promised remuneration he is still penniless. The dissolute Marquess of Rainham is the weak corner.'

'The weak corner?'

'My father was fond of analogies when it came to business. In days of yore, when an army besieged a castle, they had two choices. Surround the fortress and starve the occupants out, whittle them down until they surrender or find the most vulnerable part of the structure and ruthlessly mine under it, then stand back and watch the impregnable stone towers collapse under their own weight. That toad is the weak corner. If *I* offer to clear his debts for him, Rainham will stand in the witness box and say anything to serve his cause. Your father sent a bad man to a penal colony for a few months to teach him a lesson, then brought him back. At the worst, he will be forced to leave society and be shunned. He will be pilloried in the newspapers. But his life will go on, as will yours. His fortune will be intact. His estate still thriving. Take it from someone with a truly dreadful reputation—it is not so bad.'

Chapter Nineteen

For a man who prided himself on always being irreverent and naughty, Hal had a habit of using logic to great effect. Lizzie plopped down on her mattress with a sigh. 'You are assuming a great deal. First we have to find him, and I doubt that will be easy. He is far too valuable to Ockendon. Even if we do, he might well have told others and then there will be no containing the gossips. The scandal will be horrific.'

Hal nodded with resignation. 'I cannot deny that.' He stood up, dragging the eiderdown with him, and came to sit next to her on the mattress and wrapping a corner around her shoulders as he pulled her head to rest against his. 'Although I remain cautiously optimistic the story can be contained. We still have over a week until Ockendon returns to town and at the very least you do not have to marry him now that I own his debt. Surely that is good news.'

'Of course it is.'

Lizzie allowed her body to relax into his. Did it really matter if the whole world knew she was a fallen woman or that Georgie was born on the wrong side of the blanket? One of these days it was bound to come out, whether by the odious Earl's hand or another's. She had always known that and had prepared for the inevitable for over a year now. Her original plan—relocate to her cottage in remote Yorkshire, assume a new name and tell the world her son's father had died in the war—would still shelter Georgie from the worst of the talk. Lizzie sincerely doubted London scandal would travel to such a rural and isolated community. She wouldn't have to give up her son. And Hal was right, her father was unlikely to be tried as a kidnapper if Rainham testified his life had been in danger and her father had, in a strange sort of way, saved him from an execution.

Unlikely. In a perfect world.

But bitter experience had taught her the world was not perfect and the current political situation was tumultuous to say the least. If the Opposition got wind of her father's actions, then they would use it mercilessly against the government. The Whigs would scream for proper justice and *proper* justice dictated a trial. Lord Liverpool might have to sacrifice his friend for the good of the nation, just as Lizzie already knew she would still sacrifice her own happiness for the sake of her papa. If she could save him that ordeal by suffering a marriage with a man she loathed, then she would say 'I do' in a heartbeat. Hal had done so much, and spent so much, to help her she did not want to diminish his herculean efforts on her behalf with a cold dose of pessimistic reality. Not tonight at any rate, when he was frozen to the bone and clearly exhausted.

Besides, she reasoned, Lord Ockendon was old. He certainly appeared much older than his years which suggested he was not in the best of health. With any luck he would leave her a widow sooner rather than later and her life would return to normal. And then again, maybe he would live another thirty years because Lizzie had nothing but bad luck when it came to men. Hal would be lost to her and would doubtless marry a pure and more deserving young lady, Georgie would still grow up without her and her ageing father... Good Lord! Her father would be dead by the time she was free.

Another sobering thought and one which made her eyes watery and her chest constrict.

'Why are you crying?'

'Relief.' The lie tripped off her tongue and she forced a smile. Hal had tried. He had bought a bank and ridden halfway across the snow-covered country overnight. It was all so tragically optimistic and hopelessly romantic. 'Thank you, Hal. How can I ever repay you for your generosity?'

His thumbs came up to brush the unshed tears away. 'Don't cry. There is no need to repay me. It has just turned Christmas Day and all I want is to see you enjoy it.'

The tears fell, about to betray her. Only at the last moment did Lizzie's expression comply as she fought to maintain the brave face she wore for him. 'But you have bought a bank...'

'An investment.' Further protest was silenced as his mouth brushed across hers. 'And if you recall, we made a bargain to protect each other till Twelfth Night. You still owe me twelve days. If you really want to repay me, then stand at my side during every interminable festive entertainment I am being dragged to, especially the tiresome ball my mother is forcing me to host, and continue to keep the hordes at bay.'

She would pretend to be happy for his sake. For her son's sake. For Papa's. Whatever happened, she would enjoy this Christmas because the realist in her still screamed it might be her last with all the men she loved. 'That hardly seems enough.'

'It's enough for me.'

On a whim, she leaned over and kissed him. Lizzie had intended it to be short, a friendly gesture of thanks, only the second her lips touched his they were in no hurry to move. Nor did his. The world was instantly a better, brighter place. Soon she might well be locked into a horrendous marriage with a man she detested or an eternity away in a desolate corner of Yorkshire. Whichever fork in the road fate took her would be without him. But Hal was here now and now might be all she ever had of him. As there was no point in fighting the temptation, she kissed him again before pulling back. 'You are such a lovely man, Henry Stuart.'

'I am more than lovely. I am irresistible. It is a wonder you can keep your hands off me.'

He had meant it as a glib remark, she knew. He was playing the flirty, charming scoundrel again to make her smile, as if his selflessness on her behalf was of no matter. But the simple truth was she very much wanted to kiss him again, realising this was her last chance. *Their* last chance. With all the misery and heartbreak cluttering the horizon she deserved this memory. One which she could cling to like a rock in a stormy sea. A real memory of what it *should* be like between a man and a woman.

They were here alone, in the dead of night, sat on her bed and wrapped in each other's arms. All at once, she ruthlessly banished all thoughts of tomorrow and the direness of her situation. Lizzie would have to face that again soon enough. For now, she had tonight. And him. The man her heart yearned for. The one who made her bare skin ache for his touch and her body want. Need pulsed in her core. Her fingers traced the day's growth of stubble on his cheek reverently. To her complete surprise, her own voice came out thickly. Breathless. 'Seeing as you have bought a bank *and* climbed the wisteria, we might as well make the visit worthwhile.'

He pulled away then. Offended. 'You know that is not what I came here for.'

Lizzie pressed one finger to his lips. 'I know. You would never come up here to seduce me. You are far too noble to use your good deeds so shamelessly.' She twisted her body to sit astride his lap, watched his eyes darken and revelled in the surge of feminine need now coursing through her veins. 'I am not so noble or good. Tonight I want to be shameless. I don't want you to leave, Hal.'

'You really don't need to...' His hands came to her waist to push her away, so she grabbed them and smoothed them shamelessly over her breasts. Pushed her pebbled nipples eagerly into his palms to prove to him he was what her body wanted. That she was serious.

'Right now all I can think about is you. Only part of that is out of gratitude. The rest is pure, un-adulterated lust.' Lust that would give her something to sustain her through the bleak years ahead. Memories of Hal. This man she loved.

'Every time you touch me, I want. Every time you kiss me, I want.' Lizzie leaned closer so that her lips grazed his cheek. 'I never thought I was capable of wanting a man again. I was done with all men...until you, Hal. We have twelve days left together and I am tired of denying myself. I'm sure a man with your reputation knows how to make love to a woman without creating a child, so what is the harm? I'm tired of feeling frightened and miserable, and I want to fully enjoy this Christmas. I want to enjoy you.'

From somewhere within, Lizzie became a seductress. It seemed to be an entirely natural state to be in with him. Natural and necessary. She trailed hot, open-mouthed kisses across his jaw and nipped at his ear. She could feel Hal warring with his own conscience as he sat still beneath her. Rigid. His breathing was erratic, but his hands still cupped her breasts even after she released them and allowed her own fingers to begin to explore the breadth of his shoulders and chest through the unwelcome barrier of his clothing.

When she brought her lips back to his mouth, he failed to respond, but his eyes closed and he allowed the pad of one thumb to circle the aching point of her nipple. When she moaned her enjoyment, then shuffled her knees forward, her nightdress riding up her thighs as she fought to get closer, she felt the unmistakable bulge of his hardness through his breeches and knew he was as desperate for the act as she was.

He wanted her, too.

All the pent-up passion and yearning she felt for him was not one-sided. It made no difference that there was no future for them beyond the next few days, there seemed little point in denying the desire which burned between them. She was long past ruined and about to be the capital's greatest scandal. One night of passion with a notorious rake would not make one whit of difference any more.

Lizzie traced the outline of his mouth with her tongue while her fingers quickly undid the buttons on his waistcoat. He made no attempt to stop her nor did he succumb to her ministrations. All the while, his thumb, the only part of him not being noble, still lazily circled her nipple until she thought she would scream from the wanting. Lord, he was stubborn! Why wouldn't he take what she wanted to freely give?

Like a woman possessed, she grabbed the hem of her nightgown and wrenched it over her head, baring herself fully to his eyes and then sat back, forcing him to look at her. His gaze caressed her body in the absence of his hands. His mossy-green eyes darkened further as his pupils dilated. They fixed on her nipples and unconsciously he licked his lips.

'I didn't come here to bed you.'

'And I won't let you leave here till you do.' She slid off his lap and walked brazenly to the window. Locked it. Closed the curtains. Then watched his eyes follow her naked body to the door. Lizzie turned the key and removed it from the lock and smiled like the most practised of courtesans as she tossed it aimlessly across the room; standing shamelessly with her hands saucily placed on her hips and a knowing smile curving her mouth.

His face was inscrutable and for several seconds he simply stared back at her, impassive... aside from his glorious erratic breathing. But then his eyes betrayed him and began to rake her body from top to bottom with barely concealed hunger. Imbued with a new sense of womanly confidence, Lizzie slowly closed the distance between them, her gaze never leaving his.

'You cannot compromise me. That has already happened. And I am not interested in trapping you into marriage like some of your baying hordes. I won't marry you, Hal. I won't marry anyone. When this surprising Christmas season draws to a close, and all of this *nonsense* is done, I am leaving London whatever happens and never plan to return. We shall have to say goodbye. It would be silly to deprive ourselves because of your misplaced nobility and your ridiculous notion that I am only offering myself to you because I am grateful, don't you think? Especially when I want you. All of you. And you know me well enough to know I am not inclined to do anything I don't want to. Now…' she stood inches away, her teeth grazed the warm skin just below his ear and she heard his stifled groan '…the burning question is: are you going to be a good boy, Hal, and give me what I want for Christmas or do I have to take it?'

Another groan; this one considerably more guttural. Almost angry. 'I think you are going to have to take it.' But his eyes were filled with need as they locked hotly with hers.

'So be it.'

He put up no resistance when she pushed his waistcoat from his shoulders. Sat impassively as she pulled his shirt from the waistband of his breeches. Almost. Because he moved his arms upwards to allow her to peel the linen from his body.

With impressive arrogance, he sat back on his hands while she tugged off each boot, then fumbled with the falls of his trousers, and watched her through passion-darkened, hooded eyes as she worked the buckskin down over his hips until he sat gloriously naked before her. Gloriously naked and completely aroused.

Just for her.

It was a magnificent sight.

Because she had to, she leaned down to kiss him. A thorough and decadent kiss which he took full part in, yet aside from the intimacy of their mouths, no other part of their bodies touched. It was the most erotic and intoxicating moment of her life. To be so close to him, both of them naked and eager, yet never to have experienced the touch of the other on their bare skin.

Lizzie caved first, smoothing her palms over his chest, and tracing the dusting of dark hair down his hard abdomen. As her fingers grazed his navel, Hal groaned. One large hand encircled her waist and tugged until she tumbled on top of him. 'You are going to kill me, woman!'

'Can you think of a better way to die?'

'Inside you. That would be perfect.'

She had to agree. She had never been more ready to give herself. Was desperate to give herself to him.

Hal rolled so their positions were reversed, then reverently pulled the ribbon from her hair. He used his fingers to tease out the plait, then spread her hair across the pillow to form a halo about her head. Satisfied with his arrangement, he lazily explored every curve of her body with one fingertip. The sensitive column of her neck. Her collarbone. Breast. The indent of her waist and the flare of her hip. The subtle undulation where her calf met her knee. Then back up again via a different route. It finally came to rest on the soft, golden triangle of curls at the apex of her thighs.

'I knew you would be beautiful. I never imagined you would be this beautiful.'

When he kissed her, Lizzie felt it everywhere and sighed into his mouth. Of its own accord her body arched towards his hand—but it was her breasts he worshipped next. Loving her nipples with his tongue until she was writhing against the mattress and begging him to take her.

But still he would not be hurried. His lips followed the same convoluted path across her fevered skin his hands had already explored. He kissed every inch of her. Rolled her on her front and nipped and nibbled his way down her back and smiled smugly when she protested before they shifted position again. The intensity of his stare emboldened her and she knew instinctively he adored what he saw. To him she was beautiful. Perhaps the most beautiful woman in the world.

'I want you now, Hal.' Every sense was heightened. Screaming for release. It was she who pushed his hand towards her sex, opening for him willingly. Shamelessly. She had never felt so deliciously unashamed before. So determined to find her own pleasure. 'Touch me.'

With the same torturously gentle motion he had used on her breasts, his fingers moved in tiny circles. Every nerve ending came alive and zeroed in on one tiny spot, and all at once she realised that Rainham had not known a damn thing about the act of love. With him it had been quick and frantic and ultimately awkward. An invasion. With Hal it was a celebration. A revelation. Utter, utter carnal bliss at the hands of a true master.

Her fingers found his hardness and explored it. So hot. So hard. Touching him was addictive. Her wits were scrambled. Limbs leaden yet quivering. Her body hovering on the cusp of something wondrous yet almost painful. She had never experienced a fiery need like it. Instinct told her to curl her palm around him and caress his length in long, firm strokes, feeling powerful when she saw the effect it had on him. His breathing became ragged and his eyes fluttered closed. Her name tumbled from his lips like a benediction. Then, with an animalistic sound he pushed her hands away from him and held them pinned gently above her head on the pillow. His gaze dropped and she allowed her thighs to fall open in invitation, no longer sure who was the seducer and who had been seduced. It made no difference. They were both too consumed with each other to think of anything except what they were about to do.

Lizzie thought he would take her quickly and put them both out of their torment, but he didn't. Their faces inches apart, they watched each other as he gently eased inside. Slowly filling her until he was buried to the hilt.

Only then did he start to move. Again, with measured, aching slowness until she could stand it no more. She wanted everything and all of him. Her legs wrapped around his waist, pinning him to her core, and she used her own hips to find the satisfaction she craved, driving them both mad. At some point, he must have succumbed to the madness, too. She had no clear memory of when that was amidst the vortex of new sensations buffeting her, before she knew it they were writhing together, wordlessly lost in each other. Moaning and kissing and frantically touching until a dazzling light exploded behind her eyes and her body shattered around him.

Chapter Twenty

Hal stared contentedly at the ceiling and enjoyed doing something he never did. Cuddling up to a sleeping woman in her bed hours after he had made love to her. Usually, when it came to sleeping, he much preferred the whole bed to himself. His own bed. Wherever that happened to be. Not that he was the sort of heartless rogue to dash out of a lady's bedchamber as if his breeches were on fire the moment the deed was done. He had too much respect for women for that and enjoyed their company immensely even when his passion was spent. He always stayed for a little while. Chatted. Made them laugh. Then pretended to bid them a reluctant farewell with whatever convenient excuse worked best to extricate him from the situation as painlessly as possible. He was fairly certain none of his former paramours had been offended by his departure.

Mind you, the women he favoured tended to be the more worldly-wise widows, the younger, neglected wives of older husbands, seasoned mistresses, actresses and opera singers. Most of them knew how the game was played. They were probably as relieved to see him leave as he was to be leaving.

Yet here he was, happily still ensconced in Lizzie's bed, his arm curled loosely about her hip while his nose nuzzled the crown of her head, feeling thoroughly pleased with himself. For the first time in his life he felt totally at home, a state he had found himself in perpetually since Lizzie had seduced him on Christmas Day.

Home.

That word and this woman seemed synonymous. No matter how many times he hauled himself up the wisteria or how many times he had made love to her since that first splendid night, try as he might he could not explain away the odd, comforting glow he had whenever he was around her. His excuses always fell ever so slightly short. Having now got to know her completely, having lost himself in her delightful body repeatedly and having spent more hours than he cared to count absorbed in her company at the numerous festivities they attended, he was prepared to acknowledge it was not just his head that he had lost.

Somewhere in the last few weeks he had lost his heart to her too. Hal genuinely lived to see her smile. He had been so preoccupied with making her happy he had quite lost sight of everything else. That was a bad case of love if there ever was one—although not quite as daunting as he had always believed it to be.

It did not matter that he was still the wrong side of thirty and still far too young to settle down. There were no more wild oats to sow. Why would he consider making love to any other woman when the only one his missing vigour wanted was right here? Thanks to a silly sprig of mistletoe, fate had decided it was time Hal took a wife. Lizzie. The most passionate, beautiful and noble woman in the whole world. Loving Lizzie, marrying Lizzie, felt intrinsically right.

Unfortunately, the stubborn wench had declared she had no desire to marry him.

Repeatedly.

A stumbling block, to be sure, but hardly an insurmountable one. When he had first met her, Hal had likened Lizzie to a fortress. Guarded. Surrounded by high battlements and with only one sturdy and unpredictable drawbridge. There were, however, no weak corners. Once the woman made up her mind, it was set. While he had basked in the euphoria of their lovemaking between bouts of fevered passion, Lizzie had talked on and on about her plans for her new life.

In the north, for goodness sake! Without him.

As if he was going to allow that to happen.

But there was no point in arguing with her when she was nobly sacrificing her own happiness—their happiness—because of the misguided belief he would be much better off without her or that the horrendous scandal she feared was about to imminently blow up in her face. Hal had even allowed her to make jokes about the future Countess of Redbridge, a woman with a reputation so pristine and shiny he would need to shade his eyes from the golden goodness radiating off her. It had soured his splendid mood until he discovered the perfect way to shut her up was to have his wicked way with her again.

As if a man like him, who had been in more strange beds than he cared to count, who was on first-name terms with the proprietors of every unsavoury gaming hell from here to John o' Groats and one who had bared himself to the amassed *ton* at the Serpentine one sunny Sunday afternoon, could tolerate an eternity with a woman so dull?

At times her determined pessimism was laughable, yet the underlying sadness he knew she masked with false gaiety for his sake—or her son's or her father's—broke his heart and, no matter how hard he tried, he could not convince her that she was not doomed because he would fix it.

She would try to distract him with passion and Hal had a talent for distracting her quite thoroughly as well. Hence she was now sleeping peacefully in his arms and he was enjoying the sight of her wistfully smiling in her sleep. Wistful smiles that he had created and that he had every intention of creating until he was dragged, kicking and screaming, from this mortal coil and buried six feet under the ground.

Fortress Lizzie was in for a shock if she seriously thought he was going to marry anyone else aside from her. And vice versa. He still had one whole day until Twelfth Night ended. One last day to breach her defences and make her see sense. In the absence of any corners to mine beneath, Hal was going to lay siege and systematically whittle the blasted woman down until she surrendered to his way of thinking. Tonight he would send the weasel Ockendon packing and they would be able to get on with their lives. It was just a shame all Hal's attempts to find Rainham had amounted to nothing. With Rainham firmly in his pocket, Lizzie would finally accept her dreadful ordeal was over and then perhaps...

He heaved a sigh and she stirred. Her face emerged from a tangle of hair and she appeared delighted to see him. Because he could, Hal ran his palm over her bottom possessively. 'Good morning. I hope you slept well.'

He watched her lips curve upwards. Neither of them had slept much last night. As the month got shorter Lizzie appeared to want to sleep less and less. Today, he knew with irritated certainty, she intended to say goodbye to him for ever at the end of his own blasted ball.

'I had a wonderful dream. A handsome rake scrambled up the wisteria and did unspeakably shocking things to me.'

'That same rake had better climb back down it swiftly before your fearsome butler wakes up and relieves him of his teeth.' Dodging Stevens had become considerably more problematic and the fellow had taken to glaring at him through menacingly narrowed eyes whenever he came to *officially* call. Hal had a sneaking suspicion he knew full well what the pair of them were up to. Knew full well, but was biding his time.

'Surely you can spare me half an hour?'

Another goodbye. Instead of grinding his teeth in irritation, Hal kissed her.

An hour later she had lost the watery glimmer of martyrdom he kept seeing in her lovely cornflower eyes—he had seen to that—and barely had the strength to wave him farewell as he gingerly lowered himself from the window.

The north! Hal wanted to shake her.

'This came for you.' Panic made him fall the last five feet and he landed with a painful thud on his bottom at Stevens's feet. The giant butler unceremoniously thrust a note in his face. 'One of your Bow Street Runners tracked you here just after midnight. I didn't want to *embarrass* Lady Elizabeth by bringing it in.'

Pride made Hal stand before he took the letter. The seal was broken. 'You opened my private correspondence?'

'You seduced Lady Elizabeth.' The butler's face

was deadpan, but his nostrils still flared. 'They've found him.'

The knots in his gut Hal had carried around for close to a fortnight suddenly loosened despite being caught red-handed, practically *in flagrante*. 'Where?'

'Seven Dials. The Runners are waiting outside where he is. I presumed you wanted to speak to them first.'

'I do!' Hal was already striding across the lawn. Perhaps it would be better if he sprinted home first? Quicker, certainly with...

'I've already got two horses waiting. I'm coming with you.'

'Suit yourself.' Having the ham-fisted brick wall next to him when he confronted Rainham the snake would be beneficial. 'But I do the talking.'

'Are *you* going to do right by *her*?'

'I'm determined to damned well marry her, Stevens!'

'Then I'll let you do the talking.'

Thanks to the horses and the fact the blanket of snow which had suffocated the city now resembled a lace shawl, the main roads were blessedly clear and empty as the sun began to rise. However, there was not enough ice to mask the stench

of the seething, reeking cess pool of Seven Dials.
The natural habitat for a rat like Rainham. They
met two Runners dressed in inconspicuous rags
loitering outside a tatty-looking brothel. The dissolute Marquess was blissfully oblivious to their
presence or that Hal was about to ruin his day.

By all accounts, a man matching Rainham's description was upstairs. He had been there since
before Christmas, when his aged companion had
paid in advance for him to stay for the next fortnight before disappearing in a 'fancy carriage' and
hadn't been seen since. He had also promised to
pay the proprietor handsomely to keep the gentleman *entertained* and his presence a secret. Because Hal had given the Runners carte blanche to
bribe whoever and however they saw fit, the proprietor was most accommodating, even going as
far as directing them to the bedchamber. Real coin
always trumped a flimsy promise. More proof that
Hal's father might have been right about the world
and coin after all, although hardly a surprise here
in Seven Dials, where poverty ruled and money
was everything.

Hal did not bother knocking on the door. He
strode in, with the beefy Stevens hot on his heels,
then stood impassively as the two lightskirts

were hastily pushed aside and Georgie's vile father pulled the sheets up to cover his nakedness. Clearly Ockendon had the measure of his accomplice to bring him here, where there was plenty to occupy someone with Rainham's debauched tastes.

'If you would excuse us, please, ladies.' He flicked two coins in their direction and waited for them to exit the room. Neither bothered dressing. They merely bundled their tangled clothes up and brazenly sauntered to the door, one winking at Hal saucily in invitation. The butler closed it with deliberate slowness, then scraped a chair across the bare wooden floor and placed it in front of it, then sat, blocking the Marquess's only escape route. He folded his arms and glared menacingly at Rainham, who looked ready to launch himself out of the single grubby window at the first viable opportunity. Hal found himself amused at the sight.

'We are three floors up, so jump out of that window if you are of a mind to. I shan't stop you. In fact, I believe I would find a great deal of pleasure seeing your broken body on the road below.'

Rainham swallowed nervously, his frightened

eyes flicking between Hal's and his giant companion's. 'What do you want?'

'I think you know… Deep down.' Because it felt like the right thing to do, Hal reached down and slid his boot knife out of his Hessian. A knife which he had only used twice. Once to cut up an orange and once to slice through the impossibly knotted laces of a lusty widow's corset—but Rainham had no idea Hal had no appetite for violence. Usually. Knowing what the snake had done to Lizzie made the thought of it significantly more tempting than it had ever been. He smiled smugly as Rainham's eyes focused on the sharp blade, then casually used the tip of his knife to clean some imaginary dirt from under his fingernails. 'You've been talking, it seems, to your new friend and *benefactor* Lord Ockendon. Telling him things that are not true. Spreading lies… Malicious lies. Isn't that right?'

'I didn't lie.' But the man blanched as he spoke, his Adam's apple bobbing repeatedly as he gulped in air. 'I promise you I didn't lie.'

'That's a shame. If you are loyal to Ockendon, then you are of no use to me. Or anyone, for that matter.'

Rainham's mouth opened and closed, then

opened again, much like a reeled salmon fighting death. 'I—I d-don't understand.' Hal turned the knife so that the weak morning light caught the blade. Smiled. 'Are you going to k-kill me?' The snake's voice was satisfyingly high. 'You can't kill me for telling the truth!'

The attempt at retaliation was wasted. His eyes were darting around, seeking a way out, and beads of damning perspiration were gathering on his pale skin. Poor Rainham. He was about to discover how talented Hal was at calling a man's bluff. A skill he had honed to perfection out of necessity to block his father. Just like his father, the Marquess of Rainham was trying to bully a woman.

Lizzie.

A woman who had been hurt enough.

He allowed the anger to ferment in his gut for a few moments before answering and found an odd satisfaction in it.

'Do you know, old boy, I rather think *I am*. Look at where we are. Slap, bang in the middle of the biggest haven of criminals and ne'er-do-wells in the whole of London. You could not have picked a place more suitable to my purpose if you'd tried. Thank you for that. Makes everything so much simpler.' The Marquess baulked and looked ready to cry. For good measure, Stevens stood and quietly flexed his fingers as if he had been brought here specifically to deal with the murdered corpse, lest the blood marred Hal's fine coat.

'If you turn up here, gutted like a fish, the residents will deny any knowledge of what happened. That is the way of things when everyone is as lawless as their neighbours. The horrendous poverty serves to make the people here ruthless. They sold you down the river for a few coins.'

Rainham gulped and the last of the air came out of his lungs in a whimper. Hal nearly had him. The man was so weak-willed, so desperate to save his own sorry skin he would be easy to completely break. What the hell had Lizzie ever seen in him?

'We will not be disturbed, by the way. The landlady was most accommodating when she learned exactly who I was and…of course… I am *very*, *very* rich.' Hal paused to allow his words to sink in, pressed his advantage when he saw realisation dawn. 'Tell me—who will mourn your passing in the *ton*? Your reputation proceeds you, as far as those who remember you are concerned, that is. You have been gone such a long time I doubt many will notice your passing…and as far as I can ascertain, your only friend in the world is that toad Ockendon and I can assure you he is next on my list. Whatever nonsense he has planned will be *ruthlessly* nipped in the bud. Of that you can be quite certain. With Lizzie's *powerful* family connections staunchly on my side, my fat purse and sudden determined appetite for vengeance, *you* don't stand a chance. So be a good boy and tell me what I want to hear. It really is your only chance of walking out of here alive.' The little colour remaining drained out of Rainham's face, so Hal paused for a heartbeat. 'Did I mention I will double whatever Ockendon promised you? And pay your passage to the Americas so you can start afresh.'

Snakes were so predictable. 'It wasn't my idea! I fully intended on keeping to the bargain I made with Lizzie's father. I knew Aylesbury would kill me if I dared to set one foot back in town.'

'Then why did you?'

Rainham gulped. 'Ockendon rescued me. Informed me that Aylesbury was dead. Said I would be safe. Said he would keep me safe if I helped him.'

'So you gave him information he could use to blackmail Lizzie. A woman you claimed to have loved.' Hal could not disguise the acid in his tone or the raw hatred in his eyes. To his credit, Hal noticed Stevens wore exactly the same expression. The world might run on coin, but it couldn't buy loyalty. True loyalty had to be earned and he was suddenly grateful she had this big brute in her corner, protecting her.

'I feel bad about that. I really do… But I had people after me, baying for blood, and there was so many stipulations and caveats on the marriage settlements. The Earl of Upminster had insisted upon them. It forced me to—'

'Steal away the Duke of Aylesbury's daughter instead because she had a fatter purse and no such caveats. *This* I *know*, Rainham. I also know you failed in that endeavour, too, and it doesn't do anything to make me feel any more lenient towards you.

The dissolute Marquess appeared to shrink as he drew his legs up and his white knuckles clutched ineffectually against the blanket. Hal was happy to let the weasel squirm and sat quietly. Waiting.

'She let me seduce her!'

Like a true snake he was blaming Lizzie rather than himself. 'What a bad girl…' His voice dripped venom. 'To allow herself to be seduced by such an accomplished and seasoned despoiler. You must be right. It was all *her* fault. Your part in the proceedings was insignificant.' Hal could picture the scene. A younger, trusting, more innocent Lizzie, bowled over by Rainham's practised charm. 'How old was she back then, Rainham? Eighteen? Barely out of the schoolroom. You had a decade of experience on her and you promised her marriage?' The temptation to drag the man out of the bed and choke the life from him was difficult to ignore. But he had to.

'You have to understand—' Hal ruthlessly cut him off with his hand.

'I understand. I understand perfectly. Be under no illusion, Rainham, that I hate you, I want to kill you for what *you* did to her, and would happily tear you limb from limb if you ever malign her or gossip about her or her family again! Right now, I will do *whatever* it takes to keep her safe. What. Ever. It. Takes. Once this is done, know that you *will* die if you ever set foot on these shores again or so much as speak her name. Do you understand!'

'Y-yes!'

Chapter Twenty-One

'I don't believe it! The blighter has won again.' Her father threw down his hand of cards in disgust.

'Believe,' said Aaron matter-of-factly. 'The blighter has the luck of the devil.'

They were wiling away time until the guests arrived for the Annual Twelfth Night Ball—a Redbridge tradition and one Hal's mother was beyond excited about. For the first time in ten days they were not in Grosvenor Square, but Berkeley Square, and for the first time in Georgie's young life he was spending the night in a house not belonging to her father. He had been having so much fun with Prudence and Grace that Lizzie had relented and allowed him to spend the night of the ball in the nursery in Hal's house with his boisterous new friends. He deserved it. Tomorrow her son would have to say a final farewell to the girls and his grandpa as they finally travelled north. A journey which had lost much of its appeal now that she also had to say goodbye to Hal—and one which might be very short lived if she had to marry the man she despised.

Hal, on the other hand, did not appear perturbed by her imminent departure at all. In fact, he had been a positive joy since his return on Christmas Eve. Thanks to the Hal and the Stuart–Wincanton clan, Georgie had enjoyed the best Christmas Day of his life. Aside from her little boy's euphoria at a whole army of lead soldiers, she had never heard him laugh so much. From the moment he'd arrived back mid-morning, Hal had taken charge of the children's entertainments and the children. For at least two hours, he organised a fearsome war between the brave and noble British and the cheese-making Frenchies, culminating in the epic Battle of the Persian Rug which everyone was commandeered to join. Hal, typically, cast himself as Wellington and forced his sister Connie to be Napoleon. Georgie controlled the Highlanders, Aaron the cavalry and her dear papa controlled the English cannons. Prudence and Grace, as hellions-in-training, were given the challenge

of being the enemy as a test of their resourceful-
ness. Lizzie was also a Frenchie as she was a girl.
Despite their best efforts, Wellington was victori-
ous and Napoleon—or rather Connie—was ceremonially rolled up in the rug as a punishment
for trying to take over the world. The children
had all slept in the nursery with Georgie after
collapsing from exhaustion. All three slept with
smiles on their faces. Smiles Hal had put there.

Hal had since become a constant companion
during the days, where he entertained the children
and led them astray, and an ardent and passionate lover every night when he climbed the wisteria and stayed till dawn. He made no mention of
their parting. The pair of them talked about the
here and now rather than the future. The one time
Lizzie had tentatively suggested he might come to
visit them occasionally, so that their final goodbye was not final and that their impossible love
affair might continue temporarily if he ever ventured north, his dark eyebrows had drawn together
and he had swiftly changed the subject. That reaction, and the fact that he had made no attempt
to renew his proposal—not that she would have
said yes—probably said it all. Theirs was a tran-
sient, mutually beneficial relationship as per the

terms of their original bargain and he had gone above and beyond. That had to be enough.

'I am surrounded by sore losers.' Hal stretched like a cat and gathered up the pile of coins in the middle of the card table. For some reason, he was wearing the same sorry-looking sprig of mistletoe which had adorned his lapel since the ill-fated Danbury house party. The one sad white berry was all shrivelled and deflated, yet he had a habit of touching it reverently whenever he was sat near his brother-in-law. 'Can I help it if fortune favours the brave?'

'My lord.' The Stuarts' austere butler interrupted. 'You have a visitor. The Earl of Ockendon. He insists you sent for him.'

Lizzie's spirits plunged. Although she had known this confrontation was due to happen tonight, she was not prepared to have it now. So early. When she was trying to enjoy her last night with Hal and desperately trying to pretend nothing was wrong, but apparently the ever-confident Hal had summoned him.

'Indeed. Show him in!' Hal was clearly eager to get the deed done but, like Lizzie, the rest of the family were suddenly all subdued.

Ockendon strode into the room with a face like

thunder, still wearing his coat and clutching his hat. 'Where is he?'

Hal stood, ignoring the hostile tone, and inclined his head like the most gracious of hosts. 'If it is your puppet Rainham you are enquiring about, I am delighted to tell you he is safely hidden and happy to be so.' He turned and smiled at her shocked face, enjoying his surprise announcement immensely.

'You found him.' Her face, her limbs, were all frozen. All Lizzie could think was, *I don't have to marry Ockendon!* The relief robbed her of breath and she gripped the back of the chair. He'd done it. Hal had saved her. Just as he had said he would.

'Of course I found him!' Hal turned back towards Ockendon. 'And my Lord Rainham was most accommodating.'

'You think you are very clever, don't you, Redbridge.' Spittle sprayed out of the Earl's mouth as he snarled. 'But I have his sworn and signed testimony which will call you both liars!' He spun and started towards the door.

Hal sat, elegantly adjusting the fabric of his trousers as if he cared about the lay of the fabric, and crossed one long leg over the other. It was such an impressive sight to see. 'About that... I'm not sure how to break this to you, old boy, but I am going to require that document.'

'You say that as if you hold all the cards, Red-bridge, when we both know I have the means to destroy the entire fêted Wilding family in one fell swoop.' For the first time, Ockendon's gaze took in the rest of the room, his cold eyes settling determinedly on Lizzie. 'Are you going to sit here and watch this buffoon make idle threats to your betrothed on your behalf? Be warned, madam, you will pay for every slight.'

Lizzie went to speak, only to feel Connie's hand on her arm. 'Let my brother deal with him. Hal obviously has the situation well in hand.' And apparently, nobody else, her own father included, appeared to want to contradict this statement.

'If you say one thing to malign Lizzie, her father or her son, I will happily destroy you.' Hal's voice was icy calm. His eyes colder. 'The Marquess of Rainham will *not* testify against Lord Upminster. In fact, he is now of the earnest belief he put himself on the boat bound for Botany Bay to escape the tangled mess he had made of his life. If you use that testimony, he will stand in the witness box and say you obtained it under duress, when he was out of his wits in a stinking gaol, and that you told him exactly what to write in order to blackmail the Wildings.'

Aaron and Connie smiled at this news. Her father visibly sagged with relief, a little overcome. All Lizzie could do was slump back into her chair.

Again Ockendon chose to ignore Hal and snarled at Lizzie instead. 'Am I to assume you will not be announcing our engagement tonight?'

'I would prefer complete ruination than a single day spent as your wife.'

His eyes narrowed. 'So be it.'

Ockendon turned on his heel and stalked towards the door. 'When I leave here, I am going to tell the world about your bastard!'

Quick as a flash, Hal was out of his chair and hot on his tail. One large hand grabbed the Earl's collar and pulled him back, then shoved him ruthlessly against the wall. 'If you ever speak to her like that again, they will be the last words you ever say.'

The older man's rheumy eyes widened in fear as Hal lifted him from the ground by his lapels, but he still spat and clawed like a cat. 'Unhand me! I do not dance to your tune, Redbridge.'

'Actually. You do.' Hal let go and stood back simultaneously, so swiftly and unexpectedly that

Ockendon was not ready and dropped on to his bottom on the carpet. Instantly, Hal was all lazy charm again. 'I assume you are familiar with the Norwich Municipal Bank? You should be, seeing as you owe them a great deal of money...'

'I am sure I have no idea what you mean!' Ockendon scrambled to his feet, tried and failed to appear nonplussed.

'Come now...' Hal began to straighten the Earl's crumpled lapels '...they lent you eight thousand pounds. Eight thousand pounds you are struggling to pay back. Eight thousand pounds which would render you bankrupt if the loan was suddenly called in.' Fear made the tendons in the Earl's scrawny neck stand out. Made him lick his vile lips nervously. 'I suppose now is as good a time as any to inform you that *I* am now the majority shareholder of the Norwich Municipal Bank. I hold sixty-eight per cent, in case you were wondering. *Sixty. Eight. Per. Cent.* So you see, you *do* dance to my tune, Ockendon. And you will continue to dance to my tune. If you utter one word about Georgie or what happened to Rainham—just *one* word—I will call in that loan. I will take your precious town house and raze it to the ground and have *you* thrown into debtors' prison.' The

Earl of Ockendon's face was ashen as Hal strode to the door and opened it. To everyone's surprise Stevens was filling the doorway. 'Throw this odious man out, Stevens, would you? He won't be coming back. And be a good chap and bring back Lord Rainham's testimony.'

One meaty hand grabbed the Earl by the collar and within a split second he was gone, the door clicked quietly shut behind him. Hal simply sauntered back into the centre of the room like the cat who had all the cream.

'Who's up for another hand of whist?'

The room had erupted and while they celebrated, Lizzie tried not to focus on the sad reality. This scandal might be over but, at best it was a respite. Unless she left society, Georgie and her dear papa were still at risk and that meant Lizzie still had to face the heartbreak of doing what she knew was necessary. She couldn't stay. Another stolen day, or week or month was merely delaying the inevitable—and the delay would make leaving so much harder in the long run. She had already tumbled head-first into love with Hal. With every day that love only grew deeper. If her heart was going to withstand the pain, she had to cut all ties quickly.

This was it.

Her last night with Hal.

For ever.

Their eyes met across the noisy room and she saw the pride in his at his achievement on her behalf. When she smiled back at him, his stare became even more intense and that pride turned to joy. All he ever seemed to want was to make her happy so Lizzie did not want his last memories of her to be anything other than that.

For his sake, one last time, she would sparkle. So she celebrated with everyone, and when Stevens returned with that damning document she threw it on the fire laughing, toasting Hal's victory with the champagne he had opened, enjoying the giddy relief of freedom until the first guests began to arrive and they all had to behave as if the end of the world had not just been narrowly averted.

As expected, the ball was an unmitigated success. Everyone was having a wonderful time—except Lizzie. The closer she got to midnight, the more the confused and tangled warring emotions drained her. Relief. Joy. Disbelief. Sadness. Love.

Pain.

Pain so intense she had to fight the hovering tears constantly. Every time she glanced in Hal's direction and he gave her a secret, intimate smile back, it ripped through her and she wished with all her heart things could be different.

But how could they be? Lizzie had responsibilities. She did not have the luxury of concerning herself solely with her own selfish happiness. Georgie could not be hidden away in Mayfair for ever and the alternatives were impossible. She would never allow him to be banished to the country and could see no way he could suddenly magically appear in Mayfair without his existence ruining her father. How did one explain away a four-soon-to-be-five-year-old child? Or a ten-year-old one. A sixteen-year-old one. With each passing year, fresh lies would have to be heaped on more lies and her innocent boy would have to suffer.

'Waltz with me.'

Hal's warm breath caressed her neck and the tears threatened to spill. Soon the guests would leave and so would she. 'Of course.' Another memory to store away in a box now full of them.

One last dance to go with the last kiss they would share in the morning before she drove away. The last time she saw him as her carriage would pull out of sight.

Hal led her on to the floor and tugged her into his arms. Typically, too close for propriety, but not so close to scandalise. Lizzie was past caring about the latter and stepped closer still, allowing herself the pleasure of feeling their bodies touching.

One last time.

'Where are you taking me?' He had twirled her across the floor and was headed towards the door.

'The hall.'

'The hall. And that, I suppose, is explanation enough?'

He smiled and slowly brought the dance to a stop. 'Come. I wanted to show you something.'

They seemed to stroll for an age. His town house was impressive, even by Mayfair standards, the entrance hall vast and filled with milling couples who had gathered to escape the crowds and the heat of the ballroom. Hal led her past all of them and then through another door into a deserted, firelit parlour.

'Are we having a tryst? Because if we are I have

already seen what you are going to show me.' Flirting covered the pain.

He simply smiled enigmatically and went to the sideboard. He slid open a drawer and pulled out a small box. 'I put this here earlier. I want you to have it.' He placed it in her hand and stood back, uncharacteristically nervous, and her heart began to thud. Lizzie stared at it and hoped it was not what she thought it was. At her hesitation, he clasped his hands behind his back. Frowned. 'Open it.'

With shaking fingers, she did as he asked and stared mournfully at the glittering diamond nestled within. She had wanted tonight to be perfect for him and now she was about to ruin it.

'Marry me, Lizzie. Not because you are frightened or because you are grateful. Marry me because we love each other and we are meant to be together.'

'Oh, Hal…' She took one last look at the beautiful ring before slowly closing the box. He loved her? A part of her died as it clicked shut. 'I can't… You know I can't.'

He raked one hand through his dark hair in agitation and began to pace. 'For God's sake, woman! I love you!'

In her dreams, when he had said this it had been whispered, but his angry, raised voice somehow made it more heartfelt. More tragic.

'I love you, too, but my situation is untenable.'

His hands came up to grip her upper arms; despair distorted his handsome face. 'Surely you are not intent on pursuing this Yorkshire nonsense? Ockendon and Rainham cannot hurt you now. You are safe. Your father is safe. Georgie is safe...'

'Georgie is still a secret, Hal.' Lizzie broke the contact and put some distance between them. His touch would only make her falter away from what was right. 'He cannot remain a secret for ever. He deserves to live out in the open like every other child, running through fields, playing with others. If this month has taught me anything, it has shown me how he has blossomed amongst children his own age.'

'Once you marry me, he doesn't have to be a secret. I adore the boy. Are you frightened I will want him hidden away like Ockendon threatened? You can tell the world, for all I care!'

'Because that would ruin his life, wouldn't it? Everyone would realise he was Rainham's son. *Rainham's* son! I wouldn't wish that stigma on my worst enemy. Wherever he went, whatever he did, the gossip would follow him. The whispering behind fans about his fallen mother at public engagements...the pointed lack of invitations to other children's parties, the lack of acceptance in a society which puts a woman's virtue above all else! The fact that you deigned to marry a fallen woman and take on the burden of him!'

'Oh, for pity's sake—as if I care about that? I've been a scandal all my adult life—one more will hardly make a difference!'

'What about the shame it would bring to my father and the damage it would do to the reputation he has worked forty years to achieve? He was complicit in hiding my baby. Good grief, Hal... What if the truth about his hand in Rainham's disappearance is questioned?'

'I'm paying for passage and a new life for that man in the Americas. You do not need to worry about him...'

Lizzie held up her hand and slowly backed towards the door. She had to fight the overwhelming urge to believe he could be right. 'We escaped the scandal this time. Next time we might not be so lucky. You know what the gossips are like. My way is better... I am better on my own. In the north I can invent a new past for my son, which will also protect my papa, something more noble than being the dirty secret of a fallen woman and the bankrupt, dissolute Marquess of Rainham's by-blow!'

Chapter Twenty-Two

Hal wanted to grab her and shake some sense into her. The stubborn wench! Always so pessimistic and blasted noble. She denied him the pleasure by darting out of the door. No doubt she hoped he wouldn't cause a scene. Too bad. He was going to cause one.

He stalked to the door and found little comfort in noisily slamming it open. Barging past several people, he caught her by the elbow and pulled her to face him. 'We are not done!'

'Yes, we are!'

He would not be swayed by the tears pooling on her long lashes or the limpid, brave misery he saw shimmering in those fine cornflower eyes. 'You are not better on your own. Neither am I. Any fool with half a brain can see we are better together. You and I were meant to be together. You love me! You said so.' A crowd was beginning to gather. Hal didn't care. 'And I love you. Are you going to allow a silly scandal to keep us apart?'

'Weeeeeeee!'

Another sound from above.

High-pitched.

Children, nightgowns billowing. Sliding down the banister at speed towards them.

Prudence. Grace.

Georgie.

The high colour drained out of Lizzie's face as her son beamed at her proudly. She started towards him, but Hal raced to beat her. He bent and grabbed the little boy around the waist and hoisted him into the air. 'You rapscallion. You're supposed to be in bed.'

Connie had already claimed her girls and was blinking back at him with alarm. 'I can take him, Hal.'

'Nonsense. You know full well he won't sleep unless his papa tucks him in.'

It felt like the right thing to say. Especially as the crowded hall was now as silent as the grave and all eyes were on them. Georgie was staring back at him with wonder.

'We have the same dark hair.'

Hal ruffled it. 'Of course we do. And you have my handsome face, too.'

There were gasps. Murmurs. Lizzie was stood like a wide-eyed statue, the only evidence she was not made of stone the rapid rise and fall of her bosom.

'You have a son?' A rotund matron peered at him through her lorgnette.

As Hal was making this up as he went along, he nodded. 'Scandalous, I know, but hardly a surprise when I am famously scandalous. In my defence, I didn't know about him, else I would have married his poor mother—but, alas…childbirth…' He tried to look winsome, hoping that the adults would understand because he sincerely doubted he could maintain his charade if Georgie got wind of anything involving the words death and his mama in the same sentence. The boy adored his mother.

'The poor thing!' Another matron. 'But you took him in?'

'I might be a scandal, madam, but I am a noble one. Georgie is my son and I adore him.'

Remarkably, the women in the room were charmed. She could see it as one by one their faces softened. The men mostly appeared startled—but it was different for men. Many of those in this room probably had by-blows of their own and all of them hidden or ignored. Dirty secrets. Lizzie watched Hal ruffle her son's hair again. 'Why were you sliding down the bannisters, young man?'

'I saw you and Mama arguing. We thought it might make you both smile.'

Hal placed his finger over Georgie's lips. 'It's not official yet, young man. She hasn't said yes. She has this ridiculous notion that marrying me will ruin her father's reputation—but my secret is out now, so I suppose it hardly matters.' His eyes locked with hers. 'My offer still stands. I know I'm unworthy and I know I'm a scandal, but Georgie needs a mother. One who will love him as much as I do and who will treat him as her own. And I need you. I love you, Sullen Lizzie. Will you marry us?'

Two pairs of male eyes stared back at her hopefully. One pair brown, the other the most seductive green.

'If it helps, I have given him my consent. Despite his past, I am confident he has matured into a fine young man.' Her papa's eyes were watery, no doubt from a stray speck of dust in the pristine hall. Another pair of hopeful eyes.

'And I wished for it for Christmas.'

Georgie's wondrous expression undid her. She had no words. Speech of any sort was impossible, so she walked towards Hal and placed a lingering kiss on his lips. Who was she to argue against the wishes of all the men she loved.

'Is that a yes?'

She nodded and his mouth crushed hers. A few people clapped. Many were smiling. Even more were already gossiping and that was fine, too. With everything else Hal had accomplished in the last few weeks, there was no point in worrying about her talkative son giving the game away one day. Between them they would work it out. What was a little scandal in the grand scheme of things? Hal was a glorious scandal. Besides, everybody knew rakes made the very best husbands and this one was going to be a wonderful father as well—to all their children.

Hal lowered Georgie to the floor, whispered something into her son's ear that had him clamping his lips shut and kissed her again properly. When he stepped back he grinned, then plucked the single, shrivelled berry from his sprig of mistletoe and tossed it at his brother-in-law. Aaron caught it with one hand.

'Seeing as it is a night for the truth, I think it's fair to tell you I originally sought you out and wooed you because of a bet.'

'A bet?'

'Yes—the Mistletoe Wager.'

'Aaron Wincanton!' His sister's face was like thunder. 'After the Serpentine you promised...'

'It's my fault, Connie.' Hal did not appear the least bit sorry. 'I bet Aaron I could steal five kisses from Lizzie before Twelfth Night was done. I am delighted to say that I won.'

'No. You didn't.' Ignoring his wife's glare, Aaron pulled out his pocket watch and pointed at the dial. 'It's past midnight. Twelfth Night is over. As per the terms of our original arrangement, that last kiss doesn't count.'

Hal shrugged and winked at Lizzie. They both knew he had stolen more than five kisses before Christmas Day. Since then there had been hundreds and all of them splendid. And he clearly did not know that Lizzie and Hal had made their own arrangement as well. Knowing how competitive the two men were, that news was unlikely to go down well. She was going to enjoy being part of this family.

'I suppose I've lost then… Although, ironically, I also won. Although not quite what I was expecting. But a wager is a wager.' He kissed her again. Lingered. Then picked up her little boy. After a quick ruffle of his matching dark hair, Hal twisted Georgie upside down and then sensibly carried her giggling child away from the sea of gawping people, as if neither had a care in the world and being scandalous was not scandalous at all.

'Come on, Georgie. Come and help your scandalous but noble Papa in the stables.'

* * * * *